Hidden Cure

The Complete Series

ABIGAIL GRANT
FANTASY & PARANORMAL ROMANCE

Copyright 2021 © Abigail Grant

This is a work of fiction. Names, characters, places and incidents, either are products of the author's imagination or are used fictitiously.

Acknowledgements

A huge thanks to my loving husband, who inspires me to write the hunkiest of hunks! And thanks to my three little kiddos for keeping me on my toes, and never letting me get too sucked into my fantasy life!

And of course, a huge thanks to my wonderful readers! You all make my heart happy.

Contents

Chapter 1	7
Chapter 2	17
Chapter 3	27
Chapter 4	37
Chapter 5	45
Chapter 6	55
Chapter 7	61
Chapter 8	67
Chapter 9	75
Chapter 10	85
Chapter 11	95
Chapter 12	107
Chapter 13	115
Chapter 14	123
Chapter 15	131
Chapter 16	141
Chapter 17	151

Chapter 18	161
Chapter 19	169
Chapter 20	177
Chapter 21	189
Chapter 22	201
Chapter 23	209
Chapter 24	219
Chapter 25	227
Chapter 26	239
Chapter 27	247
Chapter 28	257
Chapter 29	267
Chapter 30	277
Chapter 31	287
Chapter 32	293
Chapter 33	301
Chapter 34	311
Chapter 35	317

Chapter 36	323
Chapter 37	331
Chapter 38	337
Chapter 39	343
Chapter 40	353
Chapter 41	361
Chapter 42	371
Review This Book	382
Other Books by This Author	383
About The Author	384

Chapter 1

✧✧✧

Maia

I PULL THE BACKPACK strap higher on my shoulder, looking back at the school for the last time until I need to actually walk for graduation. Thank the lord I get to leave classes early. It's only February, but my less than social life doesn't exactly make it hard to graduate early. Between school work, hanging out with my best friend Bree, and having the most overprotective father on the planet, I don't have a lot of chances to run wild.

It's not that I really care all that much though. Kids can be pretty harsh to a girl with white hair. I've tried countless times to dye my hair, but it doesn't last more than a week before the dye fades. I've learned to embrace the silky white locks I was born with. If anything, my hair makes for a great conversation starter. They can call me "freak" all they want. I'm out of here.

I can't stop the grin from stretching my cheeks as I dip into the forest that borders my little town in Vermont. I've loved these woods my whole life, but Dad rarely lets me explore them. He claims they aren't safe, full of wild animals, but I'm going to be eighteen tomorrow. I've got to disobey good old dad at least once every few years, right? He also told me not to get a tattoo, but that didn't stop Bree and I from getting matching mandala bracelet tattoos on my sixteenth birthday, symbolizing our tight bond as besties. It was all Bree's idea, but I can't deny that I was completely on board. *Sorry, Dad.*

I step through the old crunchy snow, loving the cold air on my skin. The cold is welcoming and rarely bothers me, even with only a light leather jacket and thin black leggings. I pull the crisp mountain air into my lungs as I continue along a game trail toward home. An eerie feeling begins sinking in, trailing from the back of my neck. Okay, maybe the woods are just a little sketchy.

I search for any signs of hungry animals, or axe murderers, but I'm met with only the slight crunching of month-old snowfall.

"Who's there?" I can feel my heart rate pick up, but I've never been one to shy away from a fight if it has to happen. Of course, fighting a bear would be significantly more difficult than kicking Torrie Layton's ass in the sixth grade. Still, I raise my hands and center my weight in a perfect fighting stance. *Thank you, Sensei Kenji!* If twelve years of karate classes helps me defend myself against a bear, I owe my dad a profuse apology.

Before I can start yelling at the forest, a figure dressed in purple, with curly red hair jumps at me from behind a tall bush. I scream, karate lessons going out the window as I throw my hands over my head, and I'm tackled to the snowy ground. My attacker jumps off of me and smiles down at my angry face.

"Hey, Mai. Didn't your father ever warn you about the dangers of the wild woods?"

I groan and brush the snow off of myself as I stand. "For heaven's sake, Bree! You scared the crap out of me!"

My best friend, Bree, just laughs and pushes her bouncy curls back, revealing her overly-jeweled ears. She has always worn at least six earrings on each ear daily. How she keeps from losing them all is a mystery to me.

"I'm just trying to prepare you for the inevitable wild animal attack that your adorable dad swears is around every corner. By the way, karate has failed you, girl." She raises a single blonde eyebrow at me.

I adjust my backpack and grab Bree's hand, ready to get out of the woods. I tow her after me toward home. "Please don't call my dad adorable. It's super gross, and karate hasn't failed me. I would be a great fighter if I ever had the chance to actually train. I'm too coddled!"

Bree nods beside me, pulling her thick jacket tight around herself. "Aren't you freezing, Mai? You're dressed like it's springtime, and you know as well as I do that spring doesn't happen around here until summer."

I laugh at that. She's absolutely right about the weather here. "I swear I'm not even the least bit cold. I think I have a theory about that, though."

"What theory might that be?"

I reach down and grab a stick from the ground, waving it around like a wand. "I think I'm a witch." I shout some nonsense magic word and point the stick at Bree with my best wide-eyed witchy stare.

To my surprise, she actually flinches, though her face immediately changes to a look that screams *my-bff-is-an-absolute-idiot*. "Why on earth would you think you're a witch?"

I shrug and start to tick off each of my fingers one at a time. "First, I *never* get sick. I heal incredibly fast. I don't ever get cold, though I have been too hot at times. And then there's my super weird hair. I mean, it makes sense right?"

Bree thinks over my hypothesis for a moment, but dismisses it with her words. "I think if you were a witch, you'd be a lot less afraid of cats."

I shiver, scrunching my nose up. I despise cats, and Bree thinks it's my least appealing trait. I can't help that they practically eat their own hair and then proceed to cough it up immediately afterward! It's disgusting!

"I guess you're right about the cat thing. So, what then? I'm just a weird loner girl with no special abilities? That's just too boring." I pout as we near my house.

Bree laughs again and nudges my shoulder. "You're not boring, girl. You're more unique and special than you think, trust me."

I smile at that. "Aww. Thanks, Bree." I turn my eyes to the back porch and see my dad staring at us with arms crossed and eyes narrowed. "Oh, crap."

Bree follows my gaze and snorts. "I don't know how he built a house at the edge of the woods and expected you to never wander the place." Then she raises a hand and waves. "Hey, Mathew!"

I sigh and shake my head. "Did you not hear me say *gross*, Bree?"

With a groan, she waves again. "I mean, Mr. Collins, of course." She turns to me with a wink and I'm rolling my eyes all over again. At least, thanks to Bree, my life isn't totally boring.

◊ ◊ ◊

Seth

My bones crack and slide as I land on two feet instead of four large paws. I stretch out my shoulders and look around for the pants I discarded before shifting an hour ago. They're soaked through from the snowy rock that I laid them on, and I sigh. "Great."

Now I have to go into the house completely naked in front of Dad. I don't care that he sees me in the nude, but when I run like this, it's a reminder to him that he can't shift, and I can see the hurt that it causes him to think about what he has lost.

I was only three when our wolf shifter pack was attacked by the lupercus. Those nasty cat-like shape-shifters are incredibly strong, and although they have always been an enemy to my kind, they aren't exactly known to ambush a pack in the middle of the night. They also don't normally move together in large numbers. Nobody saw it coming.

That night, many of the pack members fought back and were killed, including our alpha, Jackson Shaw. Jackson's beta and his wife were killed as well, along with their pregnant daughter. It was the biggest tragedy to happen in our pack lands in all of the Shaw pack history. That baby that was never born would've been our future alpha instead of me.

But all of that death led to Jackson's son, Nate Shaw, becoming our new alpha overnight, and my father became the new beta. When they were young, my father and Nate planned to run the pack together after they were grown, and even when my dad became paralyzed, Nate still kept him as his right hand man out of loyalty.

I was so young at the time that I've only ever known my dad to be bound to a wheelchair, his legs limp and lifeless. On that night, my mother died protecting me from the lupercus. She was my father's fated mate, and in the rage he felt from losing her, he went after three lupercus at once. It was a miracle he survived, but the pains of losing his mate and his shifting ability still haunt him. Of course, he won't talk to me about these things.

I hurry into the house and into my bedroom, slipping on a pair of sweatpants before finding my dad in the kitchen. "Hey, Dad. What are you up to?"

His tired gray eyes land on me and he continues stirring the boiling pot of pasta on the stove, having to reach high from his chair. "Did ya have a nice run?"

I chew on my bottom lip but try to hide the pity I feel for him, and I nod. "Yeah. It was great. The weather is perfect today. You should get out and enjoy it." Yeah, not happening.

Dad snorts and pushes himself higher, reaching for a jar on a high shelf. His arms are ripped, so it's not too difficult for him to push off the wheelchair, but he still struggles. I want to help him, but I hold myself back. He hates when I jump in and help. We all feel that alpha-wolf pride, but his is over the top at times.

He grunts and sits back down empty handed. "You gonna help me here, or what?" He growls the words at me, but the fact that he's asking for help means he's in a good mood today.

I hurry over and grab the red sauce from the shelf, handing it to him with a smile. "Making spaghetti? Does this mean we have company tonight?" Spaghetti is his go-to meal for company.

"Nate's coming to talk to you. He says it's time that you earn your place in the pack." Dad's eyebrows rise and he flashes me a slight smile past his thick beard. I'd like to think he's proud of me for my future place as alpha, but it's not like there were any better options. Nate never had kids, and he treated me like I was his son, training me to fight and control my wolf.

My hands start to sweat but I hide my nervousness. I know I'm strong and more than capable in a fight, but I also know I have a beast of a temper and don't do well with responsibility. I can't lie and say that I am going to make a great alpha someday. I'm only twenty, and I feel far from such an honor. And who knows if I'll ever find a mate. Most alphas-to-be are matched with a mate at birth, but the attack changed our ways after so much death and loss. I'm so out of my league.

A knock comes at the door and I run to grab it. Alpha Nate Shaw nods his head at me with a kind smile. He's taller than me by only an inch or two, standing at six-five. His skin is a dark brown, a contrast to my beige complexion. At his side is his wife, Lydia Shaw. She has always been so kind to me, and I can't stop my broad smile at seeing her. No gray has seeped into her wavy blue hair as of yet. I don't know what it is with the blue hair. She claims it's in memory of someone she once loved, but hasn't offered any further explanation. All I know is that I've never seen it in any other color. Thanks to our wolfy genes, she and Nate don't look much older than myself.

"Hey Luna Lydia. It's so good to see you." I lift her up into a tight hug and she swats at me to put her down.

"Don't you give me that Luna Lydia crap, Seth. I'm more of an aunt to you than anything. And put a damn shirt on." She winks at me with a finger pointing at my bare chest.

She has always been one to speak her mind and I love her more for it. I heard a rumor years ago that Nate and Lydia weren't supposed to be mates. Being the Alpha heir, Nate had been given a mate at birth, but nobody knows what happened to her. Nate doesn't hold me to that same tradition, thankfully. I'm glad Lydia is our Luna, though. They seem good together.

I bow to her like an obedient pup and throw a shirt on before greeting Nate. "Sir, it's great to have you both here."

He dips his head to me and pats me on the back. "I hope you still feel that way once we get down to business, Seth. An important day is here, and I'm about to tell you something that only the people in this room, and three others know."

My chin pulls back and I look at the elder shifters all watching me with worried eyes. *Well, hell. This can't be good.*

Chapter 2

◇◇◇

Maia

BE THERE IN 5.

    I send a quick text message to Bree as I walk along downtown. It's officially my birthday and I'm a woman now. And what do grown women do with their best friends? Get together for coffee.

    Yeah, so far adult life feels an awful lot like teen life. Still, it's probably just in my mind, but the new dusting of snow this morning looks crisper and the usually faint coffee smell that lingers on the street is stronger. I feel a strength today that I haven't felt before, and I am ready to face anything. Namely, coffee-time chit chat with Bree.

    I enter the small shop, but Bree is running late like usual, so I order my coffee and settle into a comfy chair by the window. Looking out onto the street with the warm cup in my hand makes me wish I would've brought along a book. Yup, day one of adulthood and

I'm still a nerd. If Bree were here she'd be mocking me right now.

I smile at the thought and look around the cozy shop. My smile falls when I spot the dark brown eyes watching me with hooded lids. A man that I've never seen before is staring directly at me, his eyes roam from my tie-dye Skechers, along my dark jeggings and overly-worn leather jacket. He locks eyes with me and I swear my heart flip flops in my chest.

Holy hell, this man is gorgeous.

If it wasn't for the pissed-off expression on his way-too-handsome face, I'd love to saunter on over to him and embarrass myself by plopping down on his lap. Not that I'm that kind of girl, but my body sure wishes I was. But his narrowed eyes and tight jaw make me look away. I chance a glance at him again and he's still staring like some murderous stalker.

His arms are large, thick against his long-sleeved sweater, and the speckle of hair on his jaw is perfectly trimmed. He doesn't care that I watch him right back, his arms crossed and unflinching. This dude has got some nerve to look at me like I'm some insolent child. I narrow my own eyes and lean forward in my seat. He should know that I'm not some blushing Barbie doll. His eyebrows raise slightly but he still doesn't look away. I shake my head, done with being creeped out, and I get up to leave.

The guy's eyes follow me all the way out the door, landing on my butt as I pass by him. He stares, completely unashamed and I want to turn around and kick him in his super hot face, but I just grind my teeth and leave without a word. I definitely shouldn't be able to smell him at this distance, but right before I shut the door behind me, a scent floats to my nose, and I swear he smells like a sexy Christmas tree.

I push down the stupid butterflies that go crazy in my stomach and I march down the sidewalk, mentally telling myself not to look back at the broody guy. I launch myself into the adjacent forest at a run, loving the breeze that flows through my hair. Bree is going to get an earful for being late today. I look down at my phone and shoot her another text.

SOME CREEP AT THE COFFEE SHOP. GOING HOME NOW.

Dad is just going to have to be okay with me going in the woods from now on. It just feels right being in here. The towering trees make me feel small, like I could just hide away from the world forever if I stayed beneath their protection. I sigh as I slow my pace toward home and I close my eyes, drinking in the serenity of the forest. Maybe I should take up camping. I could be a person who camps.

A hissing sound makes my eyes pop open and I gasp at the woman standing on the trail ten feet ahead of me. My hand flies to my chest and I laugh awkwardly.

"I'm so sorry. I am just jumpy lately." I apologize to the woman, but as I step closer, something is off about her and I feel sick to my stomach.

She is incredibly pale and skinny, wearing only a red spaghetti strap dress that falls to her bare feet. Her hair is stringy and graying, but her skin still looks clear and wrinkle-free. *Strange.* I can't judge too much with my own white locks flowing in the wind, but this lady is definitely not young.

"Hey, are you alright? Do you need some help?" I am only a few feet from her, and she still just stares at me, only a small, simple smile on her red lips.

What's with all of the staring today?

I wave my hand in front of the woman, and then I jump when she finally opens her mouth, the rest of her staying perfectly still. "I am just fine, darling. No need to worry about me." Her voice is shaky and old, but it doesn't match her young face.

I step back from her and nod. I can already see my home in the distance, so I hurry past the scary lady. "Have a good day, then," I say quickly, ready to run from this weirdo.

Before I can fully pass by her, she reaches a hand out, too fast, and grabs a hold of my arm. "Hey," I start to protest, but when I look toward the woman, she's something different.

Her eyes are sunken in and a bright yellow ring lights her irises, where they were blue just moments ago. I try to pull away, but her grip tightens, new elongated fingernails digging into me. "Do not leave just yet, young one. I only need one taste."

Oh, hell no! I open my mouth to scream for help, but my voice is cut silent in shock when the lady's mouth opens up to three times its size and two rows of sharp teeth retract from her gums like a shark.

Dear lord, I'm going to die.

Her head dips and she digs her rows of teeth into my neck, instantly sucking my blood. A choked scream escapes me as I kick and try my hardest to fight the creature off of me, but my vision starts to blur and a small tear leaves my eye. Before I black out completely, the woman is ripped from me and thrown into the trunk of a nearby tree.

I fall to the snowy ground, gasping and choking on air as I try to steady my breathing. Standing above me is the cute guy from the coffee shop. His back is to me and he's shaking like he's cold, or maybe angry? His arms flex, and it seems for a moment that the hair on his biceps grows and then shrinks back down to normal.

He watches the blood-sucking creature climb to her feet and hiss sharply at him. "Leave, dog. I am feeding!" She shouts the words at him, sounding younger than she had before. Did *my blood* do that?

The man growls and the sound is almost inhuman as it vibrates from him. "I'm only offering this once, demon. Go now, or I'll rip the little wings from your body."

Wings?

The lady hisses again before jumping into the air and transforming into a screeching owl. Her feathery wings flap hard once and she disappears into the trees. My mouth goes dry. *Great. I'm going crazy.*

I blink rapidly, trying to wake up from this horrible nightmare, but every time my eyes focus again, I'm still staring at the strange man who just threatened a blood sucking owl woman, sending her flying away.

Oh no, it's real.

The man looks down at me and instead of compassion, he's glaring again, his eyes shifting from dark brown to total black and back again as he yells at me. "What the hell are you doing out here all alone?"

Oookaaay…

◊ ◊ ◊

Seth

This is her? The girl I'm supposed to be following around? I don't know what I expected, but I didn't imagine she'd be so *helpless*. When Nate told me that a girl from town held the shifter cure in her blood, I figured she'd be stronger and more like a beast of a woman. How can this small girl protect herself from the creatures that want her blood?

Nate gave me very little information, so I came to investigate on my own. The thing that really struck me though, was the pull that I had toward her the second her eyes met mine. She stared at me in that coffee shop and I swear my body tensed from head to toe. She's incredibly beautiful, even with the snow white hair and the angry eyes. Of course, the glaring was my fault. I'm mad, and it's obvious she can see that.

I wasn't supposed to be a chauffeur to some cursed princess. I guess I don't really know what I'm supposed to be, but this doesn't seem like a task worthy of a future alpha. I follow the girl into the woods, feeling like she must be a special kind of stupid to wander off like this with something so valuable inside of her.

The sound of her garbled scream has me running faster than I ever have, like I'm not in control of myself any longer. Just her fear controls me, propelling me forward, and my wolf claws inside of me to be released. I force him down, just to feel him right at the surface when I see the bloodsucker latched onto her.

Dammit!

I've never been one to lose control of my wolf like a rogue. The rogue wolves are rare but they happen when a pack member is cast out for a crime, or rebels against the leaders and runs off. It usually drives them crazy being alone like that, and the wolf takes total control. Now, seeing this girl with her body under attack by a flippin' *bruxsa*... I can sympathize with the rogues for the first time in my life.

I grab the disgusting bruxsa demon by her stringy gray hair and throw her against a tree trunk. She's not an actual woman, just an ancient type of demon shifter, and it's not my first encounter with the type. They're nasty creatures born as sickly birds and they grow to be able to shift from owl or bat to a human form, preying on people for their blood.

I can feel myself shaking from anger as I watch the bruxsa shift and fly into the woods. My wolf growls inside of me, and when I turn around to the bleeding girl at my feet, I'm pissed and borderline feral.

She could've been killed.

"What the hell are you doing out here all alone?" I don't mean to yell at her, but my temper has a mind of its own, and I'm right on the edge of losing it.

Her hazel eyes are wet with unshed tears, but her fear and sadness morphs into rage in seconds. She blinks up at me, peering through long eyelashes and then she gets to her feet shakily, holding her head high in a show of dominance. If her human scent wasn't so strong, I'd swear she was a wolf.

"Excuse me? I don't even know you!" Her voice is strong and melodic as she yells the words at me while she wobbles on her feet, weak from blood loss.

I hold my stance, still having to press my wolf back. I can't reach out to her while I'm feeling this way.

I have never felt so out of control before, and shifting now won't help anything. "I'm the guy who just saved your life. A thank you would be nice."

She scoffs with an angry half-smile and flips her long white hair over her shoulder, covering the bite mark. "You're a freakin' psycho. You think you can just glare at me back there, and then follow me into the woods like some stalker, then save me from whatever the hell that thing was, and now I'm supposed to, what? Bow at your feet?"

Maybe she's not so fragile after all. I shake my head at her. "I wasn't stalking you, Snow! I was protecting you! Do you honestly not know how important your blood is, and then you go and let some bruxsa demon steal it from you?"

Her thin eyebrows press together and she looks at me like I'm the crazy one. "Did you just call me Snow? What does that even mean?"

I look at her long white hair and point to it. "Yeah, Snow White. Considering the white hair and the princess attitude."

Her mouth falls open in shock and she clenches her small fists. *She wouldn't try to punch me, would she?* "I'm *not* a princess, and I can say with a hundred percent certainty that I have no clue what you're talking about. I've never heard of a *bruxsa* in my life, and what on earth does my blood have to do with anything? A vampire attack wasn't on my list of to-dos today, asshole!"

Seriously? I look at her, sure she's being sarcastic, but I only find honesty in her eyes. "You have absolutely no idea what you are, do you?" Nate never informed me that she hasn't been told about this world. Who would keep this a secret from her, and why? "Wrong species, *Snow*. At least a vamp would've been a little better company than that thing."

She crosses her arms defiantly and shakes her head as she rubs at the bite mark on her neck. Her hand comes away, covered in blood and she watches it with wide eyes before quickly wiping her hand along her pants and tightening her lips in an angry line. I want to reach out and help her with the pain somehow, but I can see that she doesn't trust me. I clench my fists by my sides, my wolf finally settling down. I open my mouth to apologize for being an ass, but she holds up a red-stained hand to stop me.

She sounds defeated when she speaks. "This has been a real fun nightmare, but I'm going to go home now. Thanks for saving me from the not-vampire thing." She pauses and stares into my eyes, her hand still in the air. "And if I ever have the unfortunate *pleasure* of seeing you again, don't call me Snow."

And with that, she spins her hand around to flip me off and turns to run home. Definitely not a damsel in distress. *And, damn, why was that so incredibly sexy?*

Chapter 3

◇◇◇

Maia

OKAY. SO, A BRUXSA DEMON, or so *he* called it, just attacked me in the woods. I can handle this without completely freaking out, right? No big deal at all... Yeah, not happening. My lungs fill and empty in quick spurts as I climb the porch to my house with wobbly legs and bang on the locked door. Dad wasn't expecting me to be back yet, so being the paranoid father that he is, it's no shocker that the doors are locked.

"Dad! Let me in!" My voice is too high, and my knocking becomes quicker and desperate as I imagine that creature flying back to me for more blood. *Oh, please no.*

The door pulls open and my dad looks at me with wide eyes. Oh yeah, I almost forgot about what I must look like with the blood dripping down my neck. "Maia! What happened?"

He grabs me and pulls me into the house, scanning the woods behind us before shutting and relocking the door. Who knew Dad would be right after all of his crazy "dangerous forest" warnings? I let my father hold me in his large arms as I begin to shake.

"Dad, you wouldn't believe what my morning has been like. I was attacked by a bird vampire lady thing and this strange dude saved me, and then yelled at me!" I look into his eyes, and to my surprise, he's *not* surprised. "Did you not hear me?"

His brown eyes are worried and he shushes me, pushing my hair back from my face in his comforting way. He gestures for me to sit on the sofa as a knock comes to the front door. He grabs a tissue from the end table and places it against my neck, putting my hand on top of the bleeding spot. "Hold this here, sweetheart. I'll be right back, so try to lay back and heal."

I just watch him with my mouth hanging open as he goes to answer the door. What is happening right now? Why is my overbearing father *not* being overbearing when he actually has reason to be? He threw a hissy fit over my sprained ankle in the third grade, but not *this*?

I hear whispers coming from the front of the house, but I stay put. The whisper talking continues until footsteps enter the room. I look up at Bree and she stares down at me like I'm a poor little kid that wet her pants in class.

"What're you doing, Bree? You're not going to ask about the bleeding neck wound?" My voice is snarky, but she doesn't crack a smile. She doesn't even flinch.

"Do you want me to be honest, Mai? You're going to be mad." She looks at my dad and then back at me.

I scoff and stand up, feeling a little woozy but pushing past it. "Uh... are you kidding me right now? Since when have you *not* been honest with me?"

She flinches at that, at least. "Well, technically... as long as I've known you." She holds her hands up just as I'm about to lose my crap. "Just, hear us out."

"Us?" I yell the word, officially hysterical.

My dad sits on the couch and pulls me down beside him, his hand staying connected to mine. "Maia. I know this sounds ridiculous, alright? I was in your shoes when I met your mother, though it was a little different. She wasn't a demon, and I wasn't being attacked." He closes his eyes briefly as he mentions my mom who passed away giving birth to me. He never talks about her. "I am so sorry you're confused, and that you got hurt, and I prayed this would never happen, but it was inevitable. You're too special to keep hidden forever, and it's time we talk about it."

I'm beginning to understand why people in stressful situations crave alcohol. I've never had a drink, but I could really use one right now. I try to calm my racing heart and I pull the tissue away from my neck. The bleeding has stopped and I begin to feel a little better.

I sit back so I can look at both Bree and my dad, warring with whether I should start yelling at them, or wait for a clear explanation. "Okay. I'm listening, but I can't promise I won't flip out." *Good, calm and collected.*

Bree nods and pulls out her cellphone. "Good. I'm going to call Nate and Lydia. They'll want to be here for this." She finds the phone number on her screen and hits the call button before leaving the room.

I turn to my dad. "Why would my best friend call my aunt and uncle, Dad?"

He sighs and pats my hand. "Let's just wait for them to arrive, okay? It'll all make sense soon."

I groan and throw my head back against the couch. Nothing makes sense. My uncle Nate and aunt Lydia have always been two of my favorite people. They visit my dad and I a few times a year, always bringing gifts and teaching me new pranks. Uncle Nate and Dad are great friends, and Lydia has always been like a mother to me. She treats me like the child she never had. What could they have to say that Dad can't tell me? And why has everyone been lying to me for so long? I could really use that drink right about now.

◊ ◊ ◊

Maia

"Okay, great talk, guys. Real glad we called you over here for this." The sarcasm drips off of me as I cross my arms and lean back against the couch.

I've been sitting in the same place for half an hour with zero answers. After Bree called Uncle Nate and Aunt Lydia over, they were here in less than ten minutes, which is ridiculous because I was under the impression that they don't live nearby. But, hey. What's another lie, right? It's not like they ever invited me over to their house.

Uncle Nate's dark brown eyes narrow at me, and he clicks his tongue. Even though they never had kids, he sure has perfected the dad stare. "Now listen here, Maia. This isn't just a simple get together. I'm struggling to find the right words to gently introduce you to our world."

His forehead creases with worry, and I feel bad for him. "Why is this your job, though?" I look to my dad who stands quietly across the room. "Why can't you just tell me? You are my dad, right?" I gasp as an insane thought comes to mind. "Wait, is Uncle Nate my dad?"

Beside uncle Nate, aunt Lydia bursts into laughter as the rest of the room just watches her with wide eyes. Bree sits to my right and I can hear small giggles from her, but she keeps it under control.

Aunt Lydia reaches across the coffee table and takes my hand in hers. "Oh, hon. You are as white as they come. You do see Nate's skin color, do you not?" She winks at me, a strand of blue hair falling across her face, and I can't help my small smile as I shake my head.

I look over at my dark uncle, and she has a point. I roll my eyes and scoff. "Okay, but I'm still really confused."

Lydia pats my hand before releasing it, and I sigh from the motherly comfort she always gives me. "Since these boys seem a little slow at getting to the point today, why don't I begin?" She looks over and Nate nods to her to continue. *Odd.* "Your mother, Jade, was my best friend in the world. She and I grew up in a large community of individuals that live in the wilderness, surviving off the land."

"You guys were hippies?"

She smiles at that. "I'd say yes, but much more than that. Have you ever heard of werewolves?"

My eyebrows shoot up. Who hasn't heard of werewolves? "Of course. What about them?"

"Well, they're real, although they are not known as werewolves in their community. Instead, we are called wolf shifters." Her eyes shift to black and then back to their normal blue.

Wait, what?

"Uh... aunt Lydia. Did you just say *we*? As in, *you* are a wolf shifter?"

She nods easily, not at all concerned about how I'll react. "Yes, darling. I am a wolf shifter, and your Uncle Nate is a wolf shifter, our alpha leader to be exact." She smiles lovingly at him, and he returns her sweet smile.

Uncle Nate's eyes fall on me again and he clears his throat. "Maia, your mother was a wolf shifter, as well. She was a very strong one, too."

I want to say they're crazy and I don't believe a word, but it wouldn't be true. Somehow, I actually do believe what they're saying, so maybe I'm crazier than I thought. I did just get attacked by some bloodsucking owl lady, so wolf shifters can't be all that far off.

I nod my head, trying to accept the idea that my loved ones are supernatural beings. I look toward my dad, still standing against the far wall with his arms crossed. "Dad. What about you? Are you not a wolf shifter?"

His face is sad as he responds. "Nope. I only found out about them when I came across a beautiful wolf in the woods with bright jade eyes." He smiles softly at the memory of my mother. "However shocked you are right now, you have no idea until you see it with your eyes, baby girl."

What am I then?

I look back at Bree and she is sitting so still. She sighs and then raises her hand like a kid in school. "I'm a witch. I figured you'd ask, so there ya go."

My mouth drops open and I look her up and down, even though I've looked at her a thousand times in my life already. "Excuse me? You're a what now?"

She smiles and shakes her head, as if I exasperate her. "W-I-T-C-H," she says each letter slowly. "Witch, Maia. It's pretty much what you'd see on the Vampire Diaries. Pretty spot on, other than all of the creepy sacrificial stuff."

I close my eyes, trying to wake myself up from this trippy dream, but when they open again, everyone is still staring at me. The two wolf shifters, the witch, and my human father. *How is this my life?*

"Proof. Show me some proof." I look at everyone individually, and Uncle Nate is the one who stands.

"Okay, Maia. I'll give you some proof if it'll make you understand." He closes his eyes briefly, and when he opens them again, they are completely black, just like the guy's eyes from the woods.

He flexes his large shoulders and all along his arms, black hair grows long, and sharp claws stretch out from his fingertips. His eyes fall on me, and his lips curl up in a snarl. Razor sharp teeth shine back at me and I gasp. With the sound of my gasp, Uncle Nate shifts back to just a man standing before me.

He kneels in front of me and takes my hands. "I'm sorry if I scared you, Maia. But do you understand now?"

I nod slowly, and a heavy breath fills my lungs before I let it out, along with all of my calm. I push away from Nate and stand abruptly. "I do understand." My voice is too high, filled with panic. "I'm one of you, aren't I? This is why I was attacked, and why you guys are here?"

My dad comes to me then, his loving eyes filled with the worry that I know so well. "Maia, you are half human, and half wolf shifter. The reason we never told you is because you are the only one of your kind."

The only one? That's incredibly lonely. I step away from my dad, and I run into my bedroom, done with it all. The door slams behind me, and I finally break.

Chapter 4

✧✧✧

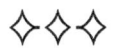

Seth

I CAN HEAR HER CRYING, but why does it bother me so damn much? I didn't have much of a choice but to follow her back home. I couldn't let her get attacked all over again, especially because she clearly doesn't know what she is. She has been lied to her whole life, and for some reason, I actually care.

How did this assignment become personal so quickly? The small whimpering cries don't help, that's for sure. I can smell alpha Nate inside. After he arrived at the house, I started to listen in. I know it's not all that ethical, but if I am to be alpha one day, I need to be in the know. Turns out, Snow White is actually named Maia, and she isn't all human like I had thought. I don't understand how a shifter can have the cure in their blood and still be alive, but I'm beginning to realize that there are a lot of secrets.

And why hadn't I just asked her name before stalking her? I'm a little backwards, I guess.

It's a struggle just sitting out here on this log, staring up at the large white house. It's a beautiful home, and I can see her growing up here. She probably spent her childhood roaming this big backyard and loving the freedoms of a normal human life. Maybe it's a good thing that she never knew about the cure in her blood. Technically, she still doesn't know, and I sure as hell won't be the one to tell her.

◊ ◊ ◊

Maia

Sure, hiding alone in my bedroom for a day isn't exactly the adult way to act, but here I am. Thankfully, the others have all left me alone for the most part. Dad comes in to leave food on my bedside table and smiles sadly at me before leaving.

My heart hurts from ignoring him like this, but I can't even begin to get into it all with him. It makes no sense to me why I've been lied to all my life. I get that I'm different, half human, half wolf, apparently. But, why is it such an issue? I would've preferred some insight into this bizarre world before getting attacked and then suddenly learning *everything.*

And what about the wolf shifter that followed me into the woods? I'm assuming that's what he is, based on his strong physique and black eyes. I want to find him and ask him what his deal is, but where would I even look?

I throw my head back into my bed, exhausted from no sleep. I've been awake since I got the news yesterday, torturing myself with too many thoughts of betrayal. A knock comes to my bedroom door and I sit up with a groan.

"Yes?" I ask, figuring it's Dad again.

"Can I come in there or are you going to hate me forever?" Bree's light voice makes me smile.

I run over to the door and yank it open. Her auburn curls are loose around her shoulders as she stands slightly shorter than me in a tight, blue knit sweater and waist-high jeans. She is gorgeous as always, the perfect mix of fit but curvy, and I wonder if it's all some witchy mirage. If so, I wish I had that power.

I raise a single eyebrow at her. "I don't hate you, but if I don't let you in, are you going to cast some spell on me?"

Her lips curve up in a wicked grin. "Only if you ask really nicely." She winks, and I can't stop the laugh that bubbles up and out of me.

"Just get in here, witch."

She follows me into the room, shutting the door behind her and pulls me into a tight hug before I can protest. "I love you, Mai. Please don't ever think less of me for what I am. I couldn't imagine life without you."

Bree's plea tugs at my heart and I pull back to see sincerity in her eyes. "Bree, I would never judge you for anything. I'm still not a hundred percent convinced you're an actual witch, but it doesn't matter to me, and it absolutely doesn't affect our friendship one way or the other."

She closes her eyes for a second and nods with a sigh. "Oh, thank the goddess!"

I sit back on my bed as she plops down onto my fluffy rug. "The lying, though. That's what's getting to me, Bree. Why couldn't you ever tell me? And how long have you known my aunt and uncle so well?"

She grimaces. "Right, the years of constant lying. Makes sense... Well, first of all, it was my grandmother's idea for me to meet you. She is the priestess of our coven, and the one that told me to keep the supernatural world a secret from you."

"So, we didn't even become friends organically? It was a set-up?" *Sheesh.*

Bree's eyes go wide as she shakes her head. "No, no, no! I was placed in your school to become your protector. I never had to be your friend, let alone your best friend, but I felt a connection with you. I *wanted* to be around you, and cause trouble with you, and talk boy talk with you. All of that was plain old friendship, no lying."

Her words calm my stress a little, but not totally. "Do I really need a protector? You were just a kid, too."

She nods. "It's pretty common for witches to form bonds at a young age with a special human, and then grow to become their protector. Now, a witch protecting a shifter isn't exactly heard of, but you aren't normal, as you know. Nobody was sure what you'd become, or if you even needed protecting." She pauses to gauge my reaction. "And to answer your other question, I didn't meet Alpha Nate or Luna Lydia until I was twelve. A witch comes into her power at the start of puberty, and my grandmother decided to introduce me to your pack, or… your mom's pack I guess. Gram said I needed to understand the shifter world in order to fully understand you."

I rub my temples. "Okay, so my aunt and uncle are actually alpha and luna of a pack of wolves, my BFF is my protector witch, and I'm some human slash shifter hybrid." Totally normal. "I know this is probably a stupid question, but why do I need protecting? Why would anyone be after a half-breed like me? That guy who saved me in the woods said my blood was important, but why mine?"

Her eyebrows shoot up. "Some guy saved you in the woods *and* talked about your blood? I'm gonna need to hear this story!" I can tell she's deliberately changing the subject. She still doesn't want to tell me everything, and it hurts. I bet if I asked that stalker guy, he'd tell me. He seemed to have no qualms about being honest.

I shake my head, clearing the guy's perfect face from my mind. "I'm thinking he was a wolf shifter, but I don't know for sure. He followed me from the coffee shop and then threw that bruxsa thing off of me." It was stupidly heroic.

She thinks for a moment and then holds a finger up. "Ooh. I bet Nate sent him to keep an eye on you. I know when you turned eighteen your wolf side was supposed to be stronger, so he was worried that others would discover what you are."

"And again, why exactly is being a half-shifter so important? I just don't get it, Bree." If anything, I shouldn't be on anyone's radar at all. Bree clams up again and looks down at her feet, so I change the subject for her. Hopefully, she'll talk when she's ready. "I'm done talking about this. What I really want to do is see you cast a spell!"

I wiggle my eyebrows and Bree's face lights up. "Yes! I've been practicing one, but I'd *love* to try it with you! It's a body switch spell." She rubs her hands together, excited.

I pull my chin back and grimace. *Why did I ask to see a spell?* "Uh... will it hurt? Is it dangerous?"

Bree shakes her head. "Not at all! If anything, it just won't work or last very long."

I sigh and wave a hand at myself. "Fine. Hit me with it, witch." I've never been one to shy away from adventure, though adventure isn't something I get handed to me often.

She giggles and kneels in front of me, taking both of my hands in hers. Her eyes close and I follow suit. It seems right for the moment. She whispers something in what sounds like an ancient language, maybe Latin, and her hands begin to heat up around mine.

Something in the air shifts, and Bree's voice breaks the silence. "Yay! It worked! Open your eyes, Mai."

I slowly open one eye, and then the other. *Holy crap on a cracker!* I'm staring back at myself, where Bree was only moments ago. The Maia copy is giving me a big toothy grin and she looks down at her, or *my* body.

When my clone's mouth opens, Bree's voice comes out and I about faint. "Do I look just like you, Mai? You look awesome! Let's go see!"

She jumps up and runs over to the full-length mirror across my room. I follow after her and when I stand in front of my reflection, I'm looking back at Bree, but *I'm* Bree. *Super trippy.*

"What in the actual hell! Bree, you really are a witch!" My Bree mouth is hanging open, and I touch the red curls hanging around my shoulders. Every detail is exactly Bree.

We actually switched bodies!

I spin to Bree, AKA *me*, and grab her by the shoulders. "I just got the best idea ever! I'm totally going to sneak out as you. Dad won't try to ask me a thousand questions, and I can actually get some fresh air for five minutes! Please, Bree?" I can't even imagine how great it'll be to avoid *that* conversation with Dad.

She shrugs and smiles back at me, rolling her eyes. "You know what, because I'm sorry for all the secrets and I love you so dang much, I'll give you ten minutes of freedom. Don't get yourself into trouble! I have a reputation to uphold." She looks sternly at me after saying the last warning, and I frown.

"Do I really look that pathetic when I try to be tough?"

She laughs and nods. "Absolutely. You're too pretty to look pissed. Now go! I don't know how long this'll last."

I jump up and down on my Bree legs and run out of my bedroom, excited for a few minutes of freedom. When I pass by my dad, sitting in his rocking chair in the front room, I give him a smile and a small wave. I don't want to talk and give myself away, so I hurry out the front door and he just lets me go without a word.

Oh, yeah. Now this is badass.

Chapter 5

✧✧✧

Seth

I'M ABOUT READY TO GO bang down the door to Maia's house. She has been locked in there for the whole night and most of today, and I'm getting anxious. Why would she hide away like that, without a word? Is she even getting any food or water?

Why do I care?

I growl low to myself and push off of the tree I've been leaning against for three hours. This job has had very little excitement so far, other than the bruxsa attack. I don't necessarily want the girl to be attacked, but just sitting here goes against my roaming wolf nature. There has to be something I can do.

I begin to stalk toward her house when a woman I don't recognize steps off the back porch and into the woods. She has curly red hair and way too many piercings for my liking. Her face is lit with a happy smile, and I wonder what's got her so cheery.

The girl's eyes fall on me and I freeze. I look like a creep standing out here in the early evening light. I just hope she doesn't start screaming and alert any enemies. To my surprise, the woman stares at me with a look of recognition and I instinctively look behind me. *No, she's definitely looking at me.*

It dawns on me that this must be the witch who has been charged with Maia's protection. I was warned about her, and told I should be friendly. My anxiety lightens, and I walk up to the witch. Her smell is different from that of the witches I have met in the past, not that there have been many. Still, I have always heard that each species has a distinct smell, but hers is unique, and mixed with the scent that was on Maia this morning. Maybe I was just smelling the witch. They are close friends after all.

"You must be Maia's protector. Is it Bree, of the Stowe coven?" I reach my hand out, and she hesitates before shaking my hand quickly.

Her brows press together before she looks down at her body and then back up at me. "Right. Nice to meet you…" She waits for my name.

"Yeah, sorry. I'm Seth Lowell, alpha heir to the Shaw pack. I've been charged by my alpha to keep an eye on Maia. He believes she may be in danger because of what her blood holds. Were you able to talk to her in there?"

I point toward the house, but my question makes the witch scrunch up her nose. "Do you actually care about Maia's well-being?"

I'm taken aback by her attitude. What'd I ever do to her? Her voice sounds forced, but also incredibly familiar. Something is not right about this witch, other than her being a witch. She's acting jumpy, and her fast heart rate tells me that she's keeping something hidden. I think about her question. Do I care about Maia?

I shrug. "It's my responsibility to care, is it not?"

She rolls her eyes and crosses her arms. "You can't just answer a question with another question, wolf boy."

Wolf boy?

I look her up and down, sure I must've known this girl before. Why else would she act like I'd wronged her in the past? Unless Maia was talking about me with her... I don't even know how to feel about that.

"Listen. I don't know what your problem is with me, but I'm not here to cause problems. I have my orders, and I care about what happens to Maia, okay?" There, I said it, and the words were more true than I thought.

Her angry eyes soften and she steps closer to me, placing her hands on my chest. It feels like a betrayal to have her touching me somehow, but at the same time, her zesty scent is similar to Maia's and the warmth of her touch is soothing. But still, it's not right.

"You know, I could turn you into a toad." Her words are steady, and I know for sure that she's lying now. *What's this chick's problem?*

I swallow hard and step away from the witch. I don't know what she's after, but I'm not playing her game. "I'm sorry, but I think some signals have been misunderstood." I look at her closer, searching her eyes, and I can't shake the feeling of wanting to be closer to her. "Have we met before?"

Her lips tilt up in a smile, but before she can speak, Maia comes running from the house, long white hair flowing behind her, and skin-tight leggings hugging every smooth curve of her hips.

"Maia!" she yells, her hazel eyes panicked. "Maia, run, now!"

She's looking directly at Bree, and my eyes go wide. *Of friggin' course!*

◊ ◊ ◊

Maia

Touching Seth's chest was an instinct. Hearing him say he cared about what happened to me wasn't exactly a confession of love or attraction, or really anything. But it still made me gravitate toward him, and it made my heart race. Plus, being in Bree's body gave me a sense of confidence that I normally don't feel. I'll need to apologize to Bree for sort of hitting on a guy in her body, though.

I didn't expect the hurt I'd feel when Seth looked at me as Bree, with that hooded gaze of attraction. Bree is gorgeous, no doubt, but I want him to look at the real me that way, even if he is a jerk.

Bree, looking like me, runs from my house like a wild chicken out of the coop. Her arms are flailing and she's yelling at me to run, but my brain doesn't catch on to the urgency with how bizarre the situation is. I turn to Seth and he's staring at me with wide brown eyes.

"Snow?" He asks, his head tilting slightly.

I grimace, trying to look apologetic, but my heart stops when his hand comes up to lay gently against my cheek, and his thumb slides along my soft skin. I suck in a sharp breath. His touch is so incredibly tender, and not at all what I expected. It's at this moment that the screeching pierces my ears.

Seth tenses, the muscles in his neck flexing. Bree stops at my side and grabs me by the shoulders. She's herself again and I look down at my own normal body. I look back up at Seth and he's staring at me, eyes wide with worry. *Was he touching me or the Bree version of me?*

"Maia! You need to run, okay? The Bruxsa are coming. At least three of them!" Bree's yelling finally reaches my ears and I gasp.

"How did you know they were coming? I am just now picking up their scent." Seth asks what I'm thinking, his eyes turning black as he clenches his large fists.

Bree scans the woods around us and begins pulling me toward the house. "I get visions. They're close now, so we need to get Maia out of here."

I let Bree pull me through my backyard and up the steps of my porch. "Why are they coming? What do they want?" I'm freaking out now. I don't want more of those freaky owl demon ladies trying to suck my blood again.

I turn to watch Seth as he paces the yard, his eyes scanning the sky. He's on guard, protecting me, and the idea sends warmth through me. "Seth, come with us!" I'm worried about him, even with his bad attitude. He turns to look at me with black eyes, but my heart clenches when the large brown owl dives from the dark sky toward Seth. "Look out!"

My scream makes Seth spin with sharp claws outstretched and he knocks the owl from the air just above him. The creature rolls along the forest floor and shifts as she rights herself. In a second, she is standing on two legs, the same woman that bit into me this morning.

Oh, no.

Fear cripples me, and I can't push myself forward. I didn't know that the attack affected me so much, but I was clearly wrong. Bree grabs me again and tries to break into my foggy mind, but my eyes are locked on Seth's battle with the demon chick.

Seth's back arches and cracks, causing my heart to stop beating momentarily. *He's dying!* A gasp leaves my mouth, but Bree jumps in front of me. "Maia. He's just shifting into his wolf form. He'll be stronger this way, okay?"

She can clearly see that I'm freaked, but nothing could've prepared me for this moment. Seth bends and twists in impossible ways before his clothes rip off of him as his body forms into a large furry black wolf. It's not a gradual change, but fast and *loud*.

He stalks toward the bruxsa with his sharp teeth flashing in the moonlight. Even though Seth's wolf is absolutely terrifying, I'm drawn toward it. No fear fills me while I watch him lunge for the creepy demon lady. Instead, I feel pride for my strong and powerful protector. *So cool.*

My dad's loud grunt brings my attention to the side of the house. To my astonishment, Dad is wielding a long and sleek sword as he battles another skinny pale lady, looking like a twin of the other, but older. He slices through the air like a pro, cutting through the creature's wrist and severing her hand from her body. A sickness fills my belly, but Bree's loud words bring me back to her.

"I'm sorry about this, Mai. I'll find you, alright?"

Bree's words fill my mind, confusing me. "What are you talking about?"

Her eyes are closed and she chants in the same old language she had before when we traded bodies. She lets go of my arms and holds her hands in front of her. The wind picks up around us, and becomes swirls of smoke, spinning around together. In the center of the spinning smoke, a hole forms, showing a separate section of the forest, like a window. Snow doesn't litter the ground here, wherever this new place is, but I can feel the chill just the same.

"What is that place, Bree?" This is a portal to somewhere, as crazy as that sounds. I've seen enough sci-fi movies to know that much.

Bree looks sadly at me, and her eyes land on a scene behind my head. I turn toward the backyard where the wolf-Seth now fights two separate bruxsa ladies. He takes a hit to the snout, and falters. One of the women shifts into an owl and begins clawing at Seth's back with her long talons.

"No, Seth!" I call out for him, worried, but my voice becomes a surprised shriek when Bree pushes me from behind, through the now large portal.

I fall onto my butt, hitting a dirt path in the middle of nowhere, but my eyes look back through the portal at Bree's sorry expression. "Stay hidden, Mai! I'll get you after we secure the house. Please stay safe!"

I try to argue, but a harrowing howl reaches me from the other side of the portal as the circling smoke swirls slam together, leaving just a fading mist in front of me. My breathing is erratic, and I look around the woods that surround me.

"Where the hell am I?" I ask out loud.

"You're in my territory, love. And that's a big problem."

The deep voice makes me jump and I spin to see the tall and lean man looking down at me from only a few yards away. His black hair is flipped perfectly on top of his head, and his pale skin shows every defined muscle beneath the surface. The man licks his lips, and when he smiles, two sharp fangs glisten back at me.

My heart sinks at the sight of him. There's absolutely no way this is happening to me, but somehow, I turned eighteen yesterday, and within twenty four hours, I got stalked by a werewolf, attacked by a bruxsa demon, and thrown through a portal by my witch BFF. *And*, my incredible luck has landed me at the feet of a friggin' vampire? *No, he can't be a vampire, right?*

The pale dude smiles wider, and I blanch. *No way is this dude reading my mind right now!*

His thick British accent practically caresses me as he speaks again. "Sorry, love, but it's true. Your luck is absolute crap."

Chapter 6

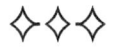

◇◇◇

Maia

I'M FACE TO FACE WITH a bloodsucking vampire. *Just be calm, Maia.* I try to steady my racing heart, but even my training in fighting can't help me in this situation. I mean, it's a real freakin' vampire!

Why does it always have to be something that sucks blood? Can't I ever be attacked by a bunny shifter for goodness sake? Though, this dude is way sexier than my last bloodsucking attacker, the bruxsa. I admire him appreciatively, even though my body is screaming at me to run.

The vamp guy raises an eyebrow as he steps closer to me where I still sit on the forest floor. I landed right on my butt after my bestie, Bree, pushed me through a portal to who-knows-where. Sexy vamp guy leans down, and his face is only inches from mine. His sharp fangs flash at me as he smiles.

Run, Maia! Stop checking the guy out!

"Didn't we already establish that I can read your mind? Will you stop thinking about touching my body? It's incredibly distracting, love."

My eyes go wide and a hot red blush fills my cheeks. *Gosh dang it. That's embarrassing.*

"I... I'm sorry. I can't exactly control my thoughts." I look away from his piercing blue eyes. "If you could just point me in the direction of Stowe, Vermont... that'd just be peachy." I look back at him with a forced smile.

The vamp grins wider and reaches a hand out to me. "You're just adorable, aren't you?" He grabs my hand and hauls me to my feet easily. "My name's James, and I'm not going to kill you or drink your blood."

Oh, so a sweet and cuddly British vamp?

James laughs, the rich sound intoxicating as he hears my thoughts. "Something like that," he says and finally releases my hand. "Though, you are on my land, and interrupted my hunt." He inhales my scent and his eyes flash red briefly before returning back to their deep blue. "What are you exactly?"

I run my hands together nervously. I might as well be honest since he can read my mind if I lie. "I'm half human, and half wolf shifter, I guess."

"You guess? Are you unsure?"

I shake my head. "I wasn't told about the supernatural world until... Well, yesterday actually." *Gosh, what a loooong weekend.* "My father is human, and he raised me that way. I just turned eighteen, and for some reason I was attacked by a bruxsa demon. I guess Dad couldn't hide the truth after that."

James scrunches his nose in disgust when I mention the bruxsa demon. "Those demons are revolting. I am sorry you had to endure that." He reaches a pale hand out to stroke my cheek, and his eyes narrow. "Are you sure of who you are? Granted, you're the first half breed I've had the pleasure of meeting, but something is… *off* about you."

I scoff and roll my eyes. "Yeah, you're not the first one to find me strange."

James smiles at that. "There's nothing wrong with *strange,* love. All the best creatures are." He gestures to himself. "Take me for example." He winks.

I can't stop my own smile, and I might just be deranged, but I really like this guy. "Well, I'm Maia. It's surprisingly nice to meet you, James." I look around at the tall trees and thick brush surrounding us. "Do you mind pointing me toward home?"

"You said Stowe, correct?" I nod. "Well, there's a bit of a problem with that. You are just shy of five hundred miles northeast of Stowe. No civilization nearby. How'd you get all the way out here on my land, Maia?"

My face pales. *Five hundred miles northeast?* I'm in Maine! I cover my face with my hands, officially freaking out now. "Why on earth would Bree drop me off in the middle of the Maine wilderness? I'm going to kill that girl!" I growl behind my hands.

I peek through my fingers at James and his eyes are wide. A small, much less cocky smile graces his lips as he begins to nod. "Bree Zoran? The little witch?"

I drop my hands and step closer to James. "Yes! She's my best friend! How do you know Bree?"

James smiles wide now, and he grabs me by the shoulders, lifting me from the ground and into his thick arms. I squeal and push against him, but he's like a stone wall. "What are you doing? Let me go!"

He just laughs and then cradles me like a baby in his arms. "Sorry, love, but if Bree sent you, then it's my duty to see you protected. Hold onto me, now."

I hesitate, but when he lurches forward at the speed of light, I tighten my grip around his neck and bury my face in his neck. He moves us so fast that I can't even take in a breath, and when we stop, I'm gasping for air. *What the hell?*

I jump out of his arms, but immediately regret it as I stumble to the dirt and the world spins around me. It feels like I just spent an hour spinning in a circle and then stopped too quickly. "Holy hell, I'm going to be sick."

James drops beside me and grabs me around the waist. "I'm sorry about that, love. I guess you haven't come into your abilities quite yet."

I groan and close my eyes, fighting back the headache that's threatening me. "I don't have any abilities, James. I'm just a girl."

He chuckles and lifts me from the ground. I'm carried into a building of some sort and James places me on a soft bed. My heart rate picks up and my breath becomes shallow. I'm completely disoriented, with a total stranger in the middle of nowhere... and now I'm on a bed. This is the type of situation that I should *not* be in. *Please don't take advantage of me.*

James growls beside me and then he lets me go. My eyes focus on him as he stands with flexed arms crossed in his tight black shirt. His eyes are narrowed at me and his foot taps angrily. "I'm not going to *rape* you, Maia. Have I given you that impression in the five minutes you've known me?"

Right. Mind-reader.

I shrug. "I've heard that it's always the charming ones, and I really don't know anything about you yet." I feel guilty from judging him so quickly. He knows Bree, and she sent me to him, so he can't be all that bad. "I'm sorry," I mumble, feeling like a jerk.

James kneels in front of me on the wooden floor and I look around the small room. It looks like a log cabin, built by hand. A small fireplace lights the room from the corner, and the furniture is just a desk, a wooden chair, and the bed I sit on with black silk sheets.

Charcoal artwork lines the walls, with drawings of the outside forest, some random beautiful women, and my eyes land on a drawing of Bree maybe a year younger than she is now. A soft smile graces her lips and she looks longingly at nothing in particular. It's a beautiful piece.

James grabs my hands and I'm torn from the drawings, back to him. "I was once a child, just like you were. Then, I became a killer, walking among the dead." I gulp. "I have done unspeakable things, and fought in wars filled with death and trauma. But, like you, I'm not *normal.* You've heard stories of my kind, I'm sure. But, I swear on my *own* grave, love, if the little witch trusts you in my care, I will *never* harm you in any way."

Holy crap.

He stands, releasing me and walks toward the door. "Now, you sleep. At dawn, we leave for Stowe."

Chapter 7

◇◇◇

Seth

BLOOD DRIPS FROM MY wolf's teeth, and I scan the large, manicured yard for any more threats. Maia's father is standing above a dead bruxsa demon, a sister to the one I just killed. His sword hangs limp in his hand as he pants from the fight. The third demon lay split in two large pieces on *and* off the tall porch where I had seen Maia only minutes ago.

But now she's gone?

My wolf growls low, feeling possessive of the girl we only met this morning. *Find.* He rumbles the word in my mind in his usual caveman way, and I agree. *Yes, we need to find her.* My body cracks and shifts back to my human self, and on two feet I run toward the porch, past the bruxsa corpse.

As I reach the top step, my eyes fall on Bree, the witch best friend, Maia's protector. She is unconscious and a large gash in her side is oozing blood. "Dammit!" I shout, and my wolf immediately surges to the surface.

I push him down and crawl over to Bree. She coughs, and looks up at me. "I sent her away. She's safe," she chokes the words out and gasps as a bright glow comes from her wound.

Maia's dad rushes to us and grabs hold of Bree, pulling her onto his body. "It's alright, Bree. I've got you. Just don't fight the healing."

The healing?

I stare at her wound as it continues to glow and slowly knit itself back together. "How's she doing that?"

Maia's dad looks at me with worried eyes. "Her grandmother has strong healing magic. She puts shields on her descendants so they can be healed when injured. Thankfully, this injury wasn't worse or it might not be working." He pulls Bree closer as she groans against the healing. "You must be Seth Lowell, the wolf protector? You're completely naked, son."

I nod, not needing to look down at my body to know he's right. "Yeah, sorry. It's kind of a hazard of the job. Are we sure Maia is alright?" I don't care that I'm naked. I'm starting to panic. The bleeding-to-death witch says Maia is safe, but how? Where is she?

The man tilts his head, watching me curiously. "I'm Mathew. Thank you for your protection, but if Bree says she sent Maia somewhere safe, then I believe her. We'll have to wait until she is healed before we can find out where, though." His dark eyes are sad for his daughter. This man, Mathew, is surprisingly calm for a human faced with the supernatural. I can see Maia's bravado in him.

How have I only known this girl for a day and I can't clear my mind of her for even a second? I need to find her. I look down at Bree, but she is unconscious again as her body heals. Finding Maia will need to wait.

◊◊◊

Maia

I toss and turn all night in James' bed. I need to know if my family is okay. Last I saw of Dad, he was fighting the bruxsa with a sword, and it looked like he was winning. *Gah, I hope he won.*

And then there was Seth in his wolf form. He was so incredibly powerful, and I bet he could take down any creature. Still, I can't help the pang in my gut at the thought of him being hurt. And as for Bree, I'm mad at her for pushing me away when I could've tried to help. Maybe I'm too frail to battle demon creatures, but I don't need to be forced away. I want to see them all again.

"Hey, love. Would you like some breakfast?" James stands at the door to the small cabin. His mouth is curved in a half smile and he has a plate in his hands, piled high with fried eggs.

I run my fingers through my tangled hair. *Stop trying to look cute for the vampire!* I yell at myself in my mind and then my eyes bug out when I remember he can hear my thoughts. I look up at James and his cocky smile is back, fangs aglow in the orange firelight.

I smack my hand over my forehead and silently curse at my girlish thoughts. "Thanks, James. I'd love some breakfast," I murmur through clenched teeth.

He laughs and brings me the plate of still steaming eggs along with a wood-carved fork. "Don't worry about your thoughts, love. I've heard things that can't even be repeated in a lady's presence. Your thoughts are refreshingly tame."

I shake my head, taking a bite of the delicious food. I hadn't realized how hungry I was until this moment. "I'm just sorry you're stuck hearing everyone's inner rambling. Isn't it exhausting?"

He sighs. "Why do you think I built a little cabin in the middle of nowhere? No people out here..." He eyes me, "Well, normally."

I take another bite of the breakfast and moan appreciatively. "Where did you get eggs all the way out here?" I probably should've questioned the eggs before digging in, but what's done is done.

James sits beside me on the bed, very close. "You've never had wild turkey eggs before? I hear they're just like chicken eggs." His eyes follow the food to my mouth and focus on my lips as I chew.

I lick my lips. "Are you not going to eat?"

He smiles again, his blue eyes finding mine. "I'm on a... *special* diet." His eyes flick to my throat as I swallow. They flash red and then back to blue, so fast I feel like I imagined it.

I nod in understanding. "Oh, right. I'm in the home of a blood sucking vampire in the middle of the woods... eating wild turkey eggs." *You can't make this crap up.*

James laughs and stands from the bed. "The sun is rising now. Should we head out, love?"

Love. I'm really starting to like that. Yeah, I know you can hear me, so shut it.

I roll my eyes at his wicked grin. "You're not going to carry me at lightning speed again, are you?"

He shakes his head. "It would get us there significantly faster, but I don't believe your human body could handle it. We'll simply hike toward civilization and then borrow a car."

Relief fills me. "Good, 'cause that sucked." I stand from the bed and grab my leather jacket from the bedpost. I start to imagine the loneliness James must feel out here, but I hurry and try to change my thoughts so I don't offend him.

He grabs my hand, his skin cold against mine. "If you're so worried about me being lonely, love, then you can stay longer and keep my bed warm." His eyes lock onto mine and he stands in front of me with a hooded gaze.

My breath hitches and I stutter. "I... I should get back to my family." *How is he so good at making me flustered?*

James leans in closer to me. "As you wish, love," he says smoothly, his gaze falling to my parted lips. *It's gotta be the accent, right?*

I try to imagine his lips touching mine, and to my astonishment, it's Seth's face that flashes through my mind. His brown eyes fill my thoughts instead of James' blue ones. *What the heck?*

James' eyebrows raise and he leans away from me. "Well, that's a mood killer, isn't it? How can I possibly kiss you now with some other bloke's face in your head?" He tsks and shrugs. "And I was sure we'd have something good here."

He winks with a disappointed smile and pulls me toward the door, thoughts of kissing thrown out the window. We exit through the front door while Seth's face continues to fill my mind, and I slam into James' back when we reach the cool morning air outside.

"Owww! What the..." I start to protest, but when I look past James, there's Seth, in the flesh. And he's about to shift into a wolf.

Chapter 8

◇◇◇

Seth

I STARE AT BREE, her wound completely healed now, at least outwardly. She should be waking up. A wolf can normally smell injury, but hers is gone now. "Why isn't she waking up?" I growl the words into the large living room area of Maia's house.

Mathew steps to my side and hands me a warm cup of coffee. "Here. She just needs rest."

I nod and mutter a thanks, but I can't stop staring at Bree. As soon as her eyes open, I'm going to demand to know where she sent Maia. The waiting is torture. It has been eight hours since the fight with the bruxsa demons. Mathew carried Bree into the house and laid her out on a sectional couch after she passed out on the porch. He then offered me some clothes, which I gratefully accepted.

Mathew and I cleaned up the dead bodies in his yard and burned them in a bonfire. I have a lot of questions about the man's knowledge of the supernatural, but it doesn't feel right to ask. His daughter is missing, and it was my job to keep her safe. *Gosh, I hope she's safe.*

I've been staring at Bree since then, hoping that every flutter of her eyes is the one when she wakes up. She groans and turns to her side, but continues sleeping. I throw my head back and try to calm my rising wolf. My wolf has been just below the surface, obsessing over finding Maia.

Mathew nudges my arm gently. "You haven't slept and it's nearly sunrise. You need sleep as much as the rest of us."

I sigh and close my eyes. "I know. I just can't stop worrying. What if she's lost and scared?" There's no hiding the whine in my voice.

I open my eyes again and Mathew is staring at me with his eyebrows pressed together. "It seems like you care an awful lot about my daughter. You understand what's inside of her, right?"

What does that mean!? I nod. "Well, yeah. She has the shifter cure inside of her blood."

Mathew shakes his head and sighs. "She doesn't just have the cure inside of her blood, Seth. Maia's blood *is* the cure. She so much as bleeds on your wounds, and you die."

My heart sinks at that thought. How can I truly protect her if I have to be so careful with her blood? Just last night I had open wounds all over my body from fighting the creatures who are after Maia's blood.

Would I have been unable to save her at that point if she was bleeding?

A small groan pulls my attention back to Bree. She turns onto her back and her eyes open, scanning her surroundings. I rush to her side with Mathew. Bree looks at us worrying over her and her eyes go wide.

"Oh my goddess! How long have I been out?" She sits up fast, not even getting dizzy in the process. *Wow. Go witchy grandma.* The healing spell worked wonders.

Mathew feels her forehead and grabs her wrist as he counts her pulse. "You slept all night. It's just about sunrise."

Bree smacks her head and looks at me with sorry eyes. "I sent Maia to Maine. I have a vampire friend there who I trust with my life. She is safe with him, I'm sure of it."

My jaw tightens and I bite my teeth together hard to keep from sprouting fur in the middle of the living room. "A *vampire?*" I practically shout at her through my teeth. Vampires are known to be seductive and lure women in with charm so they can drink from them. Why would Bree send her to one of *them?*

Bree glares at me. "Yes, a *vampire.* I'm not stupid, wolf. I know this vampire personally and he doesn't drink from humans." Her narrowed eyes are steady and I have no choice but to trust her decision.

"Fine. Send me there and I'll bring her back." It's a command from me, and I can't help the alpha voice that comes out. She doesn't deserve to get snapped at, but I'm about to lose it.

Bree sits higher and closes her eyes. She begins chanting some words and waving her arms in the air. Her body is strong after the miracle healing, and I can sense her excitement as she uses her magic.

In the center of the room, a circle opens up in the air, a window to another world; Maine apparently. As soon as the door is big enough for me to climb through, I don't hesitate. I fall to the other side, onto rocky ground, and I can hear Bree's heavy panting words just before the portal closes again.

"My power is depleted. Just bring her home."

◊ ◊ ◊

Maia

"Snow." Seth's voice is low as he uses his pet name for me. His dark brown eyes are locked onto my hand where it's wrapped tightly in James'. Fur ripples down his arms and disappears like a wave crashing back into the sea. I try to wrench my hand free but James keeps it in his grasp.

"Stay back, love. There's a wolf out here and he looks murderous." James glances back at me but stays put, guarding me.

Seth growls, the sound menacing and deep. "Let her go, bloodsucker. She's *my* charge." Seth's voice isn't entirely human, causing my knees to shake. Anger rolls through me at Seth's possessive claim but I tamp it down.

James laughs and then pulls me to his side. "I do believe she can make her own choices, chap. She hasn't needed you while she's been here with me *all* night."

My mouth drops open. *What is he doing?!*

Seth starts to shake and black flashes across his eyes. *Oh, damn.* I finally pull my hand free from James and step closer to Seth. I hold my hands up trying to calm his anger. I don't know what has him so wolfish, but I can't let him try to hurt James. Even though he probably deserves it after goading him like that.

"Seth, I'm fine, okay? Calm down. James has kept me safe." I step closer to him and finally he pries his black eyes from James. They turn brown again and scan my body, maybe for injury.

Seth's breathing slows and he closes his eyes briefly before nodding and sighing. "Good. Now let's go." He grabs onto my hand and drags me behind him, not waiting for my approval.

I dig my heels into the ground and yank my hand out of Seth's. "Excuse me?" I'm mad now. How dare this man grab me and pull me around like a freakin' caveman? If I knew I could get away with it, I'd punch him right in the face.

Seth spins on me with narrowed eyes. "We're going back to my pack where I can keep my eyes on you. I'm *your* protector."

I scoff and cross my arms. "I don't give one tiny piece of crap about your assigned position as my protector, wolf boy! I'm grateful for your help and everything you've done for me, but if you try to command me like I'm some little pup under your control, I will not hesitate to kick your wannabe-alpha ass!"

Seth's eyebrows raise, lessening his intense glare and his lips twitch. *Is he about to smile at my admittedly pathetic threat?* I turn to look at James but he's just grinning from ear to ear and leaning against his cabin door like he's taking in a good show.

When my eyes fall on Seth again, my heart flutters at his nearness. He's standing just a foot from me and his hand is clenched in the air between us. "You're right, Snow. I'm sorry, okay? I promised your father and Bree that I'd get you home, but I'll give you a few minutes to say goodbye to the… to *him*."

He swallows hard and then walks a few yards into the forest to wait for me. I take a deep steadying breath and have to pry my eyes away from his large muscular back. Even in the winter cold, he only wears a t-shirt and fitted jeans. *And it's way too sexy.*

I turn back to James and I have to roll my eyes at his stupid, gorgeous, cocky grin. Of course he heard my private thoughts about Seth, and I should be mortified, but I can hardly care anymore. *Stop looking at me like that, vampire.*

I glare at him and he only smiles wider. He steps close to me and grabs both of my hands in his cold ones. "Oh, we would've been so good together, love. Too bad your heart is taken."

He whispers the last part so quietly that I almost don't hear it. I shake my head and speak in my mind so Seth doesn't hear. *My heart isn't taken, James. I don't even know him, just like I don't know you.* "Are you not coming with us?" I ask out loud.

James shrugs. "I think it would be best if I stay here. You have a decent guide to get you back home, and I wouldn't do well near humans anyways." He leans into my ear and whispers softly, "Don't believe what the angry wolf says. He's in denial about his feelings, and because I am who I am, to speed things along…"

He pulls back just enough to look into my eyes before his lips crash into mine. His kiss takes me off guard, but I let him press deeper for a moment, feeling the warmth in my belly grow into a flame. The low growl from behind me makes me pull away from James, my breath heavy.

Best kiss I've ever had, I say in my mind, causing James to smile a perfectly happy smile. I've only been kissed twice before, by the same boy at school. Once in eighth grade and again in ninth. The boy eventually decided I was too weird to come back for a third. But kissing James felt like a whole new level of kissing, even if it was only a few seconds.

James looks past me and then stands up straight. "You should get going then, love, before the angry wolf tries to kill me." He raises a single eyebrow and then turns me toward Seth's death glare. *Can a wolf shifter kill a vampire? Best I don't stay to find out.*

Chapter 9

✧✧✧

Maia

WELL, HE'S MAD AGAIN, of course. I don't know how Seth can be constantly seething with anger, but it must be a wolf thing. I've always had a temper, but Seth's is far beyond my own. He stalks ahead of me, hiking easily through the woods.

I'm not bad at keeping up, but he's purposely making me fight to stay on his tail. "Do you even know where we're going?" I call after him and he just grunts as he continues forward.

We've been traveling west for at least five hours and all I've gotten from him is a couple of grunts and shouts for me to keep up. He'd make a sucky trail guide, probably leaving the elderly behind for slowing him down.

I'm crashing now, having only had small amounts of water from the streams in the area, and no food since the turkey eggs. I shout for Seth to stop, but he keeps moving forward so I stomp my foot and sit on a nearby log.

Stupid alpha jerk.

If he really does care about my well-being he'll just have to backtrack to find me. "I'm still half human, your highness!" I yell in his direction and lay my head in my hands.

Footsteps approach me and I snap my head up to see a predictable sight: Seth glaring down at me. "Oh, look. You do care," I say with a sickening sweetness.

He rolls his eyes and sits beside me on the thick downed trunk. Silence floats in the air between us, wanting to drive me crazy. I gather up my wild locks of white hair into the hair tie I keep on my wrist, tying it tightly.

I'm about to freak out from the quiet tension when Seth speaks softly. "Why'd you let that walking dead creep kiss you, Snow?"

I snap my head toward him and he's looking sadly at the ground, his broad shoulders slumped forward. I click my tongue, figuring I should take the conversation when it's given.

"James isn't a creep. He's charming, thoughtful, and kind, unlike… others." My jab at Seth's attitude is clear.

He finally looks my way, his eyes apologetic. "You're right. I've been a total ass from minute one." He rubs a large hand over his strong jaw. "I don't know how to do this, Snow."

I shrug. "How to do what? Converse politely with strangers?" I tease him and an actual smile tugs gently at his plump lips.

He nods. "Yeah, let's go with that." He chuckles quietly, his smile filling my heart with warmth.

It's quiet again for a minute, but I break the silence this time. "James is a good guy, but he's not really my type."

Seth raises an eyebrow. "What *is* your type then?"

I can feel a blush crawl up my neck as I think about what my type is. Amazingly, my type is exactly Seth, minus the attitude. But will I say that? Absolutely not. Instead, I force myself to look away from him.

"James is too cold. I guess I like… warmth." My eyes find him again and he's staring at my lips as I lick them. *Keep it together, Mai.* "And, you know. Tall, dark, hot, and rich. The four must-haves of any perfect man." I smile so he can see that I'm joking.

He smiles wide this time, and, holy cow, it is hot. He nods. "Funny. Those are the four must-haves for the perfect woman, as well." He laughs at his own joke and I shake my head at him.

"Har har," I fake laugh and shove him in the shoulder.

In an instant, he grabs the hand that just shoved him and he pulls me to my feet, so that my chest is pressed up against his. I suck in a sharp breath and I breathe in his piney scent. *Yup. Sexy Christmas tree.*

I glance up at Seth's face and he's looking out into the woods with his eyes narrowed. He sniffs the air and I can feel his entire body tense. *Please don't be a bruxsa demon!*

"What…" My words are cut off as Seth shushes me. His arms tighten around me and he spins his head to the left.

"You need to run, Snow." He looks desperately into my eyes. "Now."

Seth moves me so my body is behind him, so easily that I don't even see it happen. I finally decide to listen to his commands and I start to run, but every part of me stills when I see the incoming threat. A massive friggin' bear! I gasp and stare as the bear stands on its hind legs and growls a deep and breathy snort sound. Then it lands on all four paws, shaking the ground from the heavy force of its weight.

Seth's body starts sprouting fur and his bones crack. "Go!" he yells at me in an animalistic voice.

That snaps me out of my fog and I begin running in the same direction we'd been headed earlier. I run as fast and as far as I can while the sounds of growling and crashing bodies begin to fade with each step. A loud howl pierces the air and I slow my pace. *Was that a pained howl, or a triumphant one?*

I curse my father under my breath for not letting me experience the wolf shifter world. I feel so confused and lost. Another howl reaches me. *Definitely pain.* I spin around, ready to go head-to-head with a bear in order to help Seth, as idiotic as the thought may seem. Before I make it even three steps, I fall to the ground as I trip over something. It's not dark outside, so how did I not see whatever that was?

I look down at my ankles and my foot is caught up in a tripwire. *What on earth?* Who would put a tripwire in the middle of the woods? Before I can think too much about it, a cloud of dust explodes in my face and I scream before feeling dizzy and blacking out completely.

◊ ◊ ◊

Seth

When Maia told me that she was attracted to warmth, I could feel my entire body want to reach out to hers and bathe her in *my* warmth. Was she hinting at me with that statement? Wolves are warmer than humans, but the look in her eyes could've just been in my imagination. *Wishful thinking?*

I wanted to lean into her and take her beautiful lips between my teeth. I could hear her racing heart as we spoke, and I wanted to erase that vampire's taste from her mouth. I wanted her to only know the taste of me. I might just be a little obsessed with the half-breed princess that drives me crazy.

I pulled her scent into myself at the same time that a new scent approached us where we rested. I knew that smell, though it wasn't something I was used to. And though I wanted to keep her safe in my arms, fighting a bear shifter has to be done with the whole body.

I only hoped that telling Maia to run was the right choice. Anything better than letting a bear shifter get a hold of her. They're a ruthless species that would discover the cure in her blood and do anything to keep it for themselves. Hearing her small footsteps run away from the danger made my heart instantly lighter as I allowed my wolf to come forward and face the massive bear.

He charged me instantly, no hesitations, typical of his kind. I was ready for that, though. My wolf is good in a fight, and our minds mingled together makes us a lethal pair. I dove to the right, letting the bear stumble past, and then I spun to dig my teeth into his side.

He roared against the bite, but was stronger than I anticipated, so he rolled his body onto mine, breaking at least three bones in the process. My wolf howled into the air before wiggling out from beneath the heavy creature.

Kill. My wolf spoke only one word in my mind. He never said more than what you'd expect from a caveman learning English, but I understood completely.

Yes, kill. I agreed.

The bear slammed his head into my side, making me howl again before spinning on him with speed and agility, and finding my mark on his thick neck. My large canines sank into his throat, killing him in only seconds as my mouth filled with blood.

I sat back on my haunches, resting momentarily before I could go and find Maia. Then her piercing scream filled my soul like a knife into my chest. *No, no, no, no!*

***

Now I'm running on all fours through the trees, tracking Maia's zesty scent. She is close, but something is carrying her, unless she's running that fast. Her scent moves fast through the woods, too fast for a human. My wolf ears perk up as I listen to the forest, and I can hear multiple heartbeats and rustling in the trees.

Bingo.

I spin to the left and I spot the glowing person that has Maia thrown over her shoulder, unconscious. They're gliding above the ground, being carried by a small pair of flickering wings. It's a *faerie*! I've never seen one before but I've heard of their luminescent glow, paper-like wings, and knowledge of the wild.

Save her! My wolf shouts in my mind. He cares about her as much as I do. I obey his command and together we dive for the back of the female faerie, but another faerie slams into my side.

I roll along the ground, and the male faerie looks down at me with narrowed neon green eyes. "Stay down, wolf!"

A low growl leaves my wolf's mouth and I call upon the shift so I can speak to the new threat. Growls and snorts won't do any good against their kind. They have magic, where my wolf only has brute force.

I'll save her. Don't worry. I calm my wolf as I pull him back into myself and my body contorts until I'm standing on my two human legs again. Before I can get a word out, the male faerie throws a shawl at me so I can cover myself.

"Thank you," I say, trying to show kindness in order to bargain for Maia's freedom. I look at the female who still carries Maia like a doll over her shoulder. "Please, I need her back. I'm her protector."

The woman flicks her purple hair over her shoulder and looks over at her companion like he is a complete idiot. Whoever this chick is, she's clearly the leader. "Wilk. I was not aware that she had a protector."

The male faerie, Wilk, nods to the woman and looks back to me. He floats back to the ground and sticks a hand out for me to shake. "We are most sorry, wolf. My sister, Evin, and I came upon this woman as she was encroaching on our land. I could see that she was not a human, but I am unsure of her exact species. I thought we should take her back to our camp for investigation."

Investigation? I don't know what the faeries think Maia is, but to a wolf she seems just like a human. The cure in her blood blocks her wolf side, and the white hair makes her stand out. I can only imagine what it was like for her growing up.

I nod to Wilk. "Her father is human, but her mother was a wolf shifter. I can see the confusion, but she wasn't trying to intrude. She likely doesn't even know your kind exists. I was just returning her back to her home which is a long journey from here."

His eyebrows raise and his pale skin seems to glow brighter as he looks back at his sister. "That is so cool," he says, suddenly sounding like a human teenager and less proper than before. The female, Evin, glares at her clearly younger brother and he straightens up again. "I am sorry. Please come back to our camp and let my family feed you a proper meal before sending you on your journey."

I hesitate, but Maia's limp body makes my choice for me. I don't want to make enemies while I don't have Maia in my arms. I need to get her back. I nod to both faeries, and Wilk smiles brightly.

"Great!" He shouts and a dozen more faeries appear from behind trees and from the air. They had me surrounded, and thank all that is holy that I didn't try to attack.

Chapter 10

✧✧✧

Maia

MY EYES FEEL HEAVY AS I force them open. I'm staring at the ground, and I'm being carried by... *a glowing body?* I must be dreaming, because the green leather-bound legs in front of my face are glowing and floating above the ground. *Definitely dreaming.*

I turn my head to the right and see a half-naked Seth walking quietly beside me. His eyes meet mine and I can see him visibly sigh, but a finger comes to his lips, warning me to stay quiet. Fear fills me, and I close my eyes again. I'm actually floating in someone's arms, and they are definitely glowing.

"Would you mind if I carry her, ma'am? I am her protector and more than happy to help you lighten your load." Seth's voice is calm and collected as he speaks to whoever has me.

A boy's voice comes from somewhere ahead of us. "I will watch him, Evin. We are nearly home anyways."

The boy's words must've convinced the Evin person, because she lifts me easily off her shoulder and lays me in Seth's arms. Warmth covers me as Seth holds me close to his bare chest, and I try not to audibly sigh.

I draw his scent into my nose and have to hold myself back from licking his skin where my face rests. *Why does he have to be shirtless?*

"We are here," someone calls, a man's voice that I haven't heard yet.

I peek one eye open to see multiple beautiful, glowing people floating in two lines, creating an aisle that another one of them walks between. They all have small dragonfly-like wings on their backs and skin-tight bodysuits that cover their bodies like armor. The woman in the middle has long purple hair and pointed ears that stick out through her glowing locks. *What are these people?*

Unlike the three bruxsa chicks and one vampire that I've met so far, these supernatural creatures are almost elegant. If I had to guess, I'd say they're real-life faeries. *Freakin' insane!*

Seth carries me between the aisle of faeries, behind the purple haired woman. I watch secretly as she steps through what looks like an invisible jello wall and then she disappears mid-air. *What the frickin' frack is happening?*

I can feel my heart rate pick up, but I try to stay still. Seth hasn't told me to move yet, and I don't want to do anything to get either of us hurt. Seth rubs one of his hands along my back as if soothing me before he, too, steps through the jello wall, and we are suddenly standing beside a small stone city in the middle of the woods.

It looks like one of those ancient cities that is left standing after three thousand years, and I want to explore every last crevice of the magnificent place. It's literally a magic, invisible lost city, and I'm brought back to the story of Atlantis. Never again will I see fairytales as just that again.

Seth stops walking and I close my eyes again as I hear the same boy's voice from before. "You may go into there until she wakes. There are clothes for you to change into and a large bed for the two of you to rest if you need. My guards will be just out here when you are ready to meet us for dinner."

"Thank you for your hospitality," Seth says calmly. He lifts me higher in his arms, and behind my eyelids, I can see us entering a darker area, followed by the sound of a stone door shutting.

I'm laid down on a soft bed and warm fingers brush my hair from my face. "Snow, you can open your eyes now. We're alone."

Heat fills my belly at his words so close to me and when I open my eyes, Seth is leaning over me, his lips only inches from mine. His brown eyes roam over my face and then land on my lips before flicking back up to meet my gaze.

"We're alone?" I ask breathlessly and Seth's eyes darken, but not to black like they do when he shifts.

He nods. "Completely." His body shifts on the bed beside mine, and I can feel more warmth against my side, and his bare abdomen against the skin exposed from where my shirt rides up. "How are you feeling, Snow?"

I swallow hard and then lick my dry lips. "Good. Really good, actually." I know he's asking about how I'm feeling after being knocked out by a dust cloud, but I can only think about how good I feel being so close to him.

His face is lit by a small lantern that hangs on a nearby wall. I look away from him to check out *our* room. The place is decorated beautifully with a large carved waterfall shower on one side and antique furniture along the stone walls. The feeling is very *intimate.* And with him wearing only a shawl of some sort around his waist, the setting is almost too much for my virgin brain to handle.

I look back at Seth and he's still watching me, a small smile tugging at his lips. "The faeries know how to live," he says.

My eyes go wide, even though I already suspected what they are. "So, we're in some kind of faerie encampment? Are faeries a kind of shifter?"

Seth sits up and pulls me to sit beside him, and even though I really liked our horizontal position, I can admire his shirtless body much better from this spot. "This place is more like a city than an encampment. They can move their entire city as they travel." That's something I'd like to see in person.

He continues, "And they are more like witches, if that makes sense. They have magic similar to witches, but they also have wings that they can retract, and they wear their magic on them, making them glow with power. Because of that, they have a hard time blending into human society."

Super flippin' cool.

"Are they dangerous? Clearly they had a problem with me or they wouldn't have knocked me out. Should we be running?" If the faeries aren't friendly, I don't want to sit and chat in their home.

He shrugs. "They're a suspicious group. I don't think they meant to harm you in any way, unless they found you to be a threat. But their city and people stay safe and powerful because they are cautious of outsiders. It's honestly smart of them. I don't see a reason to run just yet. It could just make matters worse, and we don't need faerie enemies."

The thought of an army of magical flying beings hunting us down makes goosebumps rise along my skin. *Yeah, no thanks.*

My eyes flick to the waterfall shower with no shower curtain and then back to Seth. "They uh… don't have any issues with privacy around here, huh?"

He follows my gaze to the shower. "Yeah. I'm pretty sure they thought we were something more than what we are." He looks back to me with a nervous bite of his lower lip.

Something more than what we are? Am I wrong in thinking that we *are* something more?

"Right," I say. "They couldn't have been more wrong." I try to smile, but I'm pretty sure it doesn't quite hit the mark.

I stand from the bed and look away from the gorgeous hunk of man that doesn't see me the way I see him. A wooden dresser sits beside the bed and I rifle through it, digging out a large pair of men's exercise pants and a blue plain t-shirt. I turn and toss the clothes at Seth where he stands watching me. His eyes look sad, but I don't ask. I just need him to get dressed before I make a fool of myself.

"There, I'll go out so you can get dressed. You know, you should really be carrying a backpack with a change of clothes everywhere you go."

I try to step around him, but he grabs onto my arm. "Snow, you should stay here with me. I don't want to lose you again." His eyes meet mine before he adds, "Please."

What happened to the demanding jerk from the past two days? It's crazy, but it would be so much easier to not want to kiss him if he'd stay a jerk. My heart flutters as his hand slides up my arm and rests on my shoulder.

I nod and turn back toward the dresser. "Okay. I'm just going to stare very hard at this dresser then. Go ahead and cover yourself, wolf boy."

I can hear his soft chuckle and the rustling of clothing. He doesn't step further away from me as he dresses and I find it extremely difficult to not glance over my shoulder. I've never even seen a naked man before, nor have I cared to. How am I suddenly this sex-crazed person in a matter of days? It has to be a wolf thing, right?

It's quiet for a moment and I clear my throat. "You done yet or are you primping for prom?" *Oh, man, I'm hilarious.*

All of my teasing falls away as Seth's hard body steps up to stand against my back. As far as I can tell, he's fully clothed, but it doesn't stop my heart from leaping out of my chest at his warmth and nearness. One of his large hands comes up to rest on my waist and I can feel his breath in my ear as his other hand pulls my hair off of my neck and slides it over my opposite shoulder.

"You're not at all what I expected, Maia." He says my name like a caress and I swear his words actually touch the skin of my exposed neck.

The hand on my waist slides across my belly, and even though he isn't pressing, I push my back against him. I hold back the shudder that wants to roll through me when I feel Seth's stubbly cheek graze my neck. If I just turn around, I can press my lips to his. *Would he pull away?*

"Seth," his name leaves my lips in a whisper. I guess my full voice has dropped to my stomach with my heart.

I start to turn toward him, needing to be brave and let him know what I want, but the knock on the door makes me jump away from Seth's body. *So much for being brave, Mai.*

Seth's hands fall to his sides and he doesn't look at me before running to the door and pulling it open. "Yes?" he asks the short, pink-haired faerie girl. Her eyes match her hair and it's absolutely adorable, especially with her long hot pink slip dress. She looks young and has to be no older than my age.

She looks from Seth to me and nods, her small wings twitching. "Dinner is ready, and the king asks that you both attend." She looks back at me again. "Would you like me to confirm your attendance?" *So formal.*

Seth looks at me, and I nod. He smiles down at the beautiful young woman. "We will be there."

She smiles back, showing bright white teeth and deep dimples. "Great. I can lead the way, if you would like."

"Is what we're wearing appropriate for a dinner with a faerie king?" I look down at my black tank top, leather jacket, and black leggings. *Very punk chic, but not formal dinner wear.*

The cute faerie girl looks me up and down and then does the same with Seth. "I can fix that if you wish."

Seth nods to her, and she waves her glowing hand in a small circle. Her glow stretches from her fingertips to wrap around Seth and his outfit shifts from the t-shirt and pants to a forest green blazer over a white buttoned shirt and matching forest green slacks. His feet remain bare, and I realize the faerie doesn't wear shoes either. Not like she needs to, since she can float everywhere.

Seth looks drop dead sexy in his suit, and I have to hold my mouth closed so I don't drool in front of him. I look toward the girl again and she holds her hand out to me, the glow from her fingers stretching to meet me. *I guess it's my turn.*

The air around me tingles and soft fabric rubs against my skin as my clothes change. My long, black leather sleeves become tight, forest green, see-through ones, and my neckline plunges, somehow making my bra unnecessary as the tight green bodice fits firmly against my chest. I gasp as the dress magically lengthens to my feet, and my shoes disappear completely.

The dress matches Seth's suit perfectly and fits me like a second skin. It's also incredibly comfortable, like I could sleep in it and it wouldn't shift and bunch all through the night. *Faerie magic is officially the best thing ever.*

I giggle and twirl in my new digs, and I look back at the girl who is grinning from ear to ear. "Thank you, miss. Your magic is incredible."

She beams at me and bows her head. "You are very welcome, and please call me Qadira. Shall we be going?"

I look up at Seth and his eyes are traveling the length of my body, making him look like a true hungry wolf. When his gaze finds mine, he blinks quickly and clears his throat, looking back at Qadira.

"Yes, thank you, Qadira. Lead the way." I guess it's time for dinner with the faerie king.

Chapter 11

✧✧✧

Seth

I CAN'T BELIEVE I ALMOST kissed her. My body wanted Maia in a way that I have never felt before. It was like an instinct to touch her and smell her hair, her neck. She pressed her back against me and I nearly lost all control. Human women, and even shifter women for that matter, have never held my interests so much.

Though I've shared a few kisses and touches with a few females from my pack, I didn't crave them like I do Maia. I never felt the need to do more than just enjoy their company and then move on and focus on my alpha training. I can't even focus on taking a deep breath when Maia is looking at me.

And holy hell, how did that faerie girl, Qadira know exactly what to dress Maia in to drive me totally mad? I can't have her, though, can I? Even though I feel like my soul wants her as much as I do, she isn't my fated mate, and her blood is toxic to my kind.

Fate must have a hell of a sense of humor to put me in the position to be her protector and never get to make her mine. I can't keep letting my body control my actions. From now on, I need to keep my head straight, and keep Maia at arm's length. *Or maybe multiple arms lengths, just to be safe.*

◊ ◊ ◊

Maia

Walking through the faerie city has me spinning in circles just to take in all of the beauty. The tall buildings weave into nature like they grew together that way. Trees wrap around the stone walls, with flowers and vines giving them vibrant colors. It's a faerie paradise.

Faeries of various colors, shapes, and sizes pop in and out of the buildings. Some smile and wave, while others just stare. They clearly don't get guests often. Seth walks behind me and I follow Qadira into what looks like a large stone pavilion. There is a long wooden dining table in the center, and hanging twinkling lights cover the ceiling.

"It's beautiful," I say quietly, admiring the romantic setting.

Qadira nods. "Fae is a wonderful home for all of us." She looks over at a young man who is approaching us. He's maybe nineteen or twenty, and his neon green eyes are on Qadira. She blushes under his gaze and then bows her head to him. "Prince Wilk. Good evening."

"Good evening, Qadira. You look beautiful tonight." He continues to stare at the girl and I feel the need to give them some privacy, until he finally turns to me and Seth.

He smiles at me and bows his head in my direction, his shoulder-length light green hair falling in his face. "I am glad to see you awake, ma'am. My name is Wilk Arnou, prince of Fae. Thank you for joining us."

He's incredibly handsome with delicate features. For a man, he's actually quite pretty, with his neon green eyes and plump pink lips. Clearly he has Qadira's attention as she stares appreciatively at him. Seth steps beside me and dips his head back to Wilk.

I reach my hand out, not sure what the proper protocol is for meeting a faerie prince. "Thanks. I'm Maia Collins. It's nice to meet you, uh… your highness?"

Wilk's grin spreads and he laughs warmly. "I am not nearly significant enough to be called highness. My eldest sister, Evin, will soon be queen of Fae, and I will forever be a baby brother prince. Please, just Wilk." He winks at me and I instantly like the baby-face prince Wilk.

He grabs my hand and shakes it gently before doing the same with Seth. He smiles wickedly at Seth. "Your mate looks exquisite in her dress. I trust you both found your room comfortable?" There's no mistaking the suggestive gleam in his eye as he looks between us both.

Oh, dear lord. Mate??

Seth makes a choking sound and shakes his head. "I'm sorry, but Maia is my charge. I am not currently mated." *Okaaay.*

Wilk raises his eyebrows in surprise. "Oh, my mistake then." He flashes a knowing look at me and I wonder if he can read my mind like James could.

A loud male voice breaks into my awkward moment and we all turn toward the sound. "Everyone, please sit."

The voice comes from a tall man who looks remarkably similar to Wilk, but probably twice his age and with short dark blue hair. He stands at the head of the table. His wings are larger than the others I've seen and his light blue eyes seem to be all knowing as he watches us gathered around.

Wilk gestures toward a chair for me to sit, and Seth takes the spot to my right. His arm brushes against mine and I force myself not to look into his eyes. A tall, beautiful woman sits across from me, beside the man who must be Wilk's father.

The woman has long purple hair and matching purple eyes. I can see that this is some faerie trend, though the coloring is odd. I reach a hand across the table, putting two and two together. "You must be Evin, Wilk's sister? I'm Maia."

One of her eyebrows raises and she doesn't take my hand. "Yes. It is a pleasure." I don't know what's pleasurable for Princess Cranky Pants, but her face shows zero sign of enjoyment. I just smile and pull my hand back.

The seat to my left is empty so I call Qadira over to sit by me. "Qadira, please sit by me." She remains standing a few feet from the table and looks at the empty chair like she'd never seen such a thing before.

She shakes her head and smiles sadly. "Oh, I am sorry, Maia, but I am only here to serve. I am not permitted at the king's table." Her pink eyes flick toward the man at the head of the table briefly and then at Wilk who still stands beside her.

Wilk gives her a kind smile and she bows her head at him again before walking away. I spot Wilk's eyes trailing after her as she leaves the pavilion, and I wonder what their relationship is. Apparently, she is a servant and Wilk is a prince. I guess that means the same thing in all species.

The king claps his hands together and brings my attention to him as Wilk sits beside his sister. "Well, now that our guests are here, let us eat."

A faerie woman who I haven't met puts a plate in front of the king and then more plates in front of the rest of us. I look down at the dish of vibrant fruits, steaming vegetables, and what looks like cooked pheasant. My mouth waters instantly and I start digging into the delicious meal.

With a full mouth, I look up at the king who stares at me with eyes opened wide. Wilk tries to hide his smile, and his sister's eyes are narrowed at me. Seth's body scoots closer to me in a protective way.

"Uh, Snow." Back to the nickname. "It's customary in faerie culture for the king to take the first bite." I spin toward Seth and his face looks too worried for my liking.

I sit up straight and drop my fork back to the table, swallowing my huge mouthful of food. My eyes land on the large king again. "I am so, so sorry, your highness! I had no idea!"

Silence stretches across the table, until the king of Fae lets out a boisterous laugh. I look at Wilk and he is laughing along with his father while the sister just shakes her head, keeping her eyes narrowed on me. Well, at least I can entertain two of them. Seth smiles beside me, his entire body relaxing.

The king's laughter dies down and he looks at me for a long time, making me squirm under his gaze. "I am Faren Arnou, king of Fae. My subjects call me King Faren, and you are welcome to do so as well. You are a very curious creature, Maia Collins. Is it true that you are half human and half wolf shifter?"

I nod. "That's what I've been told, though I don't see any sign of my wolf side."

King Faren's eyebrows press together. "As a faerie, I can see the magic in others. My son told me that you have magic in you, but only in your blood. I see what he has seen, but I also see the magic of your shifter heritage, though it is dormant. Do you know what that could mean?"

I shake my head, confused, and I look toward Seth. His eyes are closed tight and when they open again, he looks apologetic as he watches me. He turns toward King Faren, his face showing no emotion.

"I am sorry, King Faren, but Maia does not know of the magic in her blood. And, as much as I wish it weren't so, I cannot give you the details either."

My chin jerks back at his words. *What the hell does that mean??* "What are you talking about, Seth?"

King Faren crosses his arms as he looks between me and Seth. "Well, apparently you and I will both be left wondering that very same thing, Maia Collins."

Evin, AKA Princess Cranky Pants, glares at me even deeper, if possible. "Typical. A lower species with secrets."

Seth growls low beside me and I snap my head back to him. He is glaring daggers right back at Evin, and I move my body so I'm partially in front of his line of sight. I need to have a talk with the brat.

"With all due respect, Princess Evin, I am not the one keeping secrets, and if you're suggesting that my protector is of a 'lower' species, you couldn't be more wrong. He has saved my life three times in the past forty-eight hours, where your kind has only succeeded in knocking me out and nicely taking me captive. So far, your idea of lower species sounds pretty damn *high* to me."

Evin's lavender eyes become round saucers and Wilk snorts by her side, spitting out some of his drink in the process. *Yup, I like him a lot.* Seth's hand slides under the table to rest on my thigh and I turn to see his soft smile lighting up my soul. *I like him a lot too.*

Suddenly, I remember King Faren's presence and I turn toward him with my shoulders slightly hunched in fear. To my surprise, the king is smiling just as wide as his son.

"Like I said, Miss Collins. You are a curious creature." He leans forward and stares at my forehead like he's seeing into my mind. "I can see it now. You are more than you think you are. The secret you hold in your blood. It's the shifter cure."

Seth's fingers tighten on my leg and he stands abruptly beside me, pulling me behind his back in one swift motion. "You are not supposed to know that," he says roughly.

What is the shifter cure?

Wilk lifts from his chair as his wings bring him over the table between Seth and his father. "Please, the cure does nothing for our kind. We do not wish to take it. We can help you keep it... *her* safe." His hands are held in front of him, protecting his father and king as his eyes flash between me and Seth.

Seth's chest rumbles with a low growl from his wolf side, and I reach forward to touch his arm. "Seth, don't shift. Please, just tell me what's going on."

Seth looks over this shoulder at me, and his shoulders slump. He turns his back to the faeries and grabs my hands in his. "I'm sorry, Snow. It's true. You have a cure in your blood. If your blood enters the bloodstream of a shifter, any shifter, then it will kill them. Others want to use you in a war."

I pull away from Seth. Is this why I'm needing protection from a witch *and* a wolf? My heart sinks at that thought. I'm in real danger, and nobody ever told me why. There have been too many secrets and I want to crumble from the stress of my life.

"Why me?"

Seth shrugs. "I don't have all of the details, but I'm guessing since you are the only hybrid shifter, you are also the only one capable of concealing the cure."

Oh, joy. I back away, not wanting to hear any more. "I'd like to go home now." I look past Seth toward my favorite person in the area currently. "Wilk, would you mind helping me get home?"

He straightens his shoulders and lands on the ground, letting his wings rest. He steps around Seth and nods to me with a soft smile. "It would be my honor, Maia."

Seth growls again, and I look into his blackening eyes. "You said you were here to protect me, Seth, but how can you do that while also lying to me? *Everyone* has lied to me, except for the faeries. Why would you leave me in the dark about the reason shifters are after me?"

His jaw clenches and his eyes flash from black to brown and back again. He steps closer, but my new protector Wilk quickly blocks him. Seth looks broken when his gaze meets mine again. "Snow, I was trying to keep you safe. I didn't want you to feel the way you're feeling right now."

I am feeling like garbage, and completely alone in the world, but I don't say that. I steel my features and look away from the wolf shifter that I can't get out of my head. "Wilk, I'm ready to go."

He nods and takes my hand, but his body stills when he sees the pink faerie flying toward us. "Qadira? What is it?"

Qadira lands beside me and looks toward the king. "King Faren!" She bows quickly before continuing. "We have a problem." She looks at Wilk, and then her bright pink eyes meet mine. "There is a witch trying to break into our city. She says she is a protector looking for her charge and will burn the forest down until she finds her."

Even though I'm pissed about all of the lies, relief floods me at Qadira's words. I look toward Seth and can tell he's thinking the same thing. "Bree's here."

◊◊◊

Seth

Why did I have to lie to her? I could've told Maia the truth from minute one, but I spent too much time arguing with her and letting my temper rule my actions. How could I be such an idiot?

I know it's the exact thing she hates the most about me, but I'm not about to let her get away, to pick a faerie as her protector, when I would lay down my life for her. Even if she ignores me from here on out, I'll be there by her side. Overbearing, and unmovable.

I don't care that Maia isn't my fated mate. Until I find that person, Maia is my everything. I'll keep her safe from the shifters that want her blood, and I'll figure out a way to take the cure from her so she can live her life freely. Even if it costs me my own life in the end.

Chapter 12

✧✧✧

Maia

MY BEST FRIEND IN THE WORLD doesn't look like the same girl who chased boys with me in the fifth grade. Her long red curls are floating off of her shoulders, revealing her multiple shining ear piercings. It's as if she's glowing from the power radiating from her body. *My witchy BFF.* The moon is peeking down at her, lighting up her brown eyes, but I swear a spark of magic is coming from behind them.

Bree is in tight jeans, winter boots, and a half-sleeve green sweater. Her tattoo that matches mine is on full display around her wrist. To be completely honest, she looks absolutely badass.

"I'm not going to ask again, faerie freaks! I can sense your energy, and my friend's trail ends right here. Take off your lame-ass glamour and show me Maia Collins!" Her voice is stern, with no room for argument.

Bree looks from side to side, not seeing me even though I'm standing only a few yards away. "Bree, I'm here!" I call out to her, but she can't hear me.

I turn to the faerie prince, Wilk, who brought me to the edge of his magical Fae city. The ancient-looking city can be moved around at the faeries' will, completely invisible to the naked eye, but clearly noticeable to witches like Bree.

Wilk smiles at me. "So, you know her? Would you like me to lift the wall so you can go to the witch?"

I nod. "Yes, please. She would never harm anyone here."

Wilk looks with a side-eye at my constant shadow, Seth. I don't even turn around to acknowledge him. I'm still mad that he has been acting as my protector while also lying to me about some shifter cure in my blood. I thought at least Seth would be honest with me, considering he has no filter when it comes to insulting me. I was wrong.

The sweet, pink-haired faerie servant girl, Qadira, grabs my hand as Wilk waves his arms and a wall of sparkles lights up and slowly disintegrates between us and Bree. It reminds me of a firework breaking apart and disappearing in the night sky. Once the small flickering lights are gone, Bree's eyes snap to mine, only briefly running over the creatures surrounding me.

"Oh, thank the high priestess, Mai!" She runs to me and pulls me into a tight hug, causing me to release Qadira's hand.

"It's fine, Bree. I'm not in any trouble." I try to reassure her as I step away. "Well, aside from the shifter cure running through my veins, causing a war amongst shifter-kind..." I let my words trail off as I stare knowingly at her. *Possibly glaring.*

Bree flinches and her face falls. "I'm so sorry, Mai. I don't even know what to say."

I shrug. "It's just another lie, right? I should be used to it by now." I know I'm being a brat, but I can't fight the hurt.

Bree frowns and nods without a word. She finally looks at the others surrounding me and dips her head at Seth who has made his way to my side. "I'm glad you found her. Though, I'm not totally sure why you came to the faeries." She side-eyes Wilk with a look of distrust.

What's that all about?

Wilk just smiles at her, and Qadira takes a step away nervously. I finally look up at Seth and immediately regret it as I meet his intense brown-eyed gaze. He's watching me like he can't get enough of whatever it is he sees in my eyes. I struggle not to reach out and stroke my fingers along the rapidly growing stubble on his cheek. I'm instantly very aware of the tight dress that I'm wearing, which hugs every one of my barely-there curves.

A blush fills my cheeks and I turn back to the now smiling Bree. Of course she's enjoying this. "I was just telling the faeries that I need an escort back home. Since you're here, I guess we should get going. I have a lot to discuss with Dad."

Another one of the liars.

Wilk steps closer to me and I look up at his now saddened green eyes. He looks so young with that cute puppy-dog face. "I really had hoped to get to accompany you home, Maia." He leans in to speak lower. "I am not able to get out much. I could use a vacation."

I laugh, eyebrows raising. "You consider babysitting a potential weapon of war a vacation?" *Gah, that sounds ridiculous.*

Wilk's smile grows so wide that a small dimple appears on his cheek. "Sounds like a dream."

I look at Bree again. "Would Wilk be welcome? I'm not going to pretend like I didn't hear that *tone* when you said the word '*faeries*'."

Bree rolls her eyes. "I have nothing against faeries, even though they think they're the superior magic-wielding race."

Qadira finally speaks up to my right. "Yet, witches are the ones chosen to protect human kind while we live in the shadows. I do not think you should judge us, *Sabrina*. Count yourself lucky."

My mouth drops open, along with the mouths of everyone around us, aside from Wilk. His sparkling green eyes smile along with his lips, and he winks at Qadira. There's definitely something between those two, and I want to know what it is.

Bree steps back and looks Qadira up and down. "Did you just call me Sabrina? Like, the teenage witch?"

Qadira stands taller and crosses her arms. "I did. Is that a problem?"

Bree's shocked expression becomes a full on laughing fit. She reaches out and pulls the stunned pink faerie into her arms. Bree turns to me, still holding onto Qadira. "I want her to come with us. If she comes, the other one is welcome." She points toward Wilk.

Wilk clears his throat and starts floating off the ground. "Let us go, then! Qadira and I will tell my father of this journey and return here in twenty minutes." He waves for Qadira to follow him, but it's not in a superior way, as a prince might do. He is kind to her, and she seems more than happy to trail beside him through the city of Fae.

I look back at Seth, feeling like I need to make myself clear. "You don't have to come, Seth. I have more than enough protectors now. Go ahead and enjoy your life." I'm amazed at how smooth the lie just left my lips.

His face falls and real sadness crosses his eyes. He's so incredibly handsome that I can't look away. "Snow. I'm not going anywhere. If you choose to not acknowledge me, I'll accept that." His eyes fall to my lips and then meet my gaze again. "But, I will not leave you until I'm sure you're safe from danger for good… no matter how long it takes."

My heart squeezes in my chest. *Well, damn. How can I be mad at him now?*

◊ ◊ ◊

Seth

It takes exactly twenty minutes for Wilk and Qadira to join us again. Faeries have an internal clock that amazes me, and I wish wolves had that ability. We leave the city of Fae without speaking to King Faren again, thankfully. I felt way too uncomfortable in his presence during our short dinner. I don't see any reason for him to be an enemy of Maia's, but her protection means a lot to me. Wilk assures me that his father wishes us the best and I hope we have an ally in him.

Thanks to Wilk and Qadira, Maia and I got a new magical wardrobe change. This time, I have real hiking boots and comfortable jeans, as well as a light sweater even though I don't need the warmth. Maia is in the tightest pair of fleece leggings that hug her hips just below the long-sleeved v-neck that is plenty low-cut, and her own pair of hiking boots. Qadira has a knack for dressing Maia in the things that make my eyes wander. *Stop being a creep, man.*

"Can't you create a portal back to Maia's house? You've done it at least three times now," I ask Bree, wondering why we're hiking through the woods in the dark, when we could be somewhere safe. I can't spend all night staring at the back of Maia as she easily maneuvers through the thick brush.

Bree shakes her head. "I can't transport this many people. It takes a lot of energy."

Maia's beautiful hazel eyes avoid me as she looks back at Bree, and my stupid heart clenches. She's mad at me, but I can't stop myself from wanting to be near her. She looks at the faeries with a smile that I wish was directed at me.

"You guys have magic. Can't you help Bree make a portal?"

Wilk shakes his head. "We are unable to create portals to places unknown. It happens by accident on occasion when we are unfocused, but it is a risk not knowing the final destination."

Great, I'm surrounded by a bunch of magical creatures that can't do any helpful magic. Traveling on foot it is, then. If it were just Maia and I, I'd shift and carry her on my back. What would it feel like to have her so close to me? When I wrapped my arm around her waist in that room in Fae, I nearly combusted just from the scent on her neck and the rapid beating of her heart. And then the dress didn't help my control…

I look around at the thick trees we have been walking through for over an hour. This spot is perfect for making camp, if only we had supplies. "We need to make camp so Maia can rest," I tell Wilk who walks easily beside me. "I don't have any equipment so we'll need to gather some firewood and as many ferns as we can find."

Wilk grins at me and I shake my head, confused. This faerie dude is seriously always smiling. He scans the small opening that the five of us stand in. "We do not need any of those things." He looks at his servant, Qadira. "Would you mind helping me, Dira?" *Dira?*

The pink-haired faerie girl smiles even wider and nods. The two of them wave their arms around elegantly and small sparks of light fill the darkness surrounding us. The trees that circle us begin bending inward, meeting at their tops to create a dome of protection above our heads. I can hear Maia's small gasp as she stares up in awe at the faerie magic. The trunks groan against the strain but don't break under the pressure. The floor between the trees rises to fill the openings until we are completely closed off from the rest of the forest, trapped in our own earthly igloo.

I guess now would be a bad time to tell the others that I'm claustrophobic, but it doesn't feel so bad once Wilk creates an opening between the branches at the top of the dome, letting moonlight filter in on us, and a small flickering fire starts in the very center of the floor. Well, this is far more impressive than the makeshift lean-to I had in mind. I guess the faeries joining us isn't such a bad thing.

Chapter 13

◆◇◆

Maia

"THIS IS SO FREAKIN' COOL," I say in awe as I look around the large room the faeries created for us. "Was that hard to do?"

They both shake their heads and Wilk gently touches Qadira's arm. "Together, our power is much stronger. If I were on my own it may not work this well." He smiles down at his so-called servant. He doesn't look at her in that way at all, and I want to ask so badly about how he feels about her. Another time, though.

I have a thousand questions in my mind. "Is your power endless? Do you ever get tired? I noticed you don't do spells. Why?"

Qadira shakes her head. "We get tired just as you would if you were to exercise. A little rest and nourishment keep the magic flowing."

Wilk joins in with a happy smile, as usual. "And unlike witches, faeries do not need spells. Our magic is elemental, though we have some tricks, like creating clothing or teleportation."

Bree groans and I look over to see her arms crossed and frown deep. "We don't *need* spells either. They are just useful when we need to be precise."

I giggle at their competitiveness, and a hand presses gently to my back. I look up into Seth's nervous eyes as he speaks. "Can we go somewhere and talk?"

Go somewhere alone with Seth? Yes, please.

My anger toward him has faded way too fast, and I almost can't remember why I even got so mad to begin with. *Almost.* He has never done anything to harm me, and he has protected me every step of the way, but I'm still hurt. I sigh and nod to him.

I look toward the others who are settling down on the new thick grass that the faeries pulled from the earth. Bree grins, not hiding her feelings even a tiny bit at Seth's question. *Do not blush, Mai!*

I avoid her gaze as I look toward Wilk. "Is it possible to make a door out of here?"

He smiles sweetly and waves a hand in the same way he had only minutes ago. A small rumbling comes from behind me as the earth falls back down and an opening appears between two bent trees. I don't look up at Seth as I make my way outside.

I know he's following me. His footsteps are soft and smooth, but I'm all too aware of his presence still. I stop beside a small trickling creek that snakes through the woods, having no end in sight. The air feels dry, but

I can see the moisture everywhere around us, even in the dark. I can't believe I've never been to Maine before, but I'm quickly falling in love with the wilderness.

I can smell Seth's piney scent beside me but I refuse to look up at him. "You wanted to talk?" My eyes are focused on the water flowing in front of me.

Seth's fingers reach up to me, stroking along my cheek to slide the stray white hair behind my ear. His hand continues it's caress until he's gripping my chin gently. "Please look at me, Snow."

He pulls softly so that my head tilts toward him, but I close my eyes. If I look at him, I just know I'll forgive him for his lies. *Bad idea.* My eyes are closed and I can feel his chest against mine. I'm practically asking him to kiss me.

He moves closer to me and my eyes fly open. I'm met with his deep brown gaze locked onto mine. He's looking into my eyes like he can read the unspoken words behind them. *We've been in the woods for over a day, so how does he smell so damn good?*

Seth releases my chin, but he stays close to me. "I'm so sorry, Snow. I need you to know that. I didn't know what you were when Nate had me look after you. I assumed you knew about the cure, and I should've been honest once I found out that you didn't. You were right when you called me an ass, and I won't deny that I have a temper, but I *can promise* to protect you and be *honest* with you from now on."

Aaaand, forgiven. Just like that.

I swear that my knees about crumble at his words as each one fan a warm breath against my cheeks. "Okay," I say simply. *Lame.*

Seth's smile shows all of his perfectly straight teeth. He's only inches from me and his hands leave his sides to rest on my hips. "Okay? Does that mean I'm forgiven? Because I have a lot more groveling in me."

I giggle and it feels crazy to be doing so after everything, but it also feels incredible. "No need to grovel, but I can't pretend I wouldn't enjoy it."

A low growl comes from deep in Seth's chest and I can't explain why that sound fills me with desire. Must be my animal side that is attracted to the beast in him. *Weird.*

My body gravitates toward him and I can't stop my hands from wanting to feel the hard muscles that surround the animalistic sound as I touch his chest. Seth sucks in a breath and his smile falls fast. He licks his lips and tightens his hands on my waist.

"Why do I like it so much when you growl like that?" *Oops.* I snap my mouth shut. I didn't mean to say the words out loud, but there they are.

Seth begins to smile again as his head dips toward me. "Maybe your wolf isn't so dormant after all, Snow," he whispers so close to my lips that my brain begins to malfunction.

Down girl, I tell the hidden wolf inside of me, though I doubt she'd listen when I can't seem to control my very human hands as they slide behind Seth's neck. I stare into his eyes which darken under my gaze, nearly black now. *Just kiss me!*

"Seth," I whisper as his eyes close with mine, but before I can feel the warmth of his kiss, his entire body stiffens against mine and he jerks his head away from me. He sniffs the air, making fear roll through me before I can complain about him not kissing me.

"What's wrong?" I ask as quietly as I can.

Seth shakes his head and slowly moves me around to his back. I hear the rustling in front of us, but it's too dark to tell what's making the noise. I cling onto the back of Seth's shirt, real fear gripping me. I don't even know how many terrifying creatures could be out here in the middle of the night.

"Who's there?" Seth's voice is authoritative as he speaks loudly.

The rustling grows louder and my body instantly relaxes when I see the red fox stumble into our path, seemingly wounded. The fox looks up at us, scared and shaking under Seth's gaze. I move to go help the creature but Seth stops me with an arm around my waist.

"Wait, Snow. It's not just an animal. She's a shifter."

I gasp and take a step back. How can this poor wounded creature be a shifter? My mouth drops open as the fox shifts, bones cracking and red hair disappearing to reveal a small naked woman with short black hair. Her skin is a light brown and she has to be no more than seventeen from the look of her scared round eyes and baby-soft complexion.

Seth quickly removes his sweatshirt and hands it to the shivering girl, looking away from her as he does so. He is wearing a black tank top that hugs his abs in the most delicious way, and his large bare arms glisten in the moonlight. *Yum.*

I shake my head, trying to clear the inappropriate thoughts and I have to force my eyes back to the no longer naked girl. "Are you alright? What are you doing out here?"

She dips her head to me as she continues hugging herself for warmth. "I am so sorry for scaring you. I was abandoned by my skulk days ago and I haven't been able to shift for fear of freezing to death." Tears fill her chocolate brown eyes and I can't help but reach out to her.

I pull the poor girl into my arms and rub my hands along her back. "You're alright now. We can help you. Is a skulk like a family? I'm sorry but I don't know much about fox shifters."

Seth answers for the girl. "A skulk is similar to how a pack works. They have an alpha, or leader, but they don't have a second in command like us wolves have the beta. It works more like a king or queen with a group of princes or princesses at their side." He looks at the girl in my arms and his expression softens a bit. "May I ask why they left you?"

She nods and sniffles past her slow flow of tears. "I was… orphaned at birth, only to be raised by a few of the skulk princesses. I… I was injured a week ago. It was a hunter trap." Seth growls and it makes my heart hurt, wondering if he has had that experience before. The girl continues, "My skulk left me then. I guess it was just a matter of time before they found a reason to cut me loose. I broke the trap after being stuck for two days and have been heading south since then."

I hurt for the girl. Nobody should be treated that way, and I wish her skulk leaders were here so I could give them a piece of my mind. "I'm so sorry that happened to you." I look at Seth. "Can she travel with us?"

He looks from the girl to me and I can tell he's hesitant, but he gives in with a long sigh. "Of course. I'm Seth of the Shaw pack in Vermont. This is Maia." He looks at me with a soft smile and I suddenly wish we were alone again.

The girl looks up at me. "My name is Rylee." Her smile is kind and I loop my arm with hers, hoping to ease some of her fear.

We all make our way back to camp and rest for the night. Our group is growing already, and I can't help but wonder what the future holds for this unusual pack of creatures.

Chapter 14

✧✧✧

Seth

I'M GETTING SICK AND TIRED of always being interrupted before I can taste Maia on my lips. For a future alpha, I suck at keeping my mind clear and my emotions under control. When Maia is near me, all rational thought goes out the window with every ounce of self-control tacked onto the back.

Bringing the fox girl, Rylee, back to the others went a lot smoother than I expected. I have to give it to the faeries, they're pretty easy-going. I don't mind Qadira. She is kind and attentive, even helping Rylee by providing her with fresh clothes and winter coverings. Wilk, on the other hand, is much too *friendly* with Maia for my liking.

He doesn't shy away from touching her shoulder when they speak or smiling at her every time she looks his way. I won't hesitate to knock the prince of Fae out if need be, but I hope it won't come to that.

We've been hiking for an entire day, keeping a slow pace for Maia's human body to keep up. I can tell we're nearing a town by the sweet smell in the air mixed with gasoline and tar. A sure sign of humanity.

I catch the scent of coffee and bread, causing my stomach to rumble. As an alpha heir wolf, I have this ridiculous need to keep the others around me fed and healthy as long as they're in my care. I know for a fact that Bree and the faeries don't see themselves as being in my care, but I still feel that protective instinct, as if we were a family.

This morning, I caught two wild rabbits and we cooked them for breakfast, but we haven't had food since then and it's nearly night again. I turn toward Maia where she walks beside Rylee. Maia feels protective over Rylee, as if she were a younger sister, and I love her for that.

No. Of course not love... I shake the thought out of my head and focus on speaking clear words. "We're only a mile from a town. From there it'll be easier to get back to Stowe if we can find a car."

Everyone sighs with relief and I stop beside a fallen tree to sit. I pat the seat beside me for Maia, but Rylee jumps onto the empty spot too fast for me to protest.

"I'm so glad we're resting, Seth. I could use some freshening up before we get around other people." Rylee smiles up at me and I nod with my own small smile.

My eyes look past the small fox-shifter and find Maia glaring at the back of Rylee's head. *Odd.* "Snow," I call, and her face softens toward me. "Are you okay to continue? I smell coffee, and I know how much you like coffee shops."

I can't help but tease her about our first meeting. I just want to make her smile by any means necessary. It works, and a grin forms on her perfectly pink lips.

"I used to like coffee shops, but too many creeps hang around in those places." She glares at me, but her smile is clear. "I think I'll be drinking tea from now on." She clicks her tongue and flips her long white hair over one shoulder.

Gah, she's so flippin' sassy and I love it.

I shake my head at her as I shrug. "They've got tea there too, so you're in luck."

Before Maia can throw a retort back at me, Rylee's round eyes cut into my view. "I *love* coffee, Seth. I can't wait to get some."

I nod to her. "Great." I feel around in my pockets and remember that I'm wearing magic faerie pants. "Uh, I'd say coffees on me but I'm wearing Wilk's made-up pants so I don't have my wallet."

Wilk laughs and steps closer to me to pat me on the back. *Maybe he's just a touchy guy.* "No worries, Seth. I have got plenty of money for whatever we might need. It is one of the perks of being a Fae prince." His clipped and proper tone always weirds me out, but I'm grateful we won't have to go hungry.

My eyes fly to his pointed ears and bright green eyes. His wings lay resting against his back. "Wilk, how exactly will you blend in with the humans? You and Qadira look like you're wearing Halloween costumes."

Bree chimes in after being shockingly quiet throughout our hike. "The faeries can glamour themselves."

Maia pokes her head around Rylee to land in my eyesight again. "Don't they teach you that in 'wolves-and-things 101', future alpha?"

I shake my head. "No, that's probably covered in the 305 class." She rolls her eyes at me and I find myself smiling again.

Wilk speaks again and when I pry my eyes away from Maia long enough to look at him, he is already glamoured. *Wow.*

He is the same boy, but with rounded ears, short spiky blonde hair, and a simple t-shirt with jean pants. His eyes are a completely normal shade of green. The change is so drastic that I have to take a step back. "Alright, then."

Qadira's change is slower, but much the same. She holds her hands out and a long-sleeved jacket covers her as her wings disappear within her body. Her bright pink hair shifts to a light brunette color and her pink eyes are suddenly brown.

Maia pulls her hair up into a ponytail on her head and looks from person to person. "Well, we're just a bunch of young adults strolling from the mountains and into an unknown town. No problem, right?"

Wilk winks at her and I hold back my growl. "Of course, cutie," he says, somehow not sounding creepy. "No problems will come as long as we're together."

Man, I hope he's right.

◊ ◊ ◊

Maia

"Oh my gosh, this is so good!" Bree moans through her mouth full of pepperoni pizza and I shake my head at her. For a petite little witch, my friend eats like a starved ogre.

Seth chuckles beside me and I want to sink into the sound. I look toward him as he takes a much less monster-sized bite of his own slice. He smiles at me and I can't believe I ever called this man an asshole. He's much too yummy.

The six of us continue to eat in silence at some hole-in-the-wall pizza joint in a town called Jackman. Apparently, we haven't made it all that far through Maine, even after a day and a half of traveling southwest. I don't know how much money Wilk has exactly, but when we strolled into town, he walked right up to an older man in a brand-new Lincoln Navigator and bought the vehicle right then and there.

The SUV is roomy, with eight seats for us all to ride comfortably together, but food was the main thing on our minds before taking the five-hour drive to my home in Stowe. I can't wait to hug my dad again. In my whole life I haven't been away from him for more than a sleepover at Bree's house. As mad as I was at him just three days ago, I can't hold that anger any longer.

Wilk pays for our food since he has officially become the hotshot of our little group, and we pile into the car.

"I'll drive!" Seth announces.

Rylee and I both shout "shotgun" at the same time and my head snaps toward the girl. Her grin is surprisingly cocky for a wounded animal that we found in the woods. I'm unsure what it is about the girl, but she bothers me. It could be her obvious attraction to Seth, but it's not even just that. *Though, that's plenty.*

"It's alright, hon. Sit with me in the back," Bree says, grabbing my hand and pulling me with her to the third-row seat.

My disappointment from having to sit so far away from Seth is likely all too evident on my face, but I try to hide it as I watch Rylee smile and climb into the passenger's spot. Seth smiles at her, but his sad eyes meet mine in the rear-view mirror. I don't know how I am able to feel his touch all over again with just a simple look, but I have to blink rapidly to get the inappropriate thoughts out of my head. *Chill, Mai.*

Wilk and Qadira sit in the middle row, much closer together than necessary considering it's a three-person seat, but I can't help my smile as I watch their hands rest between them, separate but longing for the other's. It reminds me of going to the movies on my first date in the eighth grade, and just wishing that Tim Daniels would grab my hand.

I sigh and sink into the plush leather. "I can't wait to sleep in my own bed."

I notice Seth shaking his head as he glances back at me while he takes us out of the tiny town. "I'm sorry, Snow, but we can't go back to your house. We'll need to go to the pack lands to stay."

My mouth drops open and Qadira tenses in front of me. Her eyes are nervous as she glances at me and then back toward the front of the car. "We are going into the wolf-shifter lands? I am not sure that is a good idea." I can hear the small quiver in her tone and it worries me.

Bree reaches forward to touch Qadira's shoulder. "Hey. It will be alright, I promise. I was a young witch when I first met the Shaw pack alpha. Nate is a kind leader and they'll all accept you both."

Rylee turns to look at us all. "Will they accept me, though? Wolves and foxes aren't exactly buddies."

Seth waves a hand as if erasing everyone's worries. "All of you will be welcome, I promise." His eyes connect with mine in the mirror and I trust his promise.

"That's so great, Seth. You're the best," Rylee says as she reaches across the center console to touch Seth's arm. I suppress the growl that starts to rise in my throat, only to end up coughing like I swallowed a spoonful of pepper. *What the hell is that all about?*

Bree reaches over and grabs my hand. Her sad smile is all too knowing, and I shrug in response. She has always been able to see right through me, and it's incredibly unfair. "You okay?" she asks in the smallest whisper.

I nod. "All good." And oh man, I wish that were true, but I have this sneaking suspicion that I might end up with a fox shifter enemy before this trip is over.

Chapter 15

✧✧✧

Maia

MY EYES FLUTTER OPEN to see bright stars shining above me. I'm laying against the window where I passed out in the back seat of the car, who knows how long ago. To my left, Bree is snoring loudly where she is pressed against her own window. Both faeries are asleep and my smile stretches when I see Qadira's fake brown hair sprawled over Wilk's shoulder where she rests quietly. *They're so cute.*

My eyes meet Seth's in the rear-view mirror and he smiles. "They're all asleep. Did you get some good rest, Snow?" His voice is soft, but floats to me easily in the quiet car.

I nod, loving how he says my nickname that I hated just days ago. "As good as sleeping against a car window can be, I guess. Bree's snoring must've woken me." I giggle and Seth joins in.

His eyes find mine again, and they trail my face before turning back to the dark mountain road, lit barely by the headlights. "Is it lame that after all of the craziness, I'm really excited to show you my home?"

My heart sighs at the sweet nervousness in his tone. He's excited to show *me* his *home*? Just me, or all of us? He was ready to kiss me only twenty-four hours ago, wasn't he? That means something. All I need is a few minutes away from everyone else to see if he would've gone through with it.

"It's not lame at all. I'm excited too. Are we close?"

He nods. "We're entering my pack's land now, actually... well, I should say *our* pack, shouldn't I?"

"I didn't grow up here, though. I was kept away because my blood is deadly... right?" What will they all think of me?

Seth shakes his head. "You were kept away for your protection and the protection of the pack, but the wolves are technically your subordinates if you think about it."

My subordinates? How? I'm only half of a dormant wolf. "But..." My words are cut off by something hitting the side of the car. My vision spins as the crunching sound of metal pierces my ears and I'm thrown against the window.

I grip onto my seatbelt, grateful for it's protection. *What just hit us?* Seth curses and spins the wheel to keep us from flipping after the hit. The car stops and dust picks up around us as the groaning of metal slows. Everyone is awake now and breathing heavily in the quiet night.

"What the hell was that?" Bree yells, but everyone stays silent, listening.

Seth looks beside him at the wide-eyed Rylee and then back at me. His eyes scan what he can see of my body. "Snow, are…" he pauses to look at the others. "…is *everyone* alright?"

Everyone mutters that they're all fine and gratefulness rolls through me. It's insane how much I care for each of them already, well, except for Rylee. "Did a deer hit us or something?" I ask Seth.

He shakes his head. "A deer can't cause that damage. I think it was a wolf."

I gasp. "Why would a wolf in *your* pack lands attack us?"

Seth removes his seatbelt and turns to see us better. "I didn't warn anyone that we'd be coming through here, especially in the middle of the night. They're probably on guard."

Wilk's fake human ears become pointed again, and his bright green eyes turn to me. "Allow me to go investigate, Maia. I am indeed one of your protectors."

Seth grunts and shakes his head. "Sorry, Wilk. I am so glad to have your support and initiative, but I should go out alone. Seeing faeries isn't exactly a common occurrence around here. They need to see *me*."

Wilk shrugs and sits back again. "Be my guest, wolf. I will be here with the ladies." He turns to give all of us *ladies* a panty-dropping smile.

Seth grunts again and climbs out of the car. "Stay here," he speaks through the open door, eyes falling on me. "If I'm not back in five minutes, take the car and drive straight north from here. Do you understand?"

I nod and the others all mumble their agreements. Seth shuts the door and the five of us look at one another in silence before Wilk speaks again. "I have heard of this game called 'spin the bottle'. Who wants to play?"

Bree snorts beside me and even with the stress of worrying over Seth, I still crack a smile. "Wilk! You little devil!"

His grin is perfection, and all of us girls swoon a little bit. The only one not smiling is Qadira as she looks around with her eyebrows squished together. "I am sorry, but I do not know this game."

Bree giggles and leans into Qadira, whispering something in her pointed ears. Qadira's pink eyes go round and a matching pink blush stains her porcelain cheeks. "Oh…" she says quietly and her eyes connect with Wilk's. "Would you really play such a game with all four of us?" I can hear the disappointment in her tone and I feel sorry for her. Even though Wilk plays the ladies-man part, I can tell he is all heart and respect.

He shrugs. "It would not work to my advantage if you did not join, Qadira." *Oooooh!*

I don't know how his proper tone works the way it does, but damn, that was so stinkin' cute. Qadira's eyes flutter and she turns away from the Fae prince with a small smile. She doesn't say another word, but Bree, Rylee, and I all look at each other knowingly. That girl is in love.

Wilk's head lifts up suddenly and he looks around us with wide eyes, searching for something outside the car. "We need to get out," he says with a heavy tone.

My heart begins to race and I look into the dark night for any potential danger. "What is it, Wilk? I don't see anything."

Bree gasps beside me and grabs my hand. "I can feel it too! They're rogue wolves!"

"What does that mean, Bree? What do we do?"

Before anyone can tell me what's happening, another hit comes to the side of the car and the whole vehicle completely flips onto its side. A scream leaves me as I'm thrown on top of Bree and glass falls along my body. My head begins to pound and I know I hit it somewhere, but I'm too scared to find out how bad the damage is.

I climb off of Bree who seems less injured than I am, even though she broke my fall. Arms grab at me from behind and I'm hauled out of the SUV. I turn to hit my captor but it's only Wilk.

"You are bleeding, Maia. Are you alright?" Wilk's eyes search my face and I nod back to him.

I can feel the warm liquid falling down my face from a cut on my head, but I feel okay considering. "I'm okay, I think."

Bree, Qadira, and Rylee climb out of the car and stand beside me, all of their eyes looking into the dark woods for danger.

Rylee turns to me and looks at my wound with sadness, or maybe disgust. "That looks bad. Let me help you." She reaches for my bleeding wound, but Bree practically tackles her before she can touch me.

"Don't touch her blood!" Bree yells at Rylee in a way I've never seen from her.

"Why can't she touch my blood, Bree?" I'm so lost, but I feel like it has to be important.

Bree continues holding onto Rylee, but looks at me. "Your blood is a weapon, Mai. We don't know how a shifter will react to touching it. If Rylee were to somehow ingest it, or let it get into an opened wound, she could die."

I gasp and look at Rylee's shaking hands. She has cuts on her arms from the crash and my heart sinks at the thought that I could've just killed the girl with a simple touch. *Why are they even helping someone like me?*

"I'm sorry, Rylee. If what she says is true, you need to keep your distance." *And so does Seth...*

Rylee shakes her head. "I'm fine. Let's just fight. I can smell them now."

She points her nose in the air and sniffs, recoiling from whatever it is that she smells. "Definitely rogues. Their scent is terrible."

Wilk turns toward the woods, floating above the ground while his wings flutter behind him. Qadira releases her wings and joins him, the two faeries guarding me. Bree tenses as well, and protects my right, while Rylee takes position a little further away to my left. They're all protecting me, but I'm ready to fight to protect them, as well.

A deep growl comes from ahead of us and my whole body stills. Out of the dark trees steps the most terrifying wolf I've ever seen. I've seen Seth in his wolf form before, but he was gorgeous and powerful. This thing is mangy-looking with matted fur, yellow eyes, and sharp broken-off teeth. Drool drips from its mouth as it snarls at us. *Oh, dear lord.*

"Get out of here, rogue!" Wilk is the one yelling, and gone is the playful tease of a boy from minutes ago.

The wolf growls louder and his massive paws step closer to our group. Bree mutters something in that Latin-like language and a shimmering dome forms around the five of us, guarding us from the rogue wolf.

"Wilk and Qadira, incapacitate him. There are three more coming in less than a minute." Bree's voice is steady as she gives the command.

How is she not absolutely flipping out?

Wilk and Qadira separate to surround the wolf. It looks from one faerie to the other, unsure of which to attack first. Wilk and Qadira's hands both stretch in front of them, causing what looks like streams of lightning to leave their fingertips and hit the animal from both sides. The wolf cries out in pain and collapses to the dark earth.

Qadira runs back to the protection of Bree's shield while Wilk pulls a small blade from a hidden sheath on his hip and approaches the dying wolf. "What are you doing, Wilk?" I ask, concerned for his safety.

He glances at me. "Close your eyes, cutie. You do not have to watch this."

My stubborn-ass self doesn't obey, and I stare wide-eyed as Wilk slides the sharp blade along the creature's throat, spilling more blood than I've ever seen. I gulp past the hard lump that wants to gag me, and take steadying breaths. Wilk wipes the bloodied blade along his tight pants and returns to my side.

"I am sorry, Maia. It is kill or be killed, as they say. It cannot be avoided with the rogue wolves. They are far gone already." He sounds sad, but it's obvious this isn't his first kill. He's a warrior, and it will be hard to tease him again after this.

A howl fills my ears and each of us whips our heads to the right toward the sound. Bree gasps and grabs my arm. "That wasn't a rogue. That was Seth. He's calling his pack."

◊ ◊ ◊

Seth

I leave the SUV reluctantly. I know Wilk and Bree will protect Maia if she needs it, but walking away while she is potentially in danger is still hard. I know exactly where I am in the pack lands. I have run these trails a hundred times, always exploring with my wolf.

I pull my wolf to the surface, needing his heightened senses as I walk deeper into the night. I smell other wolves, but I can't make out exactly who in the pack is out here.

"I am Seth Lowell, alpha heir. Show yourself."

My voice dies in the wind, only to be met with silence. I sniff again and my nose scrunches up as a foreign scent fills it. It's like a skunk, but rotten, and mixed with a sticky sweet smell. The combination is repugnant and I want to run from it.

"What are you?" I can hear the dominant wolf tone in my voice. It's my natural reaction to danger and will work to control my pack someday.

I step back when the rogue wolf appears from behind thick trees. He flashes his large, broken fangs at me, and my wolf surges forward at the silent threat. The rogue wolves are basically zombies, left without a pack and any trace of humanity, ready to hunt and kill all living things.

"Leave or die!" I shout with more growl than voice.

He doesn't take the command, instead launching himself at me. I roll to the left, barely in time to avoid his teeth on my throat. My body shifts in seconds, the clothes tearing off of me as my wolf takes control.

Kill, he says inside of our shared mind as he growls at the enemy facing us again.

Yes, kill.

We charge the rogue, and my wolf body hits him hard in the side. The rogue rolls from the hit, and my wolf goes for the kill without hesitation, sinking his teeth into the rogue's neck. One hard crunch finishes the task and we drop him back to the earth. *That was easy.*

I sniff the air for any other threats, and my whole furry body shivers from the horrid smell. There are more of them, and they're heading back toward the car. *Toward Maia.*

I throw my wolf head back and howl loudly into the night. My pack knows the sound, and if they can hear me, they'll be here in minutes. Before then, I need to fight to keep Maia safe.

Chapter 16

◇◇◇

Maia

"IS HE HURT? I KNOW I'm no wolf-howl expert, but that didn't sound good, Bree!" Yeah, I'm freaking out. A part of me wants to tear through the woods until I find Seth, but I have no clue who that part of me is. It's not the girl I grew up being, that's for sure.

Crunching branches and heavy footfalls approach us at amazing speeds. I tense, but I'm not afraid of what is to come. A new sense of rage and fight fills me as I think about Seth facing the rogues on his own.

Another large, mangy wolf dives out of the trees and doesn't slow down as it rams head-first into the shimmering protective dome. *Not the sharpest tool in the shed.*

The beast stumbles backward with a whine, but recovers too easily. It circles us, and its yellow eyes land on me. The wolf snarls and sniffs the air just a few feet in front of me. Before any of us can react, another rogue wolf runs at the dome just like the other.

Bree groans beside me and I look over to find a stream of sweat dripping from her hairline. "Are you okay, Bree?"

She shakes her head. "I'm spent, Mai. I've never held a shield for this long and they're hitting it hard."

The shimmering light flickers out and then back again. Both of the wolves make choppy growling noises, as if they are laughing at us. Bree grunts again and the entire shield disappears.

"Fight!" Bree yells, and all four of my friends crouch into fighting stances.

Rylee is the first to charge, and without shifting, she flips over the back of the larger wolf. She shakes her bangs out of her face and then does another air flip as the wolf tries to get to her. She's like a gymnast. Wilk and Qadira run at the second wolf, their hands outstretched. Wilk has his small blade, but Qadira is weaponless.

Weapons don't seem to matter, though, as Qadira shoots a stream of lightning at the rogue. The wolf howls quietly and Wilk jumps onto his large back. Bree pants beside me, crouched and ready to fight, but before I can tell her to stay back and rest, the third rogue wolf dives at me, grazing my side so that I spin and fall onto my knees.

Pain from the crack in my right knee shoots up my thigh and I gasp with a short whine. "Holy hell!" I scream, but I don't have time to throw a fit. The wolf turns to charge me again, but I jump achingly to my feet and crouch like the others had, ready to fight with my bare hands. "Come get a taste of my blood, beasty!" *Lies, lies, lies!*

The wolf pushes off of the dirt, launching himself forward, but a loud thunk shakes me as another wolf slams into his side. *Another one?*

I start to lose all bravado until I catch a glimpse of the large wolf's brown eyes. *He's not a rogue.* His fur is silky and smooth, though blood stains his muzzle. *Seth.*

I sigh a long breath of relief and follow his quick movements as he stomps down on the fallen rogue. Without hesitation, Seth bites into the rogue's neck as if he has done it a thousand times before. I whimper at the sight, but pride fills me at the same time. *Holy crap, I'm a mess.*

Seth's wolf face turns to me, scanning my body quickly, and then he turns to join in the fight with the others. His plight is pointless though, considering the other two wolves are already dead, just like their companion. The small clearing is silent for too long of a time, and I begin to shake uncontrollably.

I find Seth's comforting brown eyes in the darkness and sigh. "So, uh… I really like your home." My shaky voice breaks the silence, and to my surprise everyone bursts out in laughter.

Rylee and Bree stand over a rogue wolf body, while Wilk and Qadira wipe blood from the front of their shirts. And still, they all laugh. *And, like the maniac I am, I join in.*

With shaking hands, I wipe the tears from my laughing fit, but the humor completely leaves my body when I see Seth walking toward me on two legs again… *more* than half naked. I follow the lines of his muscled chest with a complete loss of control over my eyeballs. *Don't look down, you hussy!*

But of course, I look down and heat fills my cheeks when I see the green fern branch that Seth holds in front of his hips, covering the part of him that I am *not* ready to explore. *Yet.*

A throat clears and my eyes widen to round saucers as I remember everyone standing around. *Oh, dear lord.* Bree grins from ear to ear as she watches me ogle the naked man in front of us. Rylee has a look of indignation on her young face, but she doesn't look Seth's way as I thought she would.

And of course, Wilk snickers and whispers something in Qadira's ear that makes her giggle. I am the only one of us checking out Seth, apparently. Great. I find Seth's face, which I somehow hadn't even noticed before this moment. He's smiling at me, and even with the drying blood on his chin and neck, he is so dang sexy.

"Would anyone mind magicking me some clothes, or at least some pants?" Seth asks the faeries, but his eyes remain on me.

Wilk grunts and steps closer to Seth. "That is probably a good idea. We would not want our Maia to have a stroke."

Bree snorts to my right and my mouth drops open. I don't know how it's possible, but even more heat fills my cheeks, to the point of almost burning. I turn away from everyone, needing to calm my racing heart, but I'm face to face with a large lumberjack-looking man.

A squeal escapes me and I jump backwards, only to be caught in Seth's clothed arms. He straightens me out, and quickly steps away from me. I look back at him as he wipes my blood off of his hands and onto his shirt. I gasp at the thought that my blood could hurt him, but he shakes his head. "I'm fine, Snow. No open wounds." He shows me his now clean hands and I sigh.

How could I ever forgive myself if I killed him? I couldn't.

Seth looks up at the stranger and raises a single eyebrow. "Horas. Do you have to just appear like that?"

The man, Horas, just grins and steps fully into our little clearing beside the flipped SUV. "Sorry, Seth. We heard your call and I arrived first. Looks like the trouble's over, though." His forest green eyes scan the dead wolf bodies with a sort of appreciation.

One by one, more people step out of the dark woods, until six strangers stand before me. Four more men, not as large as Seth or Horas, and a tall, beautiful woman with long blonde hair and dark blue eyes. Seth nods to each of them and then waves a hand at our small group.

"Thank you all for coming, but it's under control. Rogues attacked our car as we were entering the lands." A few of the newbies gasp, but remain quiet. "I've brought the holder of our shifter cure. She needs a safe haven."

The tall woman looks me up and down. "*She* has the cure?" Her voice is indignant and snobbish. "And you brought... *others*?"

Wilk steps forward. "Prince Wilk Arnou of Fae, and Qadira Mage. We are glad to be welcomed in your home." So proper as always, and presumptuous.

The woman scoffs and crosses her long arms. "Right. Sure thing."

"Sasha." Seth's voice is a warning to the woman. Still, I can't stand the way her name leaves his lips, like he has said it a thousand times.

Sasha shrugs and turns around, walking away. "Let's go, then. We should probably tell Alpha Nate about this."

I look toward my friends. "Are we supposed to follow her?"

Bree rolls her eyes, and the large man, Horas, chuckles beside me. "I would if I were you. You don't want to cross that one." His eyes widen with his smile. "Seth knows."

I snap my eyes to Seth and he visibly cringes. "Uh… Yeah. Probably a good idea." He grabs my hand, and the warmth calms me slightly as we all follow the oh-so-lovely Sasha. *Very* slightly.

◊ ◊ ◊

Seth

I realize this is my first time holding Maia's hand, but I hate that I can't enjoy it. We are all headed toward Nate's massive cottage in the woods, our pack of wolves, faeries, a fox, and a witch. And then there's Maia, the unknown. Of course, it's just my luck that *Sasha* has to be leading the way.

I was only fifteen when Sasha began chasing me around the pack lands. We hadn't even shifted for the first time yet, but she was sure we'd end up being fated mates. I liked the attention, and the company, but I knew we weren't meant for one another. I was sixteen the first time Sasha and I kissed. I knew then and there that she wasn't the one for me, but she's been after me ever since.

And now my mind is all fogged up with thoughts of another girl. There's no way Sasha can hold a candle to Maia, but I can't help being worried that

Sasha will try to make Maia uncomfortable. I'll need to be ready to jump between the two if Sasha starts anything. I won't let Maia feel unwelcome in my land.

We stop at Nate's front steps and he's already coming out of the large oak door in basketball shorts and a loose t-shirt. I'm sure he has been sleeping, and he likely sensed the tension in all of us before we even arrived. Each wolf is linked to the alpha in a way that I can't imagine. I guess one day I'll know what that feels like.

"Hey Uncle Nate," Maia waves her free hand at our alpha. I've never heard anyone call Alpha Nate *'uncle'* before, but it shines a whole new light on the dark and strong Shaw alpha.

Nate's eyes fall on our entwined hands and he glares. "What's going on, Seth? What's all this?" He waves to the motley crew behind me, and I can only assume he means the faeries and our latest traveler, Rylee.

"Right," I say, feeling the usual nervousness in front of him. "Prince Wilk and Miss Qadira have decided to join us in the protection of Maia. They've already done so much for her, I believe they should stay." I glance back at Rylee. Her dark eyes are round as she stares at our alpha. "And we came across the fox shifter, Rylee, on our way home. She was hurt and needed help."

Nate's frown is deep as he studies each of our guests. "Alright, wolves, continue your patrols. Thank you for your help." He nods to Horas and the others, and they immediately disperse, going back to their nightly guard duty. His eyes fall on me. "Seth, see our guests to the visitor's cottage, and I want you, Maia, and Bree back here to stay with Lydia and I. I will give Mathew a call. He has been worried about the three of you."

With that, Nate turns back into the house, leaving me to handle the sleeping arrangements. I never thought this would be my first real alpha task, but here we are. I turn to Maia, and to my surprise she's smiling as she continues holding tightly to my hand.

"Yay. Sleepover," she says with fake enthusiasm, and I can't believe the smile that stretches across my face.

She's perfect.

Chapter 17

◇◇◇

Maia

SITTING HERE IN UNCLE NATE and Aunt Lydia's living room is surreal. I get why they never invited me to their home when I was a kid. Of course, the wolf paintings and pack quotes on the walls never would've made me guess that they'd be wolf shifters. Wolf-obsessed, sure. I suppose it was for my protection in case I ran into one of the pack members while they were shifted, but I can't help the small sting of hurt.

When we arrived in the Shaw pack lands last night, I can only imagine the thoughts running through Uncle Nate's head when he saw us. The future alpha, Seth, with a bloodied me by his side, my witch protector, our new faerie friends, and the wounded fox shifter. *How is this my life?* I have to give it up to him though, he handled it swimmingly.

The guest cottage is only a few hundred yards behind Uncle Nate's house, so it was easy settling the others in. The place is gorgeous, and roomy, as well, so it won't be hard to stick around here comfortably for a while. Seth, Bree, and I all came back to Uncle Nate and Aunt Lydia's home. They have three large bedrooms. Theirs is on the main floor, while the other two are on the second.

Bree and I shared the king-sized guest bed, leaving Seth to have the other room with the smaller bed. Poor guy is nearly six-three and sleeping in a twin bed. I can only imagine what sharing that bed with him would be like. *How could I not imagine it?*

Right now, my eyes keep falling to the floor as I try to ignore my dad's looming presence. He woke me this morning saying we need to talk, but I'm still hurt from all of his lies. It's just the two of us, and the uncomfortable tension is about to strangle me.

"Can't you even look at me, Mai? I'm still your father." His voice is pained, like it gets when he's having a hard week. He gets sad sometimes, and I think it's from loneliness. My mom died during childbirth, and Dad doesn't date. I never understood why, but now that I know they were fated mates, it makes more sense. He lost his literal soul mate, the kind of love I may never know.

I shake my head as I stare unseeingly at an uneven floorboard. "Dad, I'm just trying to wrap my head around it all. You've lied to me from day one, and I don't know how to feel about that." I lean forward and rest my elbows on my knees, combing my fingers through my white hair.

A shuffling sound comes closer to me, and I can see Dad's large frame sit down on the coffee table in front of me. "Mai. I love you more than anything else in this world. I can't begin to tell you lying was okay, but let me explain the reasoning, please?"

I hold a deep breath and release it with a long, drawn-out sigh. "Fine. I'm not about to quit being your daughter, so I guess I should learn to listen." I look up into his brown eyes and try to smile, though I'm sure it looks forced.

The lines around his eyes crease and he rubs his hands together. "Alright. I should probably tell you about your mom, and our time together before your birth."

My nose scrunches up. "You sure? I don't really need *those* details…"

Dad holds a hand up and glares. "Don't be gross, Mai! I gave you *that* talk once, and that was *plenty*. I'm talking about the events that led up to us giving you the cure." I nod and let him continue. "I was a young man, if you can believe that, when I went to the college here in town. I'd often go for hikes in the mornings before classes, out here in these woods."

I scoff and lean back, sinking further into the plush leather. "Hypocrite!" And he never let me even walk home along a perfectly carved trail?

My dad smacks me gently on my knee and sits up taller. "Stop interrupting!" A real smile stretches my lips and I nod again for him to continue. "Anyways.

One morning, it was pouring rain, so I was ready to cut my run short when I came across a large, beautiful wolf. She was unlike anything I'd ever seen, black as night with bright jade eyes." His eyes close briefly as he remembers my mom in her wolf form.

I can't even believe I had a wolf mom. I wish I could've known her. I lean forward and grab my dad's hand. "Go on, Dad. I'm still listening."

He smiles and rubs the wild beard on his chin. "Right. Your mother came to find me at the school a few days after that, in her human form, of course. I couldn't stop thinking about the wild wolf with the jade eyes, and when I saw this beautiful woman with long black hair, who smelled like wild flowers, and had the exact same eyes as that wolf, I was hypnotized." He pauses again so I interject.

"Did she tell you what she was?"

He shakes his head with a small laugh. "No, she did not. I was an idiot, and I felt this pull toward her that I couldn't understand. We were fated for one another, but I didn't know that like she did. I kissed her before even speaking one word beforehand." He laughs a real, deep laugh.

I giggle along with him as my eyes go wide. "What did she do then?" I probably would've punched a guy who did that to me… unless it was Seth.

"She punched me right in the face, and then proceeded to run off into the woods." My mouth falls open and I laugh again. My mom was a total badass wolf shifter.

Dad continues. "So, because I was an idiot like I said, I followed her into these woods, and I got the surprise of my life. I saw her with your uncle Nate, and the two of them were spying on the alpha at that time, Nate's father, Jackson. He was in a heated discussion with your mom's father, Landon. Your grandfather."

I sit up tall, suddenly feeling hopeful. "I have a grandpa?"

He shakes his head slowly as sadness fills his eyes. "You did have very loving grandparents on your mom's side. As you know, I have no family of my own, so your shifter grandparents took me in when your mom and I completed our mate bond."

"What does it mean to complete a mate bond? Did you get married?" This world is so fascinating.

Dad's cheeks actually blush and I immediately regret my question. "Uh, let's just say that completing the bond is the *event* that made you."

Oh, for Pete's sake.

I shake that thought away as fast as half-humanly possible and jump to my next question. "So, uh... what were Nate's dad and gramps arguing about?"

Dad chuckles softly before continuing. "They were discussing a possible threat to the shifter race. Others were after this ancient cure that was kept by a Shaw pack ally. That put the entire pack in danger, so they needed a place to hide the cure. Your mom and uncle Nate were young, so they didn't know about the cure, which is why they were spying."

"Why is the shifter cure so important anyway? Did they know you were there? Wolves have good senses, right?" The questions pop off without a breath and Dad holds a hand up to shush me.

"I'll get to the cure, but yes, the wolves all smelled me, but not until I had already seen your grandfather shift right before my eyes. I know you can imagine what that's like by now." He eyes me, and I give him a hard nod. I know *exactly* what that's like after seeing the owl-ladies do it, and Seth not long after that.

"Well," he says. "The wolf shifters have this rule about humans. If a human is exposed to their kind, then the human is to be executed. I was in a tough position, and not just because your jealous uncle Nate was all wolfed out and about to kill me on the spot." He rolls his eyes, but I don't miss his words.

"Umm... what? Uncle Nate had a thing for mom?" *Ewwwww*.

Dad nods. "They were actually chosen as mates for one another at birth. Nate was to be the future alpha, and your mom was the daughter of the beta. It was supposed to be a great match for the future of the entire pack."

I blink rapidly as I try to process this new information. So I wasn't all that far off when I thought

Nate might be my dad. Super weird. "So, you what? Came along and caused trouble in paradise?"

Dad shrugs, but a new cockiness overcomes him. "I couldn't help that your mom had found her fated mate. That trumps an arranged mating, that's for sure." He smiles and shakes the thought away. "Anyways, your mom saved my life that day, claiming me as her mate as she faced down the alpha heir. It was incredibly brave, like the bravado I see in you, Mai." He looks lovingly at me and I have to clear my throat to keep back the tears.

I'm like my mom.

I try to change the too-tender moment. "Okay, so you were mated then? Just like that?"

Dad sighs and shakes his head. "It was complicated. The pack wasn't okay with humans and shifters being together, so your mom gave me the option to be hers forever, or run away and not look back. She actually thought I'd run after meeting her, but I was already in love. That fast."

My heart flutters a little as Seth's face flashes through my mind. *Woah, woah, woah. Chill out crazy hormones!*

Dad continues. "I chose to be with her, and face the alpha with my head held high, and blah blah blah, bond completed." He hurries through the uncomfortable details and I have to laugh a little. "Anyways, the next day was when our lives changed in the most amazing way. A witch told us we were going to have a baby girl."

"That fast?" My eyes stretch open wide.

Dad nods and shrugs at the same time. "Yep. That fast. This witch told us that the shifter cure needed a safe hiding place, and that the only option was to place it inside of a vessel, completely out of sight. She told us you would be that vessel. According to her, the cure couldn't be destroyed since it was created by the shifter god himself who had the ability to become any animal he wanted. It was made from his blood and spelled by a powerful witch to survive anything."

My heart sinks at that thought. I was just a vessel to hide something toxic, something that will be in me forever? If my blood brings death to shifters and is impossible to destroy, how can I ever be with Seth?

My dad takes my hands in his. "Maia. Your mom and I didn't want this for you. We struggled with the decision, but just your existence has prevented a war that would wipe out shifters forever. Just after you were born, a type of shifter called "lupercus" came to the Shaw pack in search of the cure that was already hidden in your blood, and they killed your grandparents, along with many others. And as you know, your mom didn't survive childbirth. Some sort of wicked twist of fate, I guess." His voice cracks, but he continues. "The only reason you and I weren't caught up in the fight was because we were humans, living away from the pack for your safety. It's why I chose to never tell you where you came from. Being human has saved you all this time."

My mind reels and I stand from the couch, needing air. My eyes fall on the archway toward a long hallway, only to find Seth watching me with sad eyes. He twitches like he wants to move toward me, but I shake my head. I can't have him… I will never have him.

Chapter 18

✧✧✧

Seth

I JUST WANT TO HOLD HER IN my arms. I can almost feel her heart breaking as she runs out of alpha Nate's house and sits roughly on the porch stairs. It's not like she can run off, anyways. She wouldn't get far before being dragged back here for her own safety.

I heard everything Maia's father told her, and I have to say that I'm grateful somebody finally filled her in on all of the details about her past. I didn't even know most of what Mathew just spoke about. Nate was supposed to be mated to Maia's mom, and they were to run the pack as alpha and luna. Now I understand the stories I was told as a child a little better.

I knew there was a baby that was supposedly killed inside of her mother when the lupercus came, but that baby was Maia. She was born and hidden, never to be spoken of in the pack again. A half-human baby who had all of the right to rule as alpha to my pack, instead of me. Maia would be an incredible leader, even though she has so much to learn about our kind... but the wolves would never be okay with a hybrid leading them. If only they knew her like I did.

I step onto the porch, quietly watching the beautiful miracle that is Maia Collins. Her face is in her hands, and her heart is racing. I move closer to her, and before I can think any better of it, I sit behind her with my legs caging her in on the sides. "I'm here," I say, not knowing if it will reassure her in the slightest.

The warmth from Maia's back spreads across my abdomen and chest, filling me with something I've never known before. Maybe love, or maybe desire. To my surprise, Maia grabs my hands and pulls my arms around her. *Gah, this is amazing.*

I look out into the forest. The fresh snowfall glistens against the morning sunshine, and the cool breeze does little to calm the heat I feel from being this close to Maia. We sit quietly for a moment, and then she speaks.

"I don't have a future, do I?" Her voice is so heart-wrenching as she speaks the words.

I pull her closer to me and draw her zesty scent into my nose. I swear my mouth waters, but I try to control my animalistic side. Maia's head falls back to my shoulder so that my face is beside hers. Her skin is the softest thing I've ever felt, and I rub my scruffy cheek against hers.

"Snow," I can't help the silly nickname. It has become her. "What do you mean you don't have a future? You're more special than you know."

She scoffs softly and shakes her head. "Right, special. I'm a weapon of war, Seth. That's my purpose, is it not?"

My heart hurts just hearing the pain in her voice. I let go of Maia and move quickly to kneel in front of her. I can't let her feel like this. My body won't allow it. I grab her face in the palms of my hands and stroke my thumbs along her soft cheeks. A small gasp leaves her perfect lips, and my mind fogs momentarily. *Pep talk time, Seth! Not attack the pretty girl time!*

"Maia Collins. Your blood is only a weapon if you allow it to be. You have a future, but just as the rest of us, that future isn't promised. All we can do is fight for what we want to see in our lives." Her hazel eyes seem to brighten slightly, and I can't stop my smile. "I saw that, Snow."

The corners of her lips tilt up, and her eyes fall to my mouth and then meet my gaze again. "Stop cheering me up. I'm not used to this Seth, and I think I like the alpha jerk better."

I laugh and raise my eyebrows as I release her cheeks, but not before I steal a small touch of her parted lips with my thumb. "So you do like at least a part of me, then?"

"I never said such a thing!" She rolls her eyes and shoves my chest, but I grab her hand before she can pull it back. *Thank you, wolf reflexes.*

I press my lips to the palm of her hand, needing just a taste, even if I can't have all of her. Maia's smile drops and her eyes lock onto where our skin touches. "Seth," she whispers my name like a siren call, but another voice speaks behind me.

"Um… Can I have a word with Maia?"

I drop her hand and turn toward Luna Lydia. She's chewing on her lower lip as if concerned about something. If I had to guess, I'd say she's not a fan of my close proximity to her *niece.*

I stand and dip my head in respect to her like usual. "Of course, Luna Lydia. I'll go check on our guests." I look back at Maia, and her cheeks are stained a dark pink, but she avoids my eyes. She isn't sure about me, but now I've had a taste of my Snow White. There's no turning back.

◇ ◇ ◇

Maia

Dammit! Why does he have to be so addicting? I can't possibly stay away from Seth for his own safety if he keeps touching me like that. It's like I crave the alpha heir, and every time we're together I get my fix, which only makes me want more. A girl only has so much self-control… and I'm at my breaking point.

Thank heavens for Aunt Lydia and her impeccable timing. "Hey, Aunt Lydia. What did you want to talk to me about?"

Now that Seth has walked away, her serious expression softens and she sits beside me. Her blue hair practically glows against the light reflecting off the white snow. "Nate just told me that you talked to your father. He said he overheard your conversation and thinks I would be the best person to comfort you." One of her thin eyebrows raises as she stares knowingly at me. "It looked like you had plenty of comfort from Seth, though."

I shake my head and try to stop the stupid blush that wants to permanently stain my cheeks. "It's not like that. Seth is my protector, right? It's his job to help me when I'm struggling."

Aunt Lydia snorts as she laughs and my eyes go wide. I have never heard her do that. "Oh, my sweet baby girl. I love you with all of my heart, but I know you are not that naive. You are a strong woman with a good head on your shoulders. You have to see what's building between you two."

She's absolutely right, but I'm also stubborn, and a pro at the subject change. "So, what's up with Uncle Nate being practically engaged to my mom? I need to hear your side of this story."

She sighs, the sound very exasperated. "Oh, Lord. That feels like an eternity ago. I'll tell you, but I'm also not done with the Seth talk, young lady." *How is this woman not a mom?*

Her eyes close as she thinks back to before I was born. "Your mom was my best friend in the entire world, you know that?"

I shrug. "I knew you guys were close, but I thought it was because of some relation to my dad. I've never thought much about it, I guess."

She nods. "Well, your mom and I were the same age, so we grew up in this pack together. We even shifted for the first time together when we were eighteen. It was so much fun getting to run through the woods with Jade. She was so fast, though. Faster than any wolf I've ever known."

I sigh and shake my head. "You were BFFs, like me and Bree. I can't believe I never knew this."

Aunt Lydia's eyes sadden as she takes my hands in hers. "I'm so sorry, Maia. All of your life, we have tried to protect you by keeping you in the dark. It meant keeping the past a secret, and never getting to connect with you like I always wanted."

I sniff past my tears and squeeze her hands. "So, you stole Uncle Nate from mom?"

She smiles, and I'm glad for the mood change. "Well, your father stole Jade from Nate, actually. Your Uncle Nate was not happy about the fates pairing your mom with a human, when she was supposed to marry the alpha heir himself. I was so happy for Jade when I found out that she got to have a fated mate. It wasn't until after her passing that Nate and I began connecting."

"So, you two aren't fated mates, then?" They seem so perfect together that I can't imagine it not being fate.

She shakes her head with a smile. "I like to think fate had a say in our life together, but we are not technically fated mates. We just fell in love in the midst of tragedy, and when Nate was forced to be the alpha after his parents were killed, he wanted me to be by his side forever."

"Wow. So true love does exist." I want that so badly.

Aunt Lydia touches my cheek softly. "Oh, hon. True love exists in a million different ways. I had a kind of true love with your mom. It's why I had a witch spell my hair to always be blue. Your mom is the one who dyed my hair this color in the first place." She giggles at the memory, and my mouth drops open.

"I have always wondered why your hair is never any other color, but I had no idea it was a spell! That's amazing!" I grab a chunk of my white hair. "Do you think Bree could do that to mine?"

Aunt Lydia shakes her head. "Honestly, I tried to get a witch to spell your hair brown when you were just a toddler. The spell never stuck, or you'd be a brunette right now. Your father believes it's because the cure has poisoned your wolf side, causing your hair to die in a way.

"Like a disease that kills the melanin in my hair? That's super creepy."

She nods. "I would give anything to get that poison out of you, Maia..." she trails off, lost in thought so I nudge her shoulder.

"What're you thinking about?"

Her eyes are sad again. "Do you know what it means when someone has a blood disease? Like, the restrictions for them?"

I shrug, but my heart sinks at the question. "I know that my blood couldn't get into another shifter's blood stream. Bree told me it would kill them." Just the thought makes me shiver.

Aunt Lydia nods as she looks around us, as if making sure nobody is listening. *Oh no.* "Hon, you are absolutely right, but there's more. I am not about to pry into your personal life, but you need to know that you can't be with Seth, or any other shifter, for that matter."

It's not a surprise, but her implications make my skin crawl. "It's not just poisonous through blood, is it?"

She shakes her head. "I am not a doctor, but I have to warn you before your heart gets in too deep. If you were to be... *intimate* with a shifter, it could very likely kill them."

It's too late though, isn't it? My heart is in *way* too deep.

Chapter 19

✧✧✧

Maia

"HOW'RE YOU DOING, MAI?" Bree steps beside me in Uncle Nate's large kitchen.

The dark wood cupboards and granite countertops make the room cozy, and I've been spaced out staring at who-knows-what for a few minutes. I come out of my fog and look up from my chair to see Bree's concerned gaze searching my face. Standing behind her are Will and Qadira with the exact same looks of worry.

"Guys! I'll be fine. It's just a little blood, right?"

Bree nods and I grab her hand to comfort her. I'm not sure why I feel the need to comfort Bree when I'm the one who is about to get my blood magically drawn by an elderly witch. I can tell she is really worried about me, though, and I just want her to be her normal silly self.

Last night, after I spent the day depressed over all of the new information that Dad gave me, Uncle

Nate suggested that we test my blood and see exactly what it can do. Apparently, Bree's grandmother is the head witch of her entire coven, so she'll be the one running the tests. As far as I've been told, all of the shifters need to stay out of the room during the blood draw, leaving me, Bree, her grandmother, and the faeries.

Dad left back to our house today to get me some supplies since I'll be staying with the Shaw pack from now on. I didn't have any say in the matter, but here I am. Basically a prisoner. I can't really complain, though, because the land is gorgeous and everyone has been really nice. Of course, it's going to be torture having to be around Seth and knowing I can never be with him.

Wilk kneels beside me while we wait for grandma witch to arrive. He pats my knee and smiles in the way I love so much. "Did you know that a faerie has green blood that boils when it hits sunlight?"

My mouth drops open at the disturbing image. "Are you serious, Wilk?" I practically shout at him.

His neon green eyes shine brightly as his grin stretches nearly to his ears. "I am not serious. It was a joke." His clipped tone pushes me over the edge and I double over in laughter.

"Sheesh, Wilk! I was seriously mortified!"

He laughs, making a deep twinkling sound that I love, and the girls join in. Bree shoves Wilk on the shoulder. "Is that the first joke you've ever told, Wilk?"

He shrugs and steps back to Qadira's side where he seems to feel the most at home. "Joking is not something the faeries do for entertainment, right Qadira?"

She looks at him and nods. "Yes. I did not know it could be so funny."

I want to smack my head as I watch them. They're like adorable robots made of bright colored metal. "What do you guys do for entertainment, then?" I ask.

In unison, they both say, "fighting," and I'm laughing all over again.

I nod and tap Bree on the shoulder. "Okay, then. Bree, remind me to never pick a fight with the faeries."

She grins. "Same, girl."

"There's my granddaughter!" A woman's shaky voice echoes off of the high ceilings of the kitchen.

All of us spin toward a small hunched over woman with light gray hair. Her skin is wrinkled and dark from sun exposure. She smiles at Bree first, and then her gaze finds the rest of us.

"Oh, what a beautiful sight. Faeries, witches, and wolves. All together under the same roof."

Bree runs to the woman and hugs her warmly. "Grandma Em. This is Maia Collins," she waves a hand toward me and then the faeries. "And these are our good friends Prince Wilk of Fae, and Qadira."

Bree's grandma bows to the faeries in a surprising show of respect. When Bree first saw the faeries, she was more than a little hostile. "It's an honor to be around other magic-wielding creatures such as yourselves." Wilk grins from ear to ear, and then the woman looks me up and down. "And our young hybrid. You look so much like your mother, Maia."

My heart stutters. "You knew my mom?"

She nods. "I'm the one who placed that cure inside of your body on the day of your birth. Your parents struggled so hard with that decision, but I believe it was the right thing for the pack, and all of the shifters, really."

I just nod, not sure I agree, but I hold my tongue on that subject. "So, you are the powerful ally of the Shaw pack that I've heard about."

She smiles, causing the dark canyons across her cheeks to deepen. "To everyone in this room, I'm just Grandma Em, sweetheart. No more, and no less."

Maybe I do have a grandma, after all. Just being near her makes my heart feel a sense of being in the presence of family, even if we are technically a different species. If I were less of a chicken, I'd go hug her, much like Bree had, but I just stay seated, ready for my blood test.

Grandma Em steps closer to me on slow legs, and she reaches out to touch my cheek. In a voice so soft that I swear I'm the only one who can hear her, she says, "This thing inside of you is only temporary. Do not lose your spirit or hope for the future."

I can feel my eyebrows press together as my head tilts in confusion. "What do you…" My words are cut off by the sharp sting on the inside of my right elbow. I gasp and look down to see no needle, but just a thin stream of red flowing from a small hole where I've seen nurses draw blood before. I've never been poked with a needle before, but I imagine this is what it would feel like.

My blood collects inside of three small tubes that Grandma Em holds in her hand. I didn't notice those before, but this woman is sneaky for a grandma. Once the tubes are filled, she pulls out three stoppers from inside her sweater pocket, and places them inside the opening of each vial of my poisonous blood.

"That should do it, then. Who's hungry for some lunch?" She's a crazy old bat, that's for sure. Still, I can't help but love her.

Bree giggles and jabs her grandma gently. "You couldn't have warned Mai before doing the blood draw voodoo, grandma?"

Grandma Em just shrugs and looks from Bree to me like she has no idea what the problem is. "Why would I do that? A sting is a sting whether you see it coming or not. Why cause stress for the things we cannot control?" And with that, she just huffs out an exasperated breath and saunters out of the kitchen with my blood in tow.

Yup, I love her.

◊◊◊

Seth

"Hey, Snow." I stop beside her in Nate and Lydia's front yard. She's alone for the first time since yesterday, so now is my chance. Watching her be swarmed by this world that she knows nothing about makes me want to take her away from it all, or show her the good side of being a shifter.

"Oh, hey," she says, less than enthusiastic to see me. Her hazel eyes meet mine and I immediately forget why I stopped her in the first place. Damn, she's so flippin beautiful in the setting sun, and the full moon tonight is already making my senses run on overdrive. I can hardly stand so close to her and not be touching her.

Right, full moon. Cool it, idiot!

I shake my wolfish thoughts away. "So, tonight is the full moon. I know it may not mean much to you, but us wolf shifters gather during the full moon for a night run. Our senses and abilities are heightened, so it makes the experience in wolf form pretty incredible." I suddenly feel shy, which is not like me at all. "I thought you'd like to come with me. There hasn't been any sign of rogues since the other night, so we should be safe."

Please say yes.

Her eyes narrow slightly as she smiles. "You do know that I don't have access to my wolf side, right? I can't exactly shift and run in the wild below the full moon."

I step closer to her, needing just that extra inch to make me feel less cold without her. "Just because you'll be on two legs instead of four doesn't mean you can't run wild and free with the wolves. They won't hurt you, and I'll be by your side as I am now. I won't shift."

I can hear the pounding of her heart as she considers my request. Normally, I'd take that as a sign that she's flustered at the idea of being with me in a dark forest. Lately, though, I don't know how she's feeling about me.

She sighs, and nods. "That sounds really freeing, actually. I'm in."

Her answer makes me want to take her in my arms out of sheer excitement. *When did I become such a girl?* "Okay, great. Meet me back here in two hours. You can invite the others if you'd like."

Maia's smile is guarded, and I can tell she's unsure about something. I plan to show her tonight, though, that even with the cure in her blood and growing up with humans her whole life, she has a true pack. With me.

Chapter 20

◇◇◇

Maia

"YOU ARE ALL TRAITORS! You seriously won't come with me?" I glare at all four of my friends. After telling Seth I'd go on a full moon run with him, I ran back to the guest house to ask, or really beg Wilk, Qadira, Bree, and Rylee to come with us. I need a buffer between Seth and I tonight, or else I might let my stupid body control my good senses.

All of them, aside from Rylee, have told me they wouldn't come. And even though Rylee seems all too eager to join in on Seth's pack activities, one whisper from Bree has her changing her mind. "Uh, yeah. I forgot that I already promised to stay here and let Bree try some healing spells on my leg. It's getting much better, and she needs practice." Rylee lies through her teeth, and I'm shocked that Bree can convince even her to stay away from Seth for one night.

Rylee has become a little too into Seth, in my opinion. I mean, I can't have him, but I have a really hard time imagining someone else having him. Even when I let the vamp James kiss me, I couldn't imagine worrying over whether he kissed another girl in the next minute. I wouldn't have been jealous in the slightest. But when it comes to Seth, I feel this overwhelming possessiveness. I'm absolutely insane.

I look to the faeries with pleading eyes. "Let me guess, you guys have some pretend magic crap to do as well?"

Wilk shakes his head. "Nothing like that. Bree just told us not to interfere if you and Seth are to go on a date. I am guessing this is one of those dates." He smiles sweetly, and Qadira joins him, looking like an adorable pink pixie with her sweet grin.

My mouth drops open as I stare at Bree. "So, you are the traitor? My best friend." I let the hurt seep into my voice, though I can't bring myself to feel all that upset with her for being my wing-lady.

She grabs me by the arm and drags me away from the others. "Don't even start with saying this isn't a date. You two care about one another, and he is a really good person. I understand that there's stuff holding you back, but I don't see a problem with some fun."

Fun? Too much fun can lead to me killing him.

"I don't think you do understand, Bree. *Fun* on a full moon with a smoking hot guy could lead to something that I physically cannot do for fear of murdering him with my bodily fluids. Do you see what I mean?"

She raises a single eyebrow at me like I'm dumb. "Not everything leads to sex, hon. You are a woman. You have control over your body, and I think you can enjoy the company of someone you care deeply about without letting your hormones control you. You're a virgin at eighteen, Mai. Not a lot of us can say that in this day and age, so clearly you're good at self-control."

I scoff. "More like no opportunities to test my self-control while I was labeled as a freak."

She shrugs. "Just have fun for one night. For me, please."

I try to think back to the last time I let loose and had fun. The most fun I've had lately was my lip lock with James just shy of a week ago. Time has flown, and to be honest, I actually miss the half-crazed bloodsucker. The memory of a painting done of Bree by James makes a question pop into my mind.

"Speaking of you not having self-control. What's the story with you having a certain vampire recluse wrapped around your witchy finger?"

A soft pink blush fills Bree's cheeks and my eyes go wide. Before I can comment, she holds a hand up. "Long story short, and then you have to go out with Seth."

I nod as I roll my eyes, and she continues. "I accidentally made my first portal to somewhere in the

Maine wilderness, and there was James. I was fifteen at the time, lost, and terrified, but he helped me figure out how to make a portal back home. He was kind, and really lonely." Her face softens at the memory of meeting the sexy vampire. "Anyways, I told him I'd visit him after that, and I did. I went back to see him a few times a year after that. We'd play board games and talk, becoming friends, or like I was a long-lost sister of his. After I turned eighteen, my feelings for him sort of changed, and I thought his had, too. It was last summer the last time I visited him. I tried to kiss him, but he turned me down."

My mouth drops open. "That's it? No big love story? I mean, the guy is a huge flirt."

She laughs and shakes her head. "Trust me, I know. And before you get all weird, Seth told me that James kissed you. I am not jealous or anything. I have heard plenty of James's stories about his interests in the ladies."

I cringe a little. "Yeah, I think he did it to make Seth jealous, but I'm not sure it worked."

"Oh, it worked. Trust me." She laughs again.

"When did you and Seth become buddies?" And why didn't I know about this sooner?

Bree waves a hand at me. "We're both your protectors, Mai. We have talked a few times about your safety."

Doesn't sound like talks about safety to me.

"If you want to get deep into girl talk, we can do that later, maybe when you have something juicy to tell me." She winks, and my heart sinks even further as I contemplate this so-called *date* with the alpha heir of the Shaw pack.

What have I gotten myself into?

◊◊◊

Maia

The moon is high above the trees, and completely full. I stare at the hazy glow it casts over everything the blue light touches, and my body feels looser. It's as if I'm captured in some sort of spell by the moon's beauty. Never in my life have I given even a second thought to the sun or the moon, or the stars for that matter. I've taken a look and moved on, but tonight is something entirely different.

"It's beautiful, isn't it?" Seth's deep voice speaks softly behind me, pulling me from the moon's trance.

I spin around to see him standing in a plain gray t-shirt, dark jeans that hug his large thighs tightly, and no shoes. *Gah, how does he always look so sexy?* He gives me a cocky smile as if he knows exactly what I'm thinking about him, and I have to remind myself that he can't actually read my mind like James can... at least I hope he can't.

"Yeah, I was just looking up at the moon. I've never seen it so full and large. It's mesmerizing."

Seth nods, and steps to my side, glancing up into the night sky. He sighs as if completely content to just stand here in silence under the moon and stars. "Can you feel a sort of pull inside of yourself? Like the moon wants to capture you and take you away from everything?" He drops his gaze to my eyes, and his eyebrows lower to give him a sort of dangerous and alluring look.

I feel as if my breath gets caught in my throat. "I do, actually. How'd you know that was what I was feeling?"

Seth's hand reaches up to slide a strand of hair behind my ear and I about turn to take a bite of his finger as he does so. Something in me feels animalistic, like I have suddenly become a wild thing with no regard for boundaries. The air between our bodies feels charged with electricity and a small whimper escapes my throat. *What the hell is wrong with me?*

I close my eyes and try to shake my sudden wildness away. "Uh... I feel a little... weird." I open my eyes again and Seth is watching me with hunger in his eyes.

He licks his lips and steps away from me abruptly. "Yeah, sorry. I wasn't expecting the moon to affect you, considering your wolf side should be totally dormant. I also wasn't expecting it to make me feel so…" he trails off, but I desperately want to know how he's feeling right now, and if it's anything like what's going on inside of me.

I step closer and reach my hands up to stroke his stubbly cheeks. The short hair is soft, but somehow rough at the same time. I don't know why I feel like I have to touch him, but for the life of me, I can't remember why this might not seem okay. Seth's eyes close and he inhales deeply through his nose.

A low rumble comes from his deep chest, and he quickly grabs my wrists in his hands. "Snow, I shouldn't let you do this. You don't understand what's happening, and I should've warned you earlier."

I shake my head. I don't want to stop touching him, but I'm also incredibly confused. "You're right. I don't understand at all what's happening right now, but I feel like I might die if I don't touch you, Seth."

Seth continues holding my wrists so that I can't move my hands closer to him. His eyes darken under the moonlight. Even though I can't touch him with my hands, I move my body forward until it's pressed against his. Every inch of him is solid and warm, and I can't help but sigh. "Kiss me," I say before I can stop myself.

Seth grips my wrists tighter but doesn't release them. I can tell that he's trying to restrain himself, but I'm not having it. "Please," I beg, completely gone from myself now.

Seth doesn't hesitate anymore as his lips crash into mine. He drops my wrists, and his large hands slide around my waist, hoisting me higher to capture his mouth more fully. I moan against the taste of him that I have been waiting for since the moment we met. My hands dip into his hair, and I press my body harder against his.

Seth growls somewhere inside of him, and the vibrations from it reach my lips, causing any control I may have had left to break. "Seth," I whisper against his mouth, and in seconds, I'm lifted away from him and placed firmly on my feet.

Seth's eyes flash black and then back to brown again, and he's breathing as heavily as I am. "Snow, I can't do this with you right now. Please try to understand."

My eyebrows drop, and I can feel my control coming back to myself. "Um... why am I feeling so insane right now?"

Seth sighs and licks his lips. "It's a wolf thing. The full moon sort of heightens our senses, particularly our hormones, and sexual drive. It's nature's way of encouraging procreation for our kind. I'm really sorry you have to go through this without someone guiding you."

I wrap my arms around myself, trying to understand what he's saying. *Oh, dear lord! I'm sex crazed and I just attacked Seth!* The realization brings me back to reality and a hot blush fills my cheeks. Now that I know what's happening, it's as if I have slightly more control, and I am incredibly embarrassed.

"I'm so sorry, Seth! What did I just do? I seriously begged you to kiss me." My face heats up even more, and I cover the warmth with my hands, wishing I could hide forever.

Seth actually laughs, and I peek through my fingers to see his teeth shining in the bright night. "I don't know why you're sorry, Snow. I can't lie and pretend I didn't enjoy that, *a lot,* or that I wouldn't want much more of that in the future. Under these circumstances, though, it doesn't feel totally right."

My heart clenches at his words. He wants more with me? I want that so bad, but I can't, can I? Maybe he doesn't know the consequences if we were to be intimate with one another. I run a hand through my hair and shuffle back and forth between my feet. *This conversation sucks so bad.*

"Seth, I think we need to talk. You know that we can't..." I wave a finger between us, really hoping I won't have to say the word out loud. "I mean, if we were to..."

Thank all that is holy that Seth raises a hand to stop me. His shoulders slouch slightly, and he tilts his head at me. The look is almost shy, and incredibly adorable. "Snow, I know very well what the cure in your blood keeps us from doing. I can't deny that I have thought about it... a lot." He chuckles softly. "But I also can't just ignore the way I feel about you."

A warmth fills me at his words, as if I just snuggled into the warmest blanket beside a roaring fire. "How do you feel about me, exactly?" The urge to touch him only grows, and I *accidentally* step toward him again. *Oops.*

Seth looks at the six-inch gap between us, and then back up at my eyes. "You know how you feel when you look up at that full moon? Like it's drawing you in, and you just want to be nearer to it? Like if you could just touch it, or disappear inside of its embrace, you could be content forever." I gulp and nod, understanding the feeling completely. "Well, that's how I feel every single time I look at you, Maia."

Did he just call me Maia? Holy hell.

Seth reaches one of his large hands up to rest just below my ear, against my neck. I shiver at his touch and the hazy moon spell comes over me again, or is that just my own wildness? "Seth, I'm practically a poison to you. Nothing about me is a smart decision, or a safe one at that." Even as I say the words, I barely feel truth in them. I have very little common sense right at this moment and I can still feel his lips against mine.

Seth nods in agreement. "You are right, Snow. It's not safe at all." His head tilts toward mine, and he breathes in my scent with his wolf senses. I don't know what he smells on me when he does that but thank goodness I showered today. "You know, I've never shied away from danger." His eyes show the truth in what he says.

"What about death? Shouldn't you shy away from that?"

Seth seems to think on my words for a moment, and then a long howl fills the night sky somewhere deep into the forest. Seth's lips tilt up in a grin and he stands up taller. "It's time to run with the pack, Snow. Are you up for a little danger tonight?"

A nervous laugh comes out of me. I have a feeling that he's not just talking about running, but my heart races at the thought anyways. "Absolutely," I say, and Seth grips my hand in his as he takes off toward the howl.

Chapter 21

◇◇◇

Seth

MY WOLF IS RIGHT AT THE SURFACE as I run through the pack lands with Maia by my side. She is fast, and decently agile in the trees, thanks to the full moon lighting our path. I could be running at five times her speed right now, but I keep pace with her so that she can experience this even with her wolf side shut away.

I'm surprised to find that she still feels the effects of the full moon, even though she shouldn't have access to that side of herself. Just knowing that she feels the need to touch me like I do with her nearly causes me to forget all of my cautions and sense, just to claim her as mine under the shining moon. And now that I know what it feels like to kiss her, and hear her moan against me, how can I ever want to do anything other than that again?

These are always the nights that many of my kind lose their virginities. Normally, it's only with their fated mate, but that's not always the case. It's not uncommon for two shifters to fall in love with one another even though it's frowned upon if they aren't fated. Maia may not be my mate, but I can't help the way I feel about her already.

I turn to watch her white hair fly behind her as she runs, the moon light reflecting off it perfectly. Her beautiful face is lit with a smile, and she focuses on the woods in front of her with such concentration. Even with my wolf driving me forward with incredible balance, I could easily lose focus and trip just from the inability to take my eyes off of Maia.

And I wouldn't give a single damn.

Maia gasps as a gray wolf runs beside her for a moment before taking off at full speed ahead of us. She starts to stumble, but I grab onto her and slow us to a stop. "Did you see that wolf? It was gorgeous!"

She's breathing heavily, and her eyes go wide as more wolves run past us. I point to three smaller wolves that run side by side. "Most of the wolves out tonight are newly shifted, and having some fun under the full moon, or looking for their fated mate. It's like a big party once a month."

Maia stares after the two wolves that slow down to tumble over the other playfully. She smiles and looks up at me. "When did you first shift?"

"Every wolf shifter turns for the first time during their first full moon after they reach eighteen. For me, it was two days after my eighteenth birthday."

I can still remember that first shift as if it were yesterday, and it has been nearly two years.

Maia nods. "I wish I could do that, Seth. What's it like? Does it hurt?"

"It doesn't hurt at all anymore. The first few times feels like you're stretching a muscle too far, or the feeling of overextending, only all over your body. It's incredibly uncomfortable, but not excruciating."

She grimaces. "Ooh. Maybe I don't wish for that." She laughs softly, and the sound causes my wolf to stir. He likes the sound as much as I do.

I squirm a little, and Maia eyes me. "Are you okay, Seth?"

I rub a hand along my face as I look up at the moon through the parted trees. "I'm fine. My body just wants to shift. It almost feels uncomfortable to not shift on a night like this."

Maia's eyes go wide and she steps away from me. "Do it, then! Please, don't deny your instincts just because of me."

I deny my animal instincts every time I'm near her, but I'm not about to creep her out like that. I think about it, and maybe she's right. "You wouldn't be scared to see me like that?"

She shakes her head, and something behind her eyes shows excitement. "I haven't had the chance to really see you as a wolf up close. Each time, I've been running for my life. I'm actually kinda curious."

Excitement fills me with her words. My wolf has been ready for this since the sun went down. I nod and step further back from Maia. "Alright, Snow. Don't freak out."

I let the wolf come forward and take total control. A new energy fills me, and my clothes tear into pieces as the change comes on fast, completely unlike the first time. I drop onto all fours as a wolf, and my focused eyes find Maia's round hazel eyes instantly. *How can she be so incredibly beautiful?*

◊ ◊ ◊

Maia

He's a huge freakin' wolf! Clearly, I knew this already, but right now, standing here with him makes it so much more real. Seth's brown eyes watch me as his wolf nose sniffs the air between us. His head tilts from side to side, making him look like a curious pup, and I can't help but smile.

"Wow," I say breathlessly. I reach my hand out toward him and his eyes close when my fingers dive into the thick black hair along his head. "You're incredible, Seth."

He makes a snorting sound and then presses his snout into the center of my chest. I giggle and continue petting him. "Woah, woah. Just because you're supposedly a wild animal, doesn't mean you're allowed to get frisky with me. I see into your eyes and I know the human side of you is plenty in control."

I swear he smiles, if that's possible. I slide my fingers along Seth's silky neck and he gives a big shake. His head nuzzles into my side, and he's so warm that I sigh. "If only I could feel what it's like to have that much power."

Every inch of the massive wolf is layered in muscle and thick fur. He's so powerful. Seth lowers his head to the ground as if he's bowing, and he nudges me with one giant shoulder. "What?" I ask, confused.

He tries to press himself underneath me, nearly taking my feet out from under me. No way does he want me to get onto his back right now. "Do you want me to ride you like a horse, Seth?"

His wolf head nods and he nudges me again. My heart is racing as I imagine what it would be like to ride a werewolf. I guess I'm about to find out. I grip the hairs on his neck, making sure not to pull too tightly, and I throw one of my legs over his back.

Without hesitation, Seth rises with me half on top of him and shifts me to the side so that I am fully resting on the center of his back. "Holy cow, this is so crazy. I don't want to pull your hair."

His head shakes, and he starts walking through the trees after the other wolves. I hold on for dear life as he picks up the pace. I can feel every one of his muscles beneath me as he runs. The strength from within him is incredible, and I want to be even closer to him if that's possible.

Please do not tell me that I am sexually attracted to a wolf.

I shake that thought away and try to focus on the trees flying past us. Seth is running nearly as fast as James did when he first carried me to his home. I don't feel sick or dizzy this time, though. I feel grounded with Seth's warm wolf body against me. My heart is beating out of control, and I feel free for the first time in my life. I can't believe I considered not doing this tonight.

I tilt my head back and throw my best howl into the night, laughing as the sound trails off. Seth copies me with his own low howl, though his is innately more impressive. More howls circle me from different places in the woods, and I can't stop my giggles at what I started. I want this life, even though I know it's not a possibility. It feels like home.

Seth's ears pick up and he stops abruptly, nearly throwing me over his shoulder. "What's up, Seth?" I ask, hoping I'm not hurting him.

His head turns from side to side, and my whole body feels the deep rumbling growl that ripples through him. My skin turns cold at that sound. Something isn't right. I climb off of his back, but Seth doesn't leave my side. He backs up to me as he looks into the dark forest for something I can't hear or smell. *Stupid human senses.*

Another growl fills the night, but it doesn't come from Seth this time. Through two evergreens, a wolf nearly as big as Seth steps out of the shadows and into the moonlight. I know instantly what this is. It's a rogue wolf, and just like the ones from the other night, it's out for blood.

The wolf's wide jaw drips with saliva, and he snaps his broken teeth at Seth. Seth snarls back at the animal, and I know Seth is stronger than the rogue. I just hope more don't come. Seth dives at the wolf, and a scared squeal leaves my throat. I clench my fists, wishing Seth didn't always have to be the one in harm's way because of me.

The rogue blocks Seth's initial attack and rolls a few feet away. It jumps back up and lunges at Seth's neck, barely missing him. I gasp, and back myself against a thick tree trunk. "Please win this fight, Seth," I mutter under my breath. "Please, please, please."

It hits me as I watch the wolves snap at one another, grazing the other with superficial scrapes and cuts. Seth has my heart in his hands. Somehow, somewhere along our journey, I have fallen for him, and if I lost him… I would be broken forever.

Tears fill my eyes as Seth howls in pain from the rogue's teeth sinking into his hind leg. "No!" I scream into the night. The only sounds are the breaking of branches and growls from the two wolves. I freeze though when another noise meets my ears.

A deep growl comes from my right, and I snap my head toward the incoming rogue wolf. *Not another one.* My heart sinks as I realize I'm completely defenseless. Seth is fighting for his life, and I'm left to fight my own battle for once.

"Get out of here!" I yell with a surprising amount of force at the new threat.

The rogue shakes its body and in seconds, it becomes a man. A completely naked man, but that's the least of my concerns. His skin is pale and littered with scratches and scars. His long hair is wild and dirty, and his dark red eyes narrow at me as he sneers. "Meat," he says simply, and a chill rushes down my spine.

Holy hell, he's hungry.

"Not meat. Go before my protector finishes with your friend!" I try to reason with the shifter, but he continues moving slowly toward me where I'm backed into the tree.

"No," he says, and his half human, half wolf fangs flash at me.

I gulp and try to remember my karate training. I can fight a man. He's just a man right now at least, but I can do this. I psych myself up and crouch into my fighting stance. I can still hear Seth and the other rogue wrestling through the forest, but I keep my eyes trained on the naked shifter in front of me.

He steps within my reach and I attack first, kicking my leg at his knee. He grunts, but it doesn't stop him in the slightest. I swing out with my right arm, trying to connect with his jaw, but the man grabs my wrist and throws me to the ground with a force like nothing I've ever felt. I hit the earth hard, but turn onto my back so I can keep my eyes on the threat. The man bends over me and drops his knee onto my chest.

"Die," he says in his caveman-like voice, and claws stretch from his fingertips. He swipes at my chest above where he kneels on me, ripping through my shirt.

Blood pools from the scratches and I cry out in pain. I look down at the red staining my shirt and dripping onto the man's bare knee. *That's it!* My mind kicks into full gear and I remember that this man is just another shifter, and my blood is a toxin to him.

I wiggle, trying to get myself out from under him. He growls again, pressing me deeper into the dirt, so I just do what's available to me, and rub my hand along the blood on my chest. I take my hand and shove it against the shifter's mouth, hoping to get some of the cure inside of him. The disgusting creature greedily licks my blood off of his lips and smiles like he's having the best meal of his life.

I want to vomit, but I continue trying to wiggle out of his hold. It only takes a few moments for the shifter to start shaking, and fall off of me onto the ground. I gasp as his whole body writhes and flops against the dirt. His eyes go wide and latch onto me as he gasps for breath. In seconds, his claws shrink back to human fingernails, and his red eyes turn a normal shade of dark green.

He looks just like another human as he dies in front of me, taken by the cure in my blood. My body trembles at the sight. I just killed this man, and I could do the exact same to Seth if I'm not careful.

◊ ◊ ◊

Seth

"Maia!" I call out her name as I run back to her after my fight with the rogue wolf. It took too long to take down the rogue, and I've lost sight of Maia.

I catch her perfect scent in the breeze and take off running toward her. She's standing a few yards away from a dead body, and she's shaking like she's freezing. I reach out to grab her, but she holds her hands out between us.

"Stop! Don't come near me!" She screams the words at me, and my whole body stills.

I take in the sight of her. She's covered in blood, and I know it's all hers from the gashes across her chest. I can feel anger rising in me, and I begin to shake just like her.

"Snow, what happened? I'm so sorry I left you." I try to step closer again but she backs up with tears streaming down her face.

"Seth! You can't touch my blood. Please, just get away from me before I kill you too." She sobs between her words, and everything that once made up my heart crumbles to a million pieces.

I look down at the man. He has what looks to be Maia's blood on his mouth. He ingested her blood and died from the cure. "Was he a rogue, Snow? Did he give you those cuts?"

She nods, and sniffles without a word. Her arms wrap around herself, and damn, how I wish it were my arms instead of hers. Maia tries to avoid looking at me, probably because I'm standing naked in front of her, but I couldn't care less about that right now. I run my hands through my hair, feeling more lost than I ever have before.

"We need to get home, Snow. How can I do that if I'm not touching you? We're too far away for you to get back on your own two feet with so much blood loss."

She opens her mouth to speak, just as a bright light fills the space between us. A portal opens up directly in front of Maia, and I can see Bree on the other side. Bree's eyes go wide when she spots Maia bleeding, and she reaches through the portal to grab her friend's hands.

"Seth," Bree says when she sees me. "Come on. I've got her now."

She pulls Maia into her arms, safely inside what looks to be Alpha Nate's guest house. I shake my head, knowing I shouldn't follow Maia. She doesn't want me near her right now. "I'll shift and come to Nate's. Just please take care of her, Bree. Please."

Even I can hear the desperation in my voice. Bree nods. "She'll be okay. Hurry home, okay?"

I nod and turn away as my body cracks and I pull my wolf forward to take me home. Maia nearly died tonight, and I know one thing for sure now. I'm falling in love with her, even though she can prove to be the end of me.

Chapter 22

✧✧✧

Maia

"ARE YOU HEARING A WORD I'm saying, Mai?" Bree's voice is gentle, but I can hear the anger behind it.

It's understandable, really. She has been trying to talk to me and I don't hear a single word. I'm completely ignoring her, though I'm not trying to. I think I'm in shock in a way, but maybe if I really were in shock, I wouldn't think I was in shock. I don't even know anymore.

I look at Bree where she sits beside me in the Shaw guest house. She has her feet tucked under her and wears a large sweater that hugs her like a dress all the way to her knees. She looks cozy, and not traumatized like myself. I wish I were as carefree as Bree.

She waves a hand in front of my face, and I finally look into her eyes for the first time this morning. "I'm sorry, Bree. I just feel lost, or maybe even damaged. Something broke in me out in those woods last night, and I can't seem to put it back together." I groan. "Hell, I don't even know what it is that's broken."

Bree's small hand drops onto mine that's half covered with my too-long sleeves. I don't even remember getting dressed after Bree and Qadira cleaned the blood off of me last night. After Seth and I were attacked by two rogue wolves, Bree's witchy senses picked up that I was injured and she created a portal to pull me out of the woods. I don't know why Seth didn't come, but I'm not surprised considering I was covered in blood laced with the thing that could kill him in seconds. *The stupid shifter cure.*

I only remember bits and pieces of the events that followed my return to the guest house. I remember seeing the wide-eyed Rylee get ushered out of the living room by Wilk. His neon green eyes looked wild and his skin glowed like I've never seen before. He was speaking fast in another language, and I was sure it was a string of curse words. I wish I could understand what he was saying, but that'll be a question for another day.

Qadira and Bree were fast as they stripped my clothes off of me, and I was immediately grateful that Seth hadn't decided to join. I hazily remember him being naked in the woods, reaching out to me where I stood over the dead shifter body. The shifter that I killed. I was so afraid of hurting Seth that I yelled at him, but he doesn't deserve to be put in that situation. He deserves so much more than me and my toxic blood.

I rub at the ache on my chest where I was dripping with that toxic blood just twelve hours ago. There's only a scar there now, thanks to Qadira and Wilk using their combined faerie magic to speed up my healing. Everyone is always helping me, and all I do is cause destruction.

Bree sighs after saying more words that never register in my messed-up mind. She stands from the sofa, making me sink further into my overstuffed cushion. "You're not damaged, Maia. If anything broke last night, it was your hope. But please remember that broken things *can* be fixed."

My eyes trail after her as she leaves through the front door of the cabin. She's right. Broken things can be fixed. I just don't know if I'm capable of fixing this one.

◊◊◊

Seth

I'm pacing outside of the guest cabin behind Alpha Nate's house. Maia hasn't left the cabin yet today, and it's clear that she doesn't wish to see me. I haven't slept since the attack last night. I have two thoughts about why rogue wolves could be encroaching on pack territory. Rogues aren't ambitious enough to gather in packs and go around attacking unsuspecting shifters. Either someone hired them due to some personal vendetta, or someone out there has learned about Maia.

I hope with everything in me that this is just some pissed off rival pack and not somebody after Maia's blood. Of course, it's not like this pack to be quite that lucky. Anger rises in me as images of last night flash through my mind. Fear nearly crippled me when I lost Maia in the woods. Then, seeing her covered in her own blood had my wolf threatening to tear the world down in the hopes I'd avenge her in the process.

All I wanted was to touch her in that moment, to hold her and soothe her worries, but that wasn't possible. She was right, her blood is toxic to me, but I have such a hard time caring when she looks into my eyes. Would I really be okay with dying just to have one perfectly blissful moment with Maia? Absolutely. If only it wouldn't break her heart immediately after.

I've tried not to listen into Maia's private conversations inside the guest cabin as I carve a path through the grass with my pacing, but her soft cries find me anyway. "Dammit!" I shout into the trees. She's crying again, while I just stand out here like an idiot.

"No need to yell at the forest, wolf. I do not think it is listening." Wilk's stilted speech causes me to spin around.

The Fae prince has his arms crossed as he floats above the earth with his fluttering wings, his usual smile plastered across his porcelain face. He lands, letting his wings rest, and walks barefoot toward me. It's rare to see Wilk without Qadira by his side, but there's a first time for everything.

"Hey, Wilk. Sorry for the outburst." I dip my head at him and try to rub the worry off of my face with the palm of my hand.

Wilk's thin eyebrows raise. "Do you call that an outburst? I expected much worse considering your mate is experiencing such turmoil. Please, Seth, continue yelling if that is what you need."

I shake my head. "Maia isn't my mate, and I don't need to yell. I just need..." *What do I need?*

"You need Maia. You need to be near her, do you not?" *Damn smart faerie.*

I scoff and cross my own arms in defiance, though I don't know why this defensive feeling comes over me. "Sure, I'd like to comfort her, I guess. She shouldn't be feeling this way. She killed that rogue in self-defense." I look at the glowing faerie, noticing the smart aleck look on his face. "And how do you know what I need anyway? I thought faeries weren't good at understanding other people."

Wilk shrugs. "I cannot tell you that I am well studied in the ways of the heart. Even in our families, us Fae do not speak of love. I like to think I know of it all the same, though. I feel admiration for Maia, but I know it is different than what you feel for her. Could you explain the feeling to me?"

He wants me to explain what love is? How the hell am I supposed to know? I do know what it feels like to look at Maia, to hear her laugh, and to feel her lips against mine with the sound of her racing heart keeping pace with mine. Maybe that's love…

I sigh and raise my shoulders in uncertainty. "When you look at Qadira, what do you feel? I imagine that's love, or something close to it." I've thought there was more to the relationship between the two faeries, but I've seen no sure sign of it.

Wilk's eyebrows fall hard, shadowing his eyes in a look of confusion. He purses his lips, not smiling for once. "Oh. Now, that is something I am not sure has an explanation. I feel a need, of sorts, to look at her, to touch her, but to also protect her from the entire world, though I know she does not need that from me. If Qadira was the only person to ever again look or speak to me, I feel I could be perfectly content with that life, while if she were to ever be gone from my sight, I could just as easily die for just that reason alone." *Well, damn.*

A harsh laugh leaves me and I reach out to pat Wilk on the shoulder. "Now, I'm no expert, but that sure as hell sounds like a very deep and intense kind of love."

Wilk grins again and seems to glow even brighter momentarily. "That is good to know, brother."

He nods to me, and his neon green eyes stare off as if lost in thought.

Wilk is crazy about the little pink faerie, and I can't help but feel hopeful for his future with her. He has become my friend in this short time, though I've never really had a true friend before. I never knew I'd be able to spot love once I saw it, but it wasn't hard to know with just his words that he's head over heels. And the way he described the love he has for Qadira registered as all too relatable for me.

I shake my head in relief for finally coming to terms with my own feelings, and stalk toward the guest house with my mind made up. I'm not going to let Maia protect me from herself. I need to be near her, and it's completely selfish of me to force myself into her life when she thinks it will never work, but I cannot give up on her.

I'm stupidly in love with my Snow White.

Chapter 23

◇◇◇

Maia

I WIPE THE TEARS FROM MY EYES, hating that I am crying again. I feel like all I've done for the past twelve hours is cry and sulk. I want to smack myself for being such a girl, but I've probably had enough injury for a while. I stand from the couch, needing to face the daylight, but the front door swings open before I reach the handle.

Seth's brown eyes land on me as he enters the large cabin living room. "Snow," he says gently, like a soft caress.

I wasn't expecting to see him just yet, and why is he even here when I yelled at him to leave me alone last night? *Stubborn wolf.* I want to be mad at him for not listening to me, but as I look up at his scruffy face and hooded eyes, my whole body just wants to slip right into his arms.

I can still remember exactly what his lips feel like against mine, and I crave that feeling as if it were a drug that was only made for me. I lick my lips at the memory, and Seth's gaze drops to the movement.

"What are you doing here, Seth? I told you to not come near me." I barely hear my own words as I stare at the gorgeous man filling the door frame.

Why is he so damn distracting?

Seth steps fully into the room and the door closes behind him. He's standing mere inches from me, and I should really back away, but for the life of me, I can't make myself move. "Snow, I won't stay away from you. I know it's what you said last night, but I'm a stubborn asshole, and don't pretend you didn't call me that yourself a handful of times."

My heart lurches, but I try to stay put. "Just because it's what you are, doesn't mean you have to own it, Seth. You can choose to value your life, and protect yourself from what's inside of me." My eyes fall and I want to cry all over again. "I'm not worth the risk."

Seth's large hands are fast as he grips the sides of my head and pulls my gaze back to his. He looks pissed, but it's mixed with a dark hunger behind his narrowed eyes. "Maia, my beautiful Snow White. You are more than a physical risk to me. Yes, the cure in you could wipe me from existence, and potentially my whole race." It hurts to hear him say it out loud, but I try not to whimper. "But even if the cure didn't exist, you are still more of a risk to me than anything else on this earth. You have total control over my heart, Maia.

It's yours, do you understand? It's far too late for me to protect myself from you. My stubborn ass is in love with you, and there's no going back."

If my heart beat any faster, I'm sure I would die. Seth is in love with me? I blink back unshed tears as I stay locked in his hold, and my shaking hands climb his forearms to cover his warm hands on my cheeks. *Speak, you dummy!* I shout at myself in my mind.

"Are you really in love with me, Seth?" He nods silently, his face showing a hint of worry. I can't stop my lips from stretching into a silly grin. "I know I shouldn't be, but I am so idiotically in love with you, too... and I really want to kiss you again."

Seth doesn't hesitate. His plump lips drop to mine, and his hands slide from my face to dive into my hair. He tugs gently on the hair between his fingers, tilting my head so that our mouths fit perfectly together. His tongue strokes my lips, asking for an initiation which I willingly give as I open my mouth.

Our tongues tangle together in a heat that threatens to suffocate me, and still I want more. I dig my fingers into his thick shoulders, trying to pull him closer to me, and though he's significantly stronger than me, he goes where I tug him. Our chests slam together, both of our bodies needing to feel the others, but a sharp pain shoots across my skin at the rough contact.

I gasp and reach for the scars on my chest below my oversized shirt, just barely healed from the rogue wolf attack. The pain slowly subsides, but Seth's hungry look fades into one of worry all over again. His chest rises and falls quickly, and he rubs a hand down his face.

"Snow, I'm so sorry. I wasn't thinking about your injury at all…"

I hold a hand up, and smile through the last of the throbbing pain in my chest. I place my hand against his cheek. "Stop that right now. If while you were making out with me, you *were* thinking about my injury, then I clearly wouldn't have been doing it right." I raise a single eyebrow suggestively, and Seth's face lights up with the most adorable grin.

"Well, let me assure you. Every part of that was very, *very* right." He leans into me, and I'm ready to claim his mouth all over again when the door behind him opens right into his back with a hard thud. Somehow, Seth is unmoved by the hit, and just turns to the wide-eyed Bree with a scowl on his face.

Bree looks at the itty-bitty space between Seth and I. "As much as I am dying to, I *so* do not have the time to comment on this situation right now." She looks at me and sighs. "My grandmother is at Nate and Lydia's house. She says she had a vision… and not a good one."

My heart sinks, and Seth grabs my hand tightly in his. He nods to Bree. "We'll be right there."

Bree shuts the door again, and I close my eyes, not wanting to know what could possibly be around the next corner of this journey. Seth strokes his fingers across my cheek and kisses me lightly on the lips. The gesture is more comforting than I could have hoped for. I open my eyes to meet his loving gaze, and every part of me sighs.

"We can handle anything, okay?" Seth says with conviction. "I won't leave your side."

I nod, and the two of us leave hand in hand toward Uncle Nate's large cabin.

◊◊◊

Maia

Seth and I step into Uncle Nate and Aunt Lydia's over-crowded living room. Wilk and Qadira stand like sentinels, side by side next to the roaring fireplace. Bree sits beside Rylee on the loveseat, while my father leans against the armrest next to the fox shifter. My aunt and uncle sit closely on the larger sofa in front of Bree's grandmother who rests on an overstuffed recliner chair with her wrinkled eyes closed tight. Even the broad wolf shifter, Horas, stands against a far wall with the always glaring, blonde Sasha by his side.

I swear, all eyes fall on Seth and I's intertwined fingers, and half the room smiles while the other half tenses uncomfortably. Well, at least not all of them hate the idea, though Sasha looks as if her entire body might burst into flames, or shift into a vengeful wolf right in the middle of her alpha's house. Either way, I'm not on board with the staredown she gives me.

Grandma Em's eyes fly open, glowing a bright silver momentarily before returning to a normal shade of green like her granddaughter's. I almost think I must've imagined it, but one look at Seth's wide eyes confirms the truth.

"Good evening, Madam," Seth says to Bree's grandmother, and the old woman gives him a look that could slice through steel. Seth clears his throat before changing his approach. "I mean, Grandma Em, of course."

Grandma Em smiles at that and dips her head at us both. "I'm glad you could make it to this unexpected gathering. I know my granddaughter has told you I had a vision. Come sit and I will show it to you." She waves for me to come to her, and my eyebrows shoot up.

"Show me? What do you mean by that?"

She huffs and shakes her head as if I exhaust her with a simple question. "Just do as you're told and come."

I hurry over to the woman and kneel in front of her so we are at eye level. I'm not about to say *no* to the witch. She clearly has power that I know nothing about. Grandma Em lays her hands on my shoulders, and she leans forward until her forehead rests against mine. Her eyes close, so I follow her lead and close my own.

I draw in a deep breath, smothered in her sweet perfume, and it makes me feel like I just walked into a beauty salon. The scent is very womanly, and not at all like my own subtle pomegranate shampoo and generic soap smell.

Flashes of light appear behind my eyelids, and I flinch slightly at the sudden change. The flashes start to spread out into what looks like the first-ever moving picture with color. Slides of still images roll together to form a scene of myself standing in a vast field of frost-dusted heather in springtime. The sun is rising, and I bask in the warmth as I dance in circles through the flowers. Amazingly, my hair flows behind me, but it's a chocolatey brown color, and no longer the colorless strands that I was born with.

I can feel myself smiling as I sit in front of Grandma Em while she shows me this gorgeous vision. I open my mouth to speak, but before I can say anything, the vision changes. It shows me dancing backwards, as if on rewind. The morning becomes night, then evening, then a cloudy day, and another early morning. I don't know how many days Grandma Em's vision rewinds itself, but I find myself again, only this time I'm dripping from head to toe in blood.

My eyes are wide, and my white hair is dyed a crimson color from the death soaking it. All around me along the forest floor are dead wolves of various sizes and colors, all covered in my blood. I watch myself fall to the earth in front of a large black wolf that breathes shallowly as it succumbs to an internal injury.

My blood-stained self cries for the wolf. She grabs the beast around his neck in a warm hug and whispers to him. "I'm sorry, Seth. I couldn't save you. I couldn't save any of you." Her soft voice breaks as she sobs. "They all know about my blood now, and they won't stop. They'll never stop coming for me."

The vision of myself fades and Grandma Em pulls her head away from mine. I can feel myself shaking where I kneel on the soft carpet. I don't know when I started crying, but I reach my hand up and feel wetness along my trembling cheeks.

"What did you see, Mai? Why are you crying?" Bree's urgent voice brings me back to the room full of people, and I sniffle past my tears.

I look at all of the worried faces watching me, and find Grandma Em's knowing eyes. "Was that real? Is that what's in my future?"

She shrugs. *Very reassuring, Gram.* "Sometimes the visions show a representation of the future, but not the exact events. It could be just a metaphor, or an over-exaggeration based on your current fears. I don't know if it will look just as you saw, but I believe it does mean that the supernatural world knows of you, and a war is coming."

A few gasps reach my ears, though I don't know who from. I swallow the hard lump in my throat, and look at Bree again. "I saw death, Bree. I saw the death of the wolf shifter race..." I nearly tell the other part of Grandma Em's vision, the part where I'm happy and free... and normal.

I shake my head, deciding to keep that portion to myself, and I look back at Grandma Em who gives me a reassuring nod. I don't think she wants me to tell them the happy ending in my story. I have a feeling that that part was just for me. I turn to Seth and his gaze is clouded with a heavy worry.

Images of his dying wolf fill my mind and I want to start crying all over again, but I steady my breathing. I can't let that part of the future come true. I'll do whatever it takes to save him, and all of the others from that fate. I clench my fists in determination and look back at Grandma Em.

"What can I do? To stop this war from happening? I'll do anything, Grandma Em."

My voice is desperate, but I don't even care. Uncle Nate joins in with his own pleading. "Yes, please tell us if there's a way to save our people, Emlyn, and to save Maia. There has to be something."

Grandma Em nods and grabs my hands in hers. "I believe it's time for you to see the high priestess of the witches. It's my hope that she can destroy the cure altogether."

My father stands tall at her words. "I thought the cure couldn't be destroyed. It's why we needed a safe host for it in the first place, isn't it?"

That's me. The cure host.

Grandma Em taps a long fingernail against her lips. "I cannot tell you what the high priestess knows, Mathew. All I know is that she has the answers we need. It's important for Maia to go to her immediately." She looks at me again. "I fear your blood may have already found its way into enemy hands."

It's my turn to gasp. "How? That's impossible."

"The vials," Seth says from behind me. I spin to him, confused by what he means. "Are Maia's blood samples safe?"

No freakin' way.

My eyes fall on the frowning witch, and she shakes her head solemnly. "I'm afraid one of them has gone missing. Someone close to us has taken it, and there is no telling where it could be now."

I feel like all of the air has been sucked out of the cabin, and my heart sinks to the base of my stomach. I look around at all of the people that I care the most about in this world, minus Sasha, of course. Multiple pairs of eyes dance around the room, each accusing the others, but it couldn't be any of them. Right?

I look over at the hateful Sasha, but to my utter shock, even she looks worried. Seth's dark eyes meet mine, and I can see the anger behind his gaze. His jaw clenches tight and his eyebrows lower to a dangerous level. He's about to get a little revengey, and damn it if I'm not completely on board with that plan.

Chapter 24

◇◇◇

Seth

"IS EVERYONE READY?" I look around at all of them standing beside the waiting vehicles. The faeries stand tall and proud, side by side, and both of them nod. Bree and Rylee hold onto Maia's hands, all strong and fearless women. *Especially my Maia.*

These people have somehow become my new pack. My loyalty will always be with the Shaw pack, and I know that when the time comes, as long as I am living, I will claim my position as alpha. Right now, though, I have found a pack unlike any other, and I trust them all with my life.

This morning, Bree's grandmother warned us of the war to come, and told us to travel to Georgetown, Delaware. We're supposed to be able to find the high priestess of the witches there, but it'll be an all-night drive. I don't want to wait another minute if there's a chance to get the cure out of Maia. Maybe then, we wouldn't have to hold back.

Footsteps approach us from the woods, and I stiffen, worried that another rogue attack could be coming. I catch the scent of Horas just before he exits the trees with a big grin stretching his bearded face.

"You guys wouldn't leave without me, would ya? I'm itchin' for a vacation."

Maia smiles and runs to hug my dear friend. I have to tell my wolf to simmer down as he rises at the sight of Maia's delicate arms encircling Horas' large frame. "I'm so glad you're coming, Horas. We could always use some more muscle."

Horas steps away from her, somehow smiling even wider than before. "Don't thank me just yet, little hybrid. I'm bringing backup."

Maia's eyebrows raise, and then her face falls when she spots Horas' "backup". Sasha saunters up to our group with a little more hip shake than necessary. I want to groan in protest, but I can't turn away more willing protectors for Maia. I'd enlist an entire army of Sashas to keep her safe if I could.

Sasha throws her hands on her hips and looks at everyone's frowning faces. "What? Not happy to see me? Oh, boohoo," she says sarcastically, and flips her long blonde ponytail before climbing into the front seat of Alpha Nate's Chevy Trailblazer.

Maia turns to me with her eyebrows raised. "Well, it looks like I'll be riding in the Jeep." She rolls her gorgeous hazel eyes and climbs easily into the passenger seat of my Jeep.

I had hoped that she'd want to ride in my Jeep anyways, so I have zero complaints. I try to hide my smile as I look toward the others. "Well, I've got two spots in the Jeep. Horas, go ahead and drive the Trailblazer with Sasha and the faeries. I'll take Bree and Rylee."

Horas nods, and playfully punches Wilk in the shoulder. "Sounds good to me, boss. Come on, your highness. I'll show you how we fly without wings."

Wilk looks down at Qadira with a smile, and the two of them follow Horas into the car. "This sounds like it may be a bit of fun. Maybe I can learn how to drive, as well."

Horas laughs boisterously. "Sure thing, man."

I turn back to the girls and wave them over to the Jeep. Bree and Rylee climb into the back seat, and I settle in the driver's spot beside Maia. I look over at her, but she's staring out into the dark woods with worry creasing her forehead.

"Hey. We'll figure out how to get the cure out of you, Snow. Trust me, okay?" I reach over to grab her hand in mine, and she sighs at the contact, making my heart literally flutter in my chest.

Maia looks into my eyes. "It still won't tell us who took my blood, though." She looks back at Rylee and Bree. "Do you two have any guesses?"

Bree practically growls, which surprises me. "Whoever the hell thought they could betray us better watch out, that's for sure."

I look into the rearview mirror and catch Rylee's widened eyes. She's younger than the rest of us and has had to run too much already. I hate that we're dragging her into yet another dangerous trip.

"You can stay here with my pack, Rylee. You'd be safe and protected with Nate and Lydia."

Rylee's face lights up and she shakes her head, all fear gone in an instant. "I'm not afraid of a little adventure, Seth. This will be fun."

Maia scoffs and turns back to stare out the front window. "I don't know about *fun*, but if this road trip is anything like the last, it definitely won't be boring."

I start the Jeep, and it rumbles to life. I pull out onto the long dirt road that leaves the pack lands, with Horas' headlights shining behind us. We're only a mile away from Nate's cabin when a figure jumps into the road, causing me to slam on my breaks.

"What the hell was that?" I shout. "That wasn't human or wolf. Stay here."

I'm about to jump out and investigate, but Maia's door swings open, and all of us snap our heads in that direction.

Maia's almost-scream falls immediately. "James!"

"Mind picking up a hitch-hiker? I really hope I didn't come all this way to hang out with a wolf pack." The infuriating British vampire is smiling down at my Maia, with a wicked gleam in his dark eyes. "Hello, love."

Damn vampire.

◇ ◇ ◇

Maia

James smiles at me, and not thinking, I immediately wrap my arms around him. A low growl echoes in the jeep, and I release James like I had just been burned. *Crap!*

I almost forgot about my incredibly possessive alpha-wolf. *My wolf.* I spin around to eye Seth disapprovingly. "You stop that right now, Seth Lowell. We don't need another fight before the trip even begins."

Seth's glare fades, but I can still see the darkness in his irises, threatening to turn black. "We don't need a bloodsucker either..." he mumbles under his breath, but I pretend not to hear it. *Damn stubborn sexy wolf.*

James chuckles and I'm reminded about his little mind-reading trick. "Hey! If you want to come with us, stay out of our heads!"

James holds both of his hands up and has the audacity to look shocked. "I would never! I can't read the little witch's mind, so why don't I sit beside her?" He peers into the back seat over my shoulder. "What do ye say, Bree? It has been some time."

My eyes fly wide and I turn around to Bree. "He can't hear your thoughts? How?"

To my surprise, Bree's face flushes pink and she shrugs, avoiding James' gaze. "I think it's my grandma's protection spell over her descendants. It protects my mind as well as my body."

"Wow." I can't help but be a little jealous of that power. "Do you mind letting James squeeze in back there? Rylee?" I ask them both.

Rylee looks really uncomfortable, and doesn't look toward James, but she shrugs. "Whatever."

Strange.

"James?" Wilk's voice breaks into the darkness behind James. "Why would you be all the way out here, my friend?"

My friend?

James turns with a happy smile toward Wilk. "I found a little witch in my woods once, then a very strange hybrid lass. Consider me intrigued."

I shove him. "Hey! I'm not strange! And how do you two even know each other?"

"The faeries have lived in and out of Maine for a hundred years. We have come to a truce, and even a friendship."

Wilk laughs and pats James on the shoulder. "Definitely a friendship. I am glad we are stopped for you, and not another rogue wolf attack. Will you be joining us?"

Seth answers for everyone, less than enthusiastic. "Sounds like it. Can we skip the reunions and get on the road now?"

Wilk's bright green eyes widen in the dark slightly, but he simply nods and hurries back to the other car. "We will be right behind you."

Clearly, he doesn't want to get on the dark side of Seth's temper. Something wild inside of me wants to calm his rage in whatever way I can, or stoke the flames and see how far I can push him. I press down my psycho wolf side and gesture for James to get in the back, while he grins like a kid in a candy store.

I bet he's loving my inner struggle, and whatever is happening inside Seth's angry head. I glare back at James once more, but I find him taking a long and *hungry* look at Bree while she stares out the window.

If you eat my best friend, I will have to take extreme measures with your life, vampire.

James snaps his dark eyes to me and his smile only stretches. He nods once in acknowledgement of my threat, but doesn't respond to me.

I reach my hand out to Seth's as he drives with a death grip on the stealing wheel. He releases a long breath when his fingers curl around mine, and I wish I could hear what's happening in his gorgeous head. Whatever he's thinking, I just hope he's not worried about James and I.

Clearly, James has his thoughts on someone else.

Chapter 25

◇◇◇

Maia

"ARE WE THERE YET?" James whines from the backseat of the car like a toddler.

Bree scoffs and shoves him playfully. "You act like you've never been on a car trip before! We've only been driving for five hours."

James groans and wiggles uncomfortably. It's thrilling to see him as the uncomfortable one for once, and I can't help but smile. "I have never sat in the backseat of a vehicle in my existence, and as you know, I have lived in the woods for many years. As much as I enjoy our bodies touching for hours on end, little witch, I am incredibly antsy."

Bree's eyes widen and a new blush stains her cheek. "Oh, for hell's sake, James. Don't say things like that!"

James smiles and I catch Rylee rolling her eyes. She's not a fan of the vamp so far, and I wonder what the foxes think of James' kind. It's not like our little group is exactly orthodox, so I can understand how difficult it must be for them all to get along, especially being so close to each other.

I turn toward Seth. "Maybe we all do need some space for a few hours, Seth. We've got three wild wolves, two faeries, a fox, and a vamp that are all used to the openness of the forest. Probably best to take a breather."

Seth nods. "I think you're right. I'll find the next motel and we can sleep for the rest of the morning, just until the sun is out."

We've been driving in the dark from the pack lands in Vermont and we're nearing New Jersey. I've always wanted to explore this area, especially New York City, but Dad never took me. He said the big cities were too dangerous for a young pretty girl. *More like they're too dangerous for a young cure-carrying vessel, right Dad?*

Seth takes us off the freeway and parks at a small but clean hotel just outside the city. "I'll run in and see if they have a couple rooms." He looks back at James and sighs, seemingly defeated. "One for the guys, and one for the girls."

"Can't wait to get to know you better, mate," James speaks from the backseat, and I want to turn around and punch him for his sarcastic tone.

Seth's eyes fall on me, and the corners of his lips lift slightly. Before I know it, he swoops back into the car to press his warm lips against mine, claiming my mouth as his for the whole carload to see. As much as I want to deny his show of masculine assery, my whole body heats up from his kiss.

I hold back the moan that wants to leave my throat, and Seth pulls away with dark eyes. He licks the taste of me off his lips before winking and leaving with a hop in his step to get our rooms.

Damn, why does he have to be so sexy?

"Well, love. If I didn't know any better, I'd say the wolf has found his mate." James raises a single eyebrow in my direction.

Bree looks up at James. "Do you think their wolves could be fated for one another?"

He shrugs. "Without knowing if Maia even has a wolf, there is no way to tell. Their thoughts are incredibly possessive for just two creatures in love, though. I feel fervently warned to stay clear of his property."

"Hey!" I shout back at him. "First of all, I'm right here, so stop talking about me! Secondly, I am nobody's property." I give Bree a pointed look, hoping she'll back me up.

Bree looks apologetic as she responds. "Sorry, hon. Wolf love is a little possessive. Seth likely sees you as his property, even though it's his wolf and not his conscious mind. But, in the same way, he'd be more than happy for you to see him the same way."

I scrunch up my nose. *This is so weird.* I look at Rylee who has been strangely quiet. "Is it the same for foxes?"

She nods. "Yup. Seth practically just peed all over you for the world to see. If you were a wolf, you'd feel pretty damn lucky right now."

My mouth falls open. "Eww! Why'd you have to say it like that?"

She smiles slightly for the first time during this trip, but when she looks up at James she hurries and looks back out the window with a frown. James' eyebrows press together and his head tilts to the side as he watches Rylee. He seems confused by her, and I hope they can become friends despite their differences. If Bree and the faeries can do it, so can they.

A knock at my window makes me jump, but my fear quickly settles when I spot Qadira staring at me through the glass. I open the door and climb out with the rest of our party.

"Did you have a nice drive, Dira? The wolves are being nice, right?"

She smiles at me, flipping her long pink locks over one shoulder. "It was lovely, Maia. Prince Wilk and Horas had us laughing throughout the journey."

A small pink hue brightens her cheeks, matching the color of her eyes, and I grin out of happiness for my beautiful friend. "Fun. All we got was a complaining vampire."

Qadira giggles, and the others gather around us as Seth returns from the building. He hands me a flimsy plastic key card and holds one of his own.

"Okay," he says, taking charge as our pack alpha. "I got us two of the largest rooms they offer. There are three queen beds in each. Maia, Qadira, Bree, Rylee, and Sasha will take room 24, while Horas, Wilk, James, and I will claim the adjoining room."

All of us look around uncomfortably, except for Wilk. He practically hops as he snatches the key card from Seth's hand. "I am wonderfully excited. I have never slept in a hotel before."

"I'll take one of the queen beds. The rest of you can share." Sasha clicks her tongue and saunters off toward the long wall of doors, hips shaking in her skin-tight black leggings.

Horas makes a low whistling sound as he stares at Sasha's round hips, and Bree takes it upon herself to punch him in one of his massive arms. My eyes flick up to Seth, and unlike his pack mate, he's only looking at me.

Oh, he's too good.

"Hey, Snow. Do you mind if we have a walk while the others settle into the rooms?"

Walk alone in the dark with Seth? Yes, please.

I nod. "Sure." I hold out the key card for Bree. "I'll be there in a minute. Save me a spot before Sasha decides to push the beds together and make herself one mega bed."

James hurries and snatches the card before Bree can get it. "Sorry, little witch. You'll have to catch me first."

James grins wickedly and takes off in a run, but not fast enough. Bree throws up an invisible wall that James runs head first into with a crack, making him fall onto the asphalt.

Horas laughs so loud that it echoes in the dark parking lot, and all of the others join in with their own snickering. Even James laughs from the ground, as Bree stands over him with her hand out for the key card.

I miss what happens next, because I'm lifted off the ground and cradled in Seth's arms. I gasp, and I look up into his dark brown eyes. "You really know how to sweep a girl off her feet, wolf boy."

He playfully growls at me as he carries me away from the others. "You haven't seen anything yet, Snow."

◊ ◊ ◊

Seth

I carry Maia to the back of the small hotel outside New Jersey. I need a place where I can breathe in her scent and hear only her heart beating. Being stuck in my jeep with the others is torture when I know that Maia loves me.

At least, I hope she still loves me now that James is here. I set Maia on her feet, and cage her between my arms as I lean against the brick wall of the building. It's dark here, but I can see every detail of her with ease.

My wolf whines inside of me, wanting to smell her, or even taste her. I lean my head forward and breathe in Maia's zesty scent. She smells like an orange grove after a long rainfall. Perfectly sweet and earthy.

"Are you smelling me, Seth?" The humor in her tone has me smiling as I lean back and look into her hazel eyes.

"Is that strange to you, Snow?" It probably is. Scents are important in shifter culture, but not so much with humans.

Maia reaches her hands up to rest against my pecs. I can feel the warmth of her skin through my t-shirt. "It's not really strange. I've just never thought much about the importance of a person's scent."

I lift my chin to her in complete submission. Exposing one's neck is dangerous for wolves. It's an easy kill spot, but all I want is for Maia to bite into the flesh there. *Hell, I'm an absolute maniac.*

"Go ahead. Take a whiff and tell me what you think."

Maia giggles softly, and I can hear the thumping of her heart speed up as she leans into my neck. "I don't have your senses, but I'll give it a go." Her hot breath fans my neck and I hold back the shiver that wants to ripple through me.

Maia's nose touches my skin, just beside my Adam's apple, and she breathes in deep as she slides her nose along the skin of my exposed neck. "Mmmm," she moans as she smells me, and every muscle in my body tightens.

"I'd say... pine trees and sunshine." Her lips just barely press against my racing pulse in a feather light kiss. "Perfect," she whispers, and I'm undone.

I think my wolf growls inside of me as I grip Maia's thighs and hoist her onto my hips, pressing her back against the cold brick. She gasps, and her hands tangle into my hair, tugging hard as she scrambles to keep herself against me.

I don't wait for her permission. I press my lips against hers, and she kisses me back with just as much eagerness. Her teeth graze my skin and she sucks my bottom lip into her mouth. I'm more aware than I ever have been of the wild animal inside of me.

I press Maia harder against the wall, using it to support her as my hands explore her hips, sliding just barely under the bottom of her shirt until I feel her skin at my fingertips. I crave every part of her, and it almost hurts to keep myself from pushing her too far.

Maia's hands slide back to my chest and travel over my abdomen, making me suck in a sharp breath at the incredible sensation. She tugs at my shirt and dips her hands under the fabric to touch my skin as I did to her. She groans against my mouth, kissing me fast and hard.

If I could imagine tasting heaven, Maia taking control of my body would be it. I once thought she was delicate and weak, only human, but this assertive and possessive side of her is all alpha wolf. *My* wolf.

Maia tries to lift my shirt higher, but I reluctantly stop her as I take both of her small hands in one of mine, and slip my other one under her thighs again. She's trapped in my arms, and as much as I want her here like this, it will have to wait.

I lean my head back, breathing heavy as I scan her hooded eyes and heated cheeks. "You are so damn beautiful, Snow."

She licks her lips and smiles shyly up at me. "Then why'd you stop kissing me?"

Good question.

I laugh and slowly set her back on her feet, but stay as close to her body as possible. "You see, I'd be more than happy to never stop kissing you, and frankly to claim your body as mine right here in the dark behind this sketchy hotel… even if the cure took my life for doing so."

The reminder of the shifter cure has her smile falling. "Seth…"

I shake my head, not wanting her to feel bad anymore. "But, even as I am willing to die for the chance of pure happiness with you, I'm not willing to put the burden of my death on your head, and surely not on your heart."

I lay a hand against her chest, feeling the rapid beat beneath the surface. I'd do anything to protect that heart.

Maia closes her eyes briefly and breathes out a long breath. "I understand. We just need to get to the high priestess and see if she can remove the cure." She gazes up at me through long lashes. "Then you will be all mine, Seth Lowell."

Holy hell, that's hot.

"What about the others? Without the cure, you won't need all of this protection. I mean, I'm fine with taking James out of the picture, for sure…"

She shoves my chest playfully. "Don't hate James. The only reason he ever kissed me was to help me get you jealous enough to make a move. He could see that you were on my mind even then."

I can't help but smile, and I'm sure it looks every bit as arrogant as I feel. I never thought I'd want to talk about that kiss again, but I love that it wasn't more than just a show by the crazy vampire. *Maybe I actually like the guy.*

Maia scoffs and shoves me again, not even moving me an inch. "Stop that silly grinning, wolf boy, and if I ever see you acting all jealous again, I'll have to kick your ass."

My smile only deepens and I steal one last kiss from my Snow White before we have to join the world again. "I love you, Maia."

She smiles against my lips and whispers, "I love you too, Seth."

Chapter 26

◇◇◇

Maia

MY EYES FLUTTER OPEN AND I want to complain as I leave my Seth-filled dream. I was surprised how quickly I fell asleep in the incredibly stiff bed beside Bree. It has been too long since we shared a bed, but this is nothing like our sleepovers filled with girlish giggles and boy talk. We're in a hotel with a pack of paranormal creatures, on our way to find a super old witch leader.

What a weird road trip.

I roll over and think about that incredible kiss with Seth just a few hours ago that led to my steamy dream. I could get used to falling asleep every night with him whispering his love for me as I drift off. Thanks to Grandma Em's vision of me standing with brown hair and a smile on my face, I have hope for a normal life with my wolf shifter. *Well, semi-normal.* I just hope I can keep the ones I love safe until then.

A rustling sound brings my attention to the front door of the hotel room. I squint, adjusting my eyes to see Rylee tip-toeing out into the last dark hours of the morning. She turns just outside the room and her eyes connect with mine. She tips her head back for me to come with her, and then she disappears, leaving the door cracked behind her.

Where on earth could she be going?

I sit up and look around at the sleeping faces of my friends, *and Sasha.* Curiosity gets the better of me and I follow Rylee outside, not caring to put on my shoes or a coat. It's not like she can get very far.

"Rylee?" I whisper into the dark hotel parking lot.

I catch a glimpse of someone moving around to the side of the building, so I hurry after her. Maybe she's in trouble and needs my help, but she doesn't want to wake the others. A sick feeling settles in my stomach, but I push past it as I round the corner after Rylee.

"Rylee, where are you?"

The small alleyway where I was alone with Seth is now empty and quiet. I blow out a nervous breath, and turn to go wake up someone else. I shouldn't be out here alone, even with Rylee. Before I can turn all the way around, a large hand covers my mouth as I'm pulled against a hard body.

I try to scream, but the noise is muffled in the hand that holds me. "Shhhh. You wouldn't want to wake your friends."

I don't recognize the deep voice that whispers in my ear, and fear prickles my skin. I kick my legs out and throw my head back, trying to break free, but it's no use. Whoever has me is significantly stronger than myself.

A figure steps in front of me in the dark, and I can just make out the tall woman with perfectly straight black hair that reaches her waist. Her skin is caramel colored and her shining eyes are nearly entirely black like her hair.

"Give her the shot, Lynus, before the others come looking for her."

A shot?!

I kick back at the legs of my captor and try to break my arms out of his hold. A sharp sting hits my right arm and a tear drops from my eye. The bastard gave me a frickin shot, and I hate that I don't know what was in it. *Please Seth, wake up. Please.*

I try to push my thoughts to Seth, but it's not possible for him to hear me. I can't make a sound with the iron grip over my mouth. A fog starts to spread through my mind and I blink, trying to keep myself lucid. *No, no, no, no!*

The creepy tall woman steps closer to me, and her lips curl up in a smile. "Just rest, little one. This will all be over for you soon."

I whimper and struggle to get my body moving as sleep tries to pull me under. I flick my eyes around looking for someone, anyone to save me, but I only see one other person watching me from the dark. Someone I thought was my friend.

Rylee's eyes connect with mine, and she gives me an apologetic frown before her lips lift up into a wicked smile. She runs a hand through her short hair and stalks back toward the front of the hotel, as if she is just out for an early morning stroll.

My eyes close, and I can feel myself sinking into nothingness. Rylee is a traitor, and nobody will know what she has done to me. *Seth, I love you.*

◊ ◊ ◊

Seth

"Please Seth, wake up. Please."

I groan as I turn over on the hard hotel carpet. I wipe the nightmare of Maia's pleading from my mind. Her words felt all too real, and all I want is to go wake her up with a kiss.

Thanks to my detour with Maia last night, the other guys claimed the beds and I was stuck camping out on the floor with a thin blanket. I've slept in worse places, though. James steps over me and looks down with a smug smile.

"Sleep well, mate?"

I sit up and rub a hand along my face. "Would've preferred a bed, but they were all taken."

James shrugs. "You could have curled up by my feet like a good little doggy."

I glare back at the vampire, but even though his words are mean, I can tell he doesn't mean harm by them. *Watch it, vamp. My bite is much worse than my bark.*

He smiles wider at my thoughts, but it immediately falls when the hotel room door swings open. Qadira barges into the room with wide eyes and her skin glowing brighter than I've ever seen. Before she even speaks, James' eyes turn red and he charges out of the room in a flash of movement.

"What is it, Qadira?" Wilk asks, running to her side.

"Maia is gone! Bree and Rylee are looking for her now, but Bree said to come tell you. I reached out with magic, but I cannot feel her anywhere, Seth. She is *gone*."

No.

Every sound disappears when her words reach my mind. My vision blurs, and then suddenly I'm running. I don't know where I'm going, but I somehow shifted and my wolf is in total control. I break into the trees behind the hotel. They're not thick woods, and I shouldn't be running with the chance of humans seeing me, but all I can feel is an urgency to get my Snow back.

Howling pierces my ears, and it takes a moment for me to realize I'm the one howling. I stop and flick my head left to right with my nose in the air, searching for that mesmerizing scent, but she's not here.

"Seth! Stop running!" James yells my name, and I turn toward him.

His eyes are still red, and he's shaking with rage. "You won't find her like this, mate. We need a plan."

I hated this vampire only a day ago, and now he is here, trying to help me find the woman I love. I can't speak to him with my wolf mouth, so I reach out with the thoughts that only he can hear.

Where is she, James? How did nobody hear her leave?

"I believe she was taken. I don't know how, or by whom, but we will find her. Together."

My heart aches as I think about someone or something stealing her away in the night. I want to tear into something with my sharp teeth until it bleeds out the information I need to find Maia. The only problem is, there's nowhere to start.

Bree can find her. She has done it before, and I know she can again.

James nods and takes his leather jacket off. The red in his eyes fades as he hands the clothing to me. "Shift before a human sees you and makes a ruckus. You can wrap this around your waist."

I pull my wolf back, assuring the animal in me that we will find Maia, and I wrap James' coat around myself. It's not much cover, but it will do until I get to my clothes. James and I keep pace with one another as we run the mile back to the hotel.

I fish a pair of pants out of my bag in the back of the Jeep, and tug them on before joining the others beside the second vehicle. Bree's tear-filled eyes find me and she looks down at the ground.

"I'm so sorry, Seth. She was sleeping beside me, and I didn't hear anything. I don't understand."

I look toward the other girls, Sasha, Qadira, and Rylee. They all have sad expressions and I wonder how none of them heard a thing in the night.

"Sasha and Rylee. Both of you have exceptional hearing but you don't recall any strange sounds?"

Sasha crosses her arms in anger and shakes her head. "I swear, Seth. I don't particularly like your hybrid girlfriend, but I would have protected her and the cure with my life if needed. I heard nothing."

Her words are completely honest, and though I'm not happy about her admission of not liking Maia, I believe her. I turn to Rylee and she immediately drops her gaze to the ground just as Bree had.

"I'm sorry, too. I was asleep all night." She sniffles as if crying, and I growl in frustration.

James stiffens beside me, and I look at him curiously. *What is it?* I ask in my mind, not sure I should put the attention on his change in attitude.

James looks at me and his eyes flash from red to brown. He's angry about something Rylee said, but why? He shakes his head subtly and clears his throat.

"What do we do now? Bree, can you find her?" James looks at Bree with a gentleness he doesn't give to anyone else.

Bree wipes her tears away and straightens her shoulders. "I can track her, but not at a long distance. I can go as far as ten miles from myself, unless she's at a place I've been before. I think the best place to start is to reach out to the last place she was within ten miles from us now, and then start over again and again until we find her."

I sigh. "How long will that take?"

She frowns. "It depends on how far she was taken. That's all I can do, but we need to start now."

I look at everyone's determined faces and try my hardest not to shift all over again. I need to be patient, and I need to be a leader. I nod to Bree and reach out to lay a hand on her shoulder.

"We will all do our part to find Maia. Just tell us what you need."

Whatever it takes, Snow. I'll find you.

Chapter 27

◇◇◇

Maia

"YOU DIDN'T GIVE HER ENOUGH!"

"Nyma wants her to wake up, you idiot. We need as much blood as we can get. She can't die yet."

Their words creep into my mind, but I don't recognize the voices. I'm surrounded by total darkness, or are my eyes closed? I honestly don't know. Everything feels heavy, even my fingers. Nothing wants to move.

My eyes are definitely closed, but as hard as I try, only bits of light leak through. *Open, stupid eyes!* I can hear myself let out a raspy groan as I try to make my muscles cooperate.

The deeper voice from before speaks again. "Just let her wake up. She can't do any harm."

"I can do harm!" I try to yell the threat through my dry lips, but the sound that comes out is pathetic. *Why do I feel like I'm dying?*

The deep voice laughs, and the lighter, almost melodic female voice joins in. "Good try on the bravado, little girl. I'll give you a four out of ten."

I growl at the voice as I try to force my eyelids open again. I don't remember anything happening that would put me in the hands of strangers, but I can tell they're not the friendly kind. My fight instinct is in overdrive and I thrash to the side, trying to connect with one of the voices.

Something pulls hard on the skin around my wrists as I move, and I cry out in pain. "Wh… where am I?" Just speaking is a hard enough task.

The woman talks. "Don't worry about it. You're on vacation from all the fleabags. Consider yourself lucky."

Is she talking about the shifters? Seth?

"Where's Seth? And Bree? The faeries?" I need to know that my friends are all unharmed.

I try to draw on my last memories of them. I remember being on the road, sitting beside Seth in his Jeep. The vampire, James, was there with us, complaining about the drive. Did we get hit again, and somehow captured?

"Your weird pack of freaks are a long way from here, pup. Just forget about 'em." The man's voice has a hint of a southern drawl, but the tone holds no southern hospitality.

The woman scoffs and I hear a thud like she smacks the man. "She's not a pup, Lynus. She's barely a wolf at all."

Lynus?

Something about the man's name triggers a hazy memory. *"Give her the shot, Lynus, before the others come looking for her."*

I remember a tall woman walking toward me. I was being held by a man, Lynus, outside the hotel that the others and I were staying at. I was outside looking for... *Rylee*. My fox shifter friend betrayed me.

I try to gasp, but it only makes me start coughing. My eyes finally shoot open in the middle of my coughing fit, and I am staring down at a dirt floor underneath me. I trail my eyes along the ground and find the legs of one of my captors. I scan his dirty jeans, and loose-hanging polo shirt. He has elbow-length rubber gloves on his arms. His skin is pale, even more so than James' vampire skin, but this man is not a vampire as far as I can tell. But what do I know?

His dark blue eyes are watching me as I try to figure him out. He's clean shaven, but his shoulder length blonde hair is wild and messy. "You like what you see, pup?"

I narrow my eyes at him, trying to look strong even though my whole body just wants to sag to the dirt. "I'd like you much better buried in the ground, *Lynus*."

To my surprise, his cocky smile falls and he takes a step back. He looks to my right and I follow his gaze to a small woman who could only be twenty at the most, and maybe a hundred pounds. She has on matching blue rubber gloves that look strange against her black pencil skirt.

"Did you see that?" He asks the girl. "Her eyes?"

The woman flips her waist-length black hair over her shoulder and glares down at me. "See what? She looks half-dead already."

I try to laugh, though it sounds hoarse and weak. "You're the one who called me *little girl*? What are you, a third grader?"

Her brown eyes seem to burn as they look down on me. "Shut up, freak! Enjoy being lucid. It won't last."

The little woman grabs Lynus' arm and drags him off toward a nearby building that looks like a worn-down barn. "Wait," I call after them, but they just disappear inside.

The barn is surrounded by tall aspen trees and through the trees I can see more buildings, but the forest is so thick that not much is visible. A dirt trail leads to where I sit on the ground in a small opening between the trees. I try to turn, but the pinching pain around my wrist has me whimpering.

I crane my sore neck to the side, trying to see what's happening to my wrists, and I can just barely see them tied tightly by a bloodied rope. My arms are behind my back, wrapped around a rusty pipe that sticks out of the ground and stretches high above me. It looks like an old tetherball pole, and I have to scoff at the ridiculousness of the situation.

"What a place to tie a girl up," I mumble under my breath.

I turn to my right, trying to get a better view of the rope around my wrists, and my eyes bulge. A long thin tube is sticking out of my arm, connecting a few feet away to a slowly dripping bag of IV fluid. The bag is hanging from another metal pole that looks crudely bent and stuck into loose dirt for this purpose only.

What in the hell is going on?

I try shaking my arm in the hopes that I can wiggle the tubing from under my skin, but it only causes more pain. I'm not sure if they're giving me a drug to keep me here, or trying to hydrate me. Either way, I'm so incredibly confused.

"Hey!" I yell, but nobody responds. "Anybody! Help me!"

I keep yelling until my throat is raw, but I'm only left with silence. As far as I can tell, it's midday wherever I am. All I can do now is hope that the ones I love are okay, and not in a similar position. None of them knew Rylee would betray us, and with everything in me, I hope they have figured it out by now.

◊ ◊ ◊

Seth

I can't stop pacing. This is taking too damn long, and my wolf is about to rip this stupid car to pieces. *Just hurry up, Bree!*

I can't yell at her, though. I can see how hard she has been trying to find Maia. We all have been doing our best to get her back, but I still feel so helpless.

We left the hotel where Maia was taken early this morning, and the day is already almost over. As Maia's witch protector, Bree can track her, but only ten miles at a time, and the process is too slow for my liking. The process is odd and requires Bree to meditate in a place where Maia had been before. She says it's like she calls to the earth and the air that Maia touched, and then she has to follow the path to the next location.

All of this is done in Bree's mind while the rest of us sit in silence, just waiting. I've done all I can in the last two spots but sniffing for Maia's scent only gets me so far. Most places, I can't even smell where she had been, and it has to be because she was in a vehicle.

I bet they tied her up and stuck her in the trunk. *Stop thinking like that!* I yell at myself in my mind to calm down but I can still feel the rumbling growl roll through my chest. This waiting is agonizing.

James steps to my side where I sit half in and half out of my Jeep, staring at Bree's back as she meditates. "Do ye need a drink, mate?"

He holds out a flask for me to take, but I shake my head. "It won't do any good, James. Alcohol doesn't do much for my kind."

James shrugs. "Not for mine either, but it brings back the memories of when it did. Guess you never were human, though."

It's hard to imagine James as a normal human man. He holds himself like he knows all of the knowledge in the universe, but there was a time when he only knew his short life and nothing more.

"You have no idea how badly I wish I could relax for just a minute. I don't think I'll relax again until Maia is safe in my arms." I groan. "Damn, I'm a sissy."

James laughs. "That you are, but I do understand a bit, I think." He stares at Bree like I have been, but a smile lifts his lips. I haven't smiled since I fell asleep with Maia on my mind last night.

"Is she still not done?" Horas walks along the side of the empty highway, stopping beside James. "It's been like two hours. Sasha is becoming a pain."

The passenger door of Alpha Nate's Trailblazer flies open and suddenly Sasha is glaring up at Horas' bulky frame. "You wanna see pain, you giant oaf?" She winds back and with her wolf speed she punches Horas hard in the arm.

Horas growls and grabs his sore bicep. "Dammit, Sasha! That hurt like a mother!"

Sasha smiles wickedly and throws her hands back on her hips. "Good." She turns to me with sympathetic eyes, surprising me, and then saunters back to the waiting SUV.

James chuckles and pats Horas on the shoulder. "When they pick on you, it means they like ya, mate! Good on ye!" He snickers again and then leaves Horas and I standing in silence.

I can see the orange haze of the setting sun, and my heart only clenches tighter. "Maia's somewhere out there, and soon it'll be dark. She's probably terrified."

Horas crosses his arms. "She's a tough one, Seth. As your beta, I'll always tell you the truth, brother. I believe wholeheartedly that your little hybrid will make it through this."

I look over at my oldest friend. He has always been my first choice for my beta wolf when I become alpha, and even now I know I've made the right decision. "I hope you're right, man."

Behind Horas, my eyes find Rylee, our little fox shifter friend. She's standing at the edge of the trees that line the long stretch of highway, and she's watching Bree with narrowed eyes. Either she's just really focused, or she doesn't like what Bree is trying to do. I've never been able to get a good read on Rylee, and I'm starting to feel like I should've learned a little more about her before letting her into our trusty circle.

Her eyes flick to me and then quickly soften as she smiles sweetly. She waves at me and then turns to join the faeries where they're looking at a large map beside the road. Everyone is doing their part to find

Maia, right? I can't help the sick feeling in my gut, though.

Bree gasps and then spins toward me with wide eyes. "I've got it! I had a vision of Maia!" She turns and calls for the faeries. "Wilk, Dira, the map!"

I run over to Bree's side with the others and we all huddle around the map while Bree draws a circle on the wrinkled paper. "There?" Wilk asks, sounding unconvinced. "Is that where she is, then?"

Bree shrugs. "I saw her going through the area, I swear. But I can't say for sure if it's where they stopped."

I squint at the paper. "That's the middle of the Catskill mountains. That's like a hundred miles from here, Bree."

Rylee scoffs but quickly coughs and smiles like she didn't mean to sound upset. "What happened to a ten mile tracking distance?"

Bree shakes her head. "I don't know. My power must be growing since I've been using it more. Either way, Maia is out there somewhere. I say we get to the edge of the Catskill forest and I do another search."

I nod, and all of the others join in. "Alright. Everyone load up, and let's go find our girl."

Chapter 28

◇◇◇

Maia

"I'M READY FOR YOU TO KILL ME now!" Yup, I'm getting desperate.

I've been sitting against this stupid pole with this empty tube in my arm for hours and I just need someone to kick. My captors have been AWOL since their earlier greeting, though. Whatever was in the IV bag is completely gone, and I'm wide awake after my drugged nap this morning.

It's dark out and against my tough-girl instincts, a chill of fear ripples through my body at every small noise. Honestly, the silence is the worst part. *Someone come out here and at least pick a fight with me or something!*

A wooden door slams somewhere in the distance, and something runs toward me faster than my eyes can follow. The beefy guy, Lynus stops a few feet in front of me, picking up dirt. "Can't you just be quiet? Some of us are trying to sleep."

My mouth drops open. "Some of us? How many of you are out there exactly? And why would you be sleeping when you have a hostage tied up in your backyard? I could get away at any moment."

Except, I already tried that and failed miserably.

Lynus must know that I'm lying because his lips curl up in a cocky smile. "You think I'm worried about you running off? That's hilarious."

I growl and roll my eyes. "Can you at least answer a few questions for me while you're here? Clearly you don't want me dead or you wouldn't be hydrating me through *this* thing, right?" I try to hold up my arm but wince when the ropes around my wrist pull against my raw skin.

Lynus scrunches up his nose when he sees my bleeding wrists, and steps closer to me. Before I can even make a sound, he quickly pulls the IV tube out of my arm and tosses it to the side. "First answer. There are about two hundred of my people in this camp."

Two hundred? Why haven't I seen anyone else?

My captor fiddles around in his thick coat pocket and a new tube with a connected needle appears in his hand. My heart pounds, but I try not to show my fear as I wonder why he'd be putting a new IV in. I feel mostly fine, just hungry.

Lynus lays the tube on his bent knee and pulls out two blue latex gloves like he had on before. "Safety first," he says smoothly with a frown.

Either he's trying to stay clean, or... *He's a shifter.*

He doesn't look particularly happy with his job as Mr. Poker, but he continues forward, drawing an empty blood bag out of his other coat pocket. My mouth goes completely dry. *That's not an IV.*

"What are you doing? I've seen blood donations before. I know what that is, and I didn't volunteer for this." My voice quivers and I try to twist my hands free behind me with no luck.

Lynus clicks his tongue as he continues to connect the tube to the bag and lay it on a patch of grass beside me. "To answer your second question. No, we do not want you dead... yet."

He pops the covering off of the needle, and the sharp tip glistens in the moonlight. I can feel tears threatening to fall, and sweat covers my forehead out of fear.

Lynus continues. "We need as much blood as possible from you before you die, pup. Us lupercus used to have the upper hand in this shifter war, but without the cure, our numbers are dwindling. It's time for a weapon... AKA, you."

I flinch at his words. I've heard of the lupercus only once before. They're a group of creatures that wiped out many of the Shaw pack after I was born. "Lynus, please. If you are a shifter, any kind of shifter, you have to understand that war isn't going to help. It'll only cause more death to your kind."

He shakes his head and brings the needle closer to my shaking arm. "Lupercus aren't meant to coexist, little one. I can't imagine someone like you could understand, but we're meant to rule the shifter races, to bring them under control and stop the wild animals from overrunning the earth and killing humans."

"Aren't you a wild animal too? Just like the wolves and bears?" I don't know what lupercus shift into, but it can't be all that different from any normal animal. Apparently, they see themselves as humane and tame. I've seen nothing to convince me yet.

"Like I said, you don't understand. The lupercus aren't like the other shifters. We don't crave flesh and meat like those savages, and we don't attack innocent people. We are smarter and faster. That's how we got our hands on you, the lost cure."

I watch Lynus' hand grip my forearm while his other inches the needle closer to my skin. "It'll just be a pinch."

Is he seriously trying to soothe me right now?!

I close my eyes and every muscle in me tenses as the sharp tip pierces my skin. "No!" I yell, wanting so badly to fight back. "Let me go!"

Lynus situates the bag that begins slowly filling with my red toxic blood. "There, now just relax and let the bag fill. I'll be back in a while for more."

More?!

"Don't go. If you really care about not harming innocent people and protecting humans from beasts, you wouldn't be doing this to me. I'm just a girl." *A pissed off girl.*

Lynus peels his gloves off and rubs a hand over his face. He looks exhausted. "You have a weapon inside of you, pup. You're definitely not just a girl, and we will do what it takes to ensure the future of our people."

With that, he stands and walks back to the barn, leaving me alone in the dark as my blood slowly drains away.

I'm here, Seth. Please find me.

◊ ◊ ◊

Seth

We are finally at the edge of the Catskill mountains, and I'm dying to let my wolf loose in those woods. Maia is out there somewhere. I can almost feel it, like she's calling out to me.

I'm coming, Snow. I promise.

The group gathers around, leaving the cars behind. Bree closes her eyes momentarily. "This is where we should start. Wilk, Qadira, will you both lend me some of your power while I search for Maia?"

The faeries nod, and Wilk takes Qadira's hand. He has been touching her more than usual lately, and as much as I hope they'll work out as a couple, it makes me miss Maia even more.

The three of them find a small patch of grass that is barely illuminated by the half-moon high in the sky. It's only a few hours until morning. The drive took way too long and now Maia has been gone for an entire day already.

I look over at Horas and Sasha, my wolves. "Would you two run along the perimeter of the trees and see if you can catch any unusual scents?"

Horas dips his head to me with determination in his green eyes. "You got it, boss."

Sasha's lips are pressed into a thin line, and I can tell that even though she isn't a fan of Maia's, she is worried all the same. Even if her only worry is for the cure, I'll take it.

Rylee steps to my side and grins up at me with a smile that I'm beginning to realize is fake. "I'll go run the perimeter too, Seth..."

James interrupts and lays a hand on Rylee's shoulder. "The meditators over there are going to need someone watching their backs. Why don't you be on guard duty?"

Rylee's smile falls momentarily, but she nods and runs over to stand beside Wilk, Qadira, and Bree.

I look at James, trying to figure him out. *Do you have something you want to talk to me about?* James tips his head to the side, wanting me to follow him, so I quietly let him lead us back toward the vehicles which sit a small ways off from everyone else.

Since this morning, the cocky vampire has been almost too quiet, and he even volunteered to drive the car with the faeries and wolves, leaving me, Bree, and Rylee alone in my Jeep. Although I don't miss his British sarcasm, his behavior has made me curious.

"What's up, James?" I ask when we're out of earshot from the others, even Rylee's fox ears. "I should be out looking for Maia."

He shakes his head. "As much as I care for that little hybrid of yours, we have a pressing matter, mate." He looks back toward our friends. "The little fox girl isn't who she says she is."

"Who is she, then?"

James shrugs. "I couldn't tell ya, but I know she has been lying. Every time I try to hear her thoughts, she sort of forces me out, and will start to think the most random things like how to make cupcakes or rock climbing. She does it even when we're all talking about finding Maia. Now, who would go on thinking about baking while we're on a hostage search?"

It doesn't make any sense. Maia and I found Rylee injured and lost. She's a teenager, not a traitor, right? "How do you know she's lying, though? Maybe she's just scatterbrained."

James laughs humorlessly. "Beyond the random thoughts though, this morning, or yesterday morning, I guess, when she spoke of being asleep and seeing nothing all night… It was a lie. I could see that clearly in her eyes, if not hear it in her stuttering heartbeat." He sighs. "She's good, but not that good."

I groan. I can't argue with him. I've wondered about Rylee, but I'd hate for it to be true. "So, do you think she's the one that took Maia's blood sample? You think she was a part of the kidnapping?"

James doesn't hesitate with his rapid nodding. "I have no doubts, mate. I'm sorry to say it."

I can't believe I let her into our lives. Into Maia's life. My wolf stirs inside of me, needing to fight something, to tear into flesh, and if I let him out, I know he'll go straight for Rylee.

"What are we going to do, James? If I find out that this is true, I feel so out of control that I'll kill the girl. I've never hurt a kid before, but that's what she is."

"That's the other thing, the reason I went in the other car. I told your wolves and our faerie friends about my suspicions and the prince had an idea." He raises an eyebrow at me with a gleam in his dark eyes.

"What do I need to do?"

"You need to pull the traitor aside and have a one on one with her. If she's innocent in all this, it'll be easy to see, and maybe she was manipulated and will come clean. We'll leave her behind and continue forward… but, if you can get her talking, and get her off guard, I will be hidden, watching and looking into her head for the truth."

"What if she catches on and tries to run?" I can't go chasing her when I need to be looking for Maia.

James holds a finger up. "Wilk and Qadira are going to put an invisible wall around you two, that way she's stuck."

I try to imagine his plan, and it's perfect, but it needs to happen immediately. If Rylee was a part of Maia's capture, she may have the exact location of where they took her. I just hope we won't be too late.

Chapter 29

◇◇◇

Maia

"I'VE BEEN A TOTAL ASS FROM minute one." Seth rubs a large hand over his strong jaw. *"I don't know how to do this, Snow."*

"How to do what? Converse politely with strangers?" I tease him and an actual smile tugs gently at his plump lips.

"Yeah, let's go with that." He chuckles quietly, his smile filling my heart with warmth.

"James is a good guy, but he's not really my type."

"What is your type then?"

I can feel a blush crawl up my neck as I think about what my type is. Amazingly, my type is exactly Seth, minus the attitude. But, will I say that? Absolutely not. Instead, I force myself to look away from him.

"James is too cold. I guess I like… warmth." My eyes find him again and he's staring at my lips as I lick them. "And, you know. Tall, dark, hot, and rich.

The four must-haves of any perfect man." I smile so he can see that I'm joking.

He smiles wide this time, and, holy cow, it is hot. "Funny. Those are the four must-haves for the perfect woman, as well." He laughs at his own joke and I shake my head at him.

"Har har."

I shiver against the cold morning air and my eyes flutter open. I was dreaming of Seth. From a time before I knew I loved him. Oh, how I want to be back in that moment with him again and kiss him until I can't breathe.

I look around at the beautiful forest surrounding this terrible situation. Just once, I'd like to be in a serene place like this and enjoy it. Frost covers the plants and dew drops off of the evergreens as the sun warms them. Still, I feel too cold.

I shiver again and look down at my needle-poked arm. My skin is pale and the ground seems to spin below me. The lupercus guy, Lynus, has been back to take my blood twice in the night since the first time. It only takes about twenty minutes for the bag to fill, and then he takes it and comes back for more after a while.

Each time, I feel a little weaker, and the last *donation* must've finally made me doze off, or pass out. Who knows? It's nice not having the tube in, though I know he'll be back again soon.

As if I summoned the lupercus, footsteps make me weakly lift my head toward the barn. "Oh, it's the third grader. Do you take the morning shift before hopping along to school?"

The female lupercus woman stops a few feet in front of me with a brown bag in her hands, completing the little girl look. Her narrowed eyes lock onto me and I feel threatened with just that simple look.

"I'm surprised you're not dead yet. You've lost a good percentage of your blood." She scrunches her nose as she surveys my hunched over body.

I can't even sit up straight, but I try my best to look strong in front of my enemy. "I'm tougher than I look." *That is such a lie.*

She knows it too, so she scoffs and rolls her eyes. She tosses the brown bag on the dirt in front of me and walks around to my back. I try to follow her movements but my eyes want to close the more I try to open them. Something tugs on my wrists and I'm dropped onto my face against the hard ground.

I pull my aching arms up to wipe the grime off my face, and gasp as I stare down at my bloody hands. *I'm free.* I try to push off the ground, ready to run, but I only make it to my knees.

"Why'd you untie me?" I tilt my head up to the woman.

Her arms are crossed and she leans against a tree to watch me. "I thought I'd give you a moment of peace before you die. Eat." Something softens in her dark eyes, but she blinks it away so fast that I would've missed it if I wasn't paying attention.

I reach for the brown bag and open it to find a bright red apple, a loaded turkey sandwich, and a bag of carrots, along with a full water bottle. I gulp past the dryness in my throat and hold back the tears that want to come. I haven't eaten since the night before last and I didn't realize how hungry I was until this moment.

"Is it poison?" I ask, mostly joking. *Mostly.*

The girl laughs. "Would it make a difference? You can die from poison or blood loss. Either way, same outcome."

Against all of the sanity in me, I let out my own small laugh. "You do have a point."

I unwrap the sandwich and take a monster-sized bite, tearing through the white bread, sliced turkey, and crunching lettuce with a new found strength. I try not to moan, but who even cares at this point? I want to thank the girl, but she's a part of the creatures trying to drain me of blood, so that would be ridiculous.

She watches as I scarf down every last piece of the meal and chug the bottle of water in just a few minutes. I feel full, but still mostly lifeless, and it makes my hope sink. I guess blood loss can't be healed in a matter of minutes.

"Does my moment of peace include a nap? You can go while I rest." I try to smile innocently at the girl, and she actually looks amused momentarily.

"Nice try, but no." She comes back to me and reaches for my hands, but with all the strength I have, I spin my leg up to connect my knee with her jaw. It hits with a crack and I smile.

She falls to the side but recovers too quickly and I don't have a chance to even try standing as she grips my shoulders tightly. The girl's eyes turn completely black, and with a crackling noise, two thick horns grow out of her head. They're a dark red color but resemble a mountain goat's horns. *What the hell?!*

"Do you really think *you* can fight *me,* wolf?"

"I'm not even a full wolf! I'm a human, like the people *your* kind are supposed to protect!" I'm mad now. I'm so sick of the hate.

She shoves my back against the rusted pole. "A dog is a dog," is all she says with her black eyes shining.

She slides around me and quickly ties my wrists again while I struggle uselessly. Any gentleness she had in her is long gone. "Now, sit and stay. Your time is nearly up."

She stands, grabs the garbage from my lunch and walks back to the big barn again without another word.

"You haven't broken me yet!" I shout into the quiet woods, but the only response I get is my own echo and the quiet wind in the trees. *Peace.*

◊ ◊ ◊

Seth

"What's up, Seth? Qadira said you wanted to talk to me."

Rylee leans against the skinny trunk of a tall aspen tree. She smiles up at me like nothing could possibly be wrong, and it makes my fists clench in anger at her betrayal. I thought this girl needed help, and maybe a family.

"Yeah. I'm worried about you." *Lie.* "I know you've had a rough life, and we promised to give you a refuge, but we've brought you into a war."

She sighs and runs a hand through her short black hair. "It has been an adventure, but I like adventure. I just really hope we find Maia soon. I'm more worried about her than myself."

She is too damn good.

I try not to clench my teeth while I talk. James wanted me to keep her feeling happy and off guard, but it's so hard not to be angry. All I wanted to do when Bree finished meditating was dive right into finding Maia, but Bree could only find a small trace of where Maia *may* have been. My guess is that somehow whoever has Maia is covering their tracks. Our best hope now is to get info out of Rylee.

"You're so kind to help us, Rylee. I'm sorry we never get many chances to talk." *More lies.*

She steps closer to me with a flirtatious lift of her eyebrow. This girl has some nerve. "Well, we are alone now. What would you like to talk about?"

James steps behind Rylee, as silent as a mouse. I don't know how old he is, but he has learned a thing or two in his time. "I'd like to talk about the lupercus and your part in their kidnapping of Maia."

My eyes feel like they might bulge out of my head. *The lupercus have Maia?!* Out of all of the shifters, I never expected them, and *dammit,* I should have.

Rylee jumps, and immediately tries to run, but she slams into the invisible wall that Wilk and Qadira hold us in. The faeries step from their hiding spots, eyes glowing with power. Horas and Sasha back them up, looking like powerful bodyguards. Behind James, Bree appears with her red curls floating off of her shoulders. The last time she looked that way was when she was about to break her way into the Fae city.

Rylee spins, crouching down to fight if need be, and her brown eyes flash from black to brown as she fights off her shift. A little fox won't be a match for my wolf and she knows it.

"None of you understand. I didn't want her to be hurt, okay?" Rylee's voice shakes as she tries to defend her actions.

"I really hoped it wasn't true, Rylee. We helped you when you had no one. Or was that all just a lie?"

She shakes her head. "It wasn't all a lie. I was out to find you all, and to earn your trust, but I really did get hurt in a bear trap. You helped me, and I'm grateful."

A growl fills my chest. "How did you know about Maia? Why are you in league with the damn lupercus?" My voice rises with each question.

"I really was an orphan as a child, like I told you. The lupercus saved my life and raised me in their camps. They're my family." She pauses and looks around at all of the angry faces. "One of our members heard from a bruxsa demon that a girl in league with the wolf pack outside Stowe had the cure in her blood. We have a witch in our camp, and she found Maia somewhere out in Maine. They sent me to find out what I could. They knew that as a fox, I'd look like less of a threat. All we needed to be sure was a sample of her blood…"

"So, you stole the sample from my grandmother!" Bree shouts the accusation. As Maia's protector and best friend, she's as pissed as I am.

Rylee flinches and looks down at the ground, ashamed. "I'm sorry! I had no choice!"

I step closer to Rylee, making her look up at me. She can probably see my wolf just at the surface. "If you really didn't want Maia to get hurt, then tell us where she is."

Rylee shakes her head. "I can't do that."

Before I even make a move, James speeds between us and grabs Rylee by the throat, lifting her body off the ground and shoving her against a tree. "Tell us where she is, or you will die. My mate here may be above torture, but I'm not so civilized."

Rylee chokes past the pain in her throat. "I can't... betray... them."

James scoffs. "You betrayed everyone here just fine. I think you can find a way if you dig down deep enough."

Rylee closes her eyes briefly before giving in. "Fine." James lessens his hold on her. "The lupercus woman that took Maia is our leader, Nyma. We call her chief, and she wants to build an arsenal with Maia's blood, to kill off all shifter-kind." She pauses as tears sting her eyes. "Our camp is twelve miles west of here. Maia will be there."

James drops Rylee on the ground and looks back at me. "She's telling the truth, mate."

My heart races at the thought of finding Maia so soon. "Let's go, then. Now."

The whole group nods in agreement, and Sasha points to Rylee. "What should we do with the traitor? Want me to kill her?" *Yes, I do.*

"No. We'll tie her to a tree and leave her." I turn my eyes back to the fox shifter as she whimpers. "I wouldn't count on getting rescued a third time in your life, Rylee, but if you do, don't waste your chance to be a better person." I nod to Bree who looks ready for battle. "Let's go get our girl."

Chapter 30

◇◇◇

Maia

"WAKE UP!" THE VOICE CALLS out to me and I struggle to heed its command.

I don't even remember falling asleep. Warm hands grip my shoulders and lift me upward. *Was I lying face down?* I know I've been getting my blood drawn by the lupercus for the past day and a half.

Even though I feel weak and cold, I'm aware enough to remember that guy, Lynus, attaching a fresh blood bag to me. The extra blood loss must've knocked me out, and now somebody is holding me.

"Can you hear me?" The voice is familiar to me, and I hope it's one of my friends coming to save me.

"I can hear you," I say weakly. I flinch at the blinding sunlight peeking behind fluffy clouds as my eyes slowly open.

Seth's face appears through my blurry vision and I hear his warm voice filling my heart. "I'm coming for you, Maia. Just hold on a little longer. Please don't leave me."

I try to smile at him as I reach up to stroke his scruffy cheek. He has let the stubble on his chin grow and it's incredibly sexy. "I'm right here, Seth. You found me."

His eyebrows raise and he looks confused as he watches me. "Seth?" His voice sounds different. "Sorry, but I'm not your knight in shining armor. We just came to say goodbye."

I blink through my hazy vision and I'm no longer looking at the man I love. Lynus is the one holding me off the muddy ground. Rain falls from dark gray clouds behind his long hair, drenching him and pouring onto my face.

I turn my head from side to side, and Seth isn't here… it was only a hallucination. Just more dreams that I can't reach. I want to sob, but I'm too weak for even that.

Lynus and I aren't alone. His woman partner is beside him. The two seem to always work together. Behind her, another woman stands watching me with dark eyes. The incredibly thin woman who helped Lynus kidnap me.

"What are you doing here? Has my time finally come?" Why else would I get such a gathering? I thought I'd be ready to die, but I'm not.

The woman, who I remember Lynus calling Nyma, smiles sadly at me. "Our camp is moving, thanks to a search party looking for you. We are not prepared to launch our attack just yet, but I wanted one last sample from you first, and to tell you we are sorry."

Rain falls down her perfectly high cheekbones, and she looks too fiercely beautiful to be the one to kill me. A cold chill runs through my body and I feel nauseous. I look down at my untied arms, and see that they're already taking more of my blood. The bag is half full and I can feel my body fading.

"You're s-sorry? You know... a truly sorry person would maybe not m-murder an innocent person." My voice is clipped and my vision doubles momentarily, but I'm not done. "If you really are sorry... you could m-make it up to me by putting some of that red stuff back in me."

I try to glare, but I have no control over my expressions anymore. I just want to sleep. *Why can't I just sleep?*

I shake the thought away and try to sit up in Lynus' arms. "Let me go!"

Evil Nyma kneels in front of me. "Your blood will rid this earth of the beasts that kill for pleasure. You should feel proud that you have such an important purpose."

This is my purpose? To kill off multiple species that just want to have families and live in peace? That can't be *my* purpose.

"My f-friends will stop you." I look dead into the woman's eyes as I make my promise. "You think the other sh-shifters are the ugly and u-untame ones... but it's *you*. You will r-regret this."

Lynus lays me back on the muddy earth and I don't turn away from the rain that pelts my face. The three lupercus look down at me one last time before the younger woman unhooks the bag of blood from the end of the long tube.

She leaves the tube in my arm with blood trickling out of the end of it. The dark red color swirls into the muddy puddles filling around me and my eyelids flutter. I don't have any strength left in me.

I'm dying, but I know my pack of heroes will do whatever it takes to save the shifters. My faith is in them now, and I only wish I could tell them how much I love them all.

"I l-love you guys. I'm sorry I wasn't strong enough... Please d-don't stop fighting."

◊ ◊ ◊

Seth

Six miles... Five miles... Four miles... Three miles... Two... I can smell her blood.

Rylee said Maia would be twelve miles west of where we parked the cars. We tied up the traitor and I started running. I don't even know if the others are behind me. I just know I need to get to Maia before it's too late. I am on two legs still, trying to hold my wolf back. If I let him loose, I won't be able to think rationally enough to help Maia if she's injured.

Even now that the rain falls in heavy streams, I run through the splashing mud and freezing droplets. I'm two miles from the twelve-mile target when the coppery scent of blood stings my nose. I know it's Maia's blood.

My feet hit the ground harder as I pick up my pace, guided only by the smell of my Snow. My heavy footfalls leave my jeans brown from the mud sloshing against my legs. "I'm coming for you, Maia. Just hold on a little longer. Please don't leave me."

I know she can't hear me from this distance, but I speak to her anyway. It has been a day and a half since she was taken from me, and who knows what she has endured. My whole body shakes and I can feel the hairs sprout along my neck as I imagine Maia being hurt and alone. *Not now, wolfy.*

Her scent grows stronger and I know I'm close. I take a quick glance over my shoulder and see the faeries flying through the pelting rain, their wings beating against the air as they match my pace. Looking to my left, Horas and Sasha run easily beside James, dodging trees and focusing on the woods ahead of them. Bree is clinging tightly to James' back as he runs, and it doesn't seem to phase the vampire in the slightest. The whole pack is here.

A small clearing opens up within the trees and up ahead I can barely make out the wooden top of a large barn-like structure. We have to be close! My heart rate doubles, and in seconds, Maia's scent overwhelms me. Bree screams Maia's name from behind me, just as I spot my beautiful Snow White. And my entire body quivers with a burning anger like I've never known.

"Snow!" I drob beside her in the mud and hoist her up into my arms.

She's so frail that I worry I might break her as I cradle her against my chest. The wolves run past me toward the buildings ahead, searching for the lupercus that took Maia. They were trained for this life, and I trust them completely.

I search Maia's limp body for injury. A long tube hangs from the inside of her arm, and I yank it free of her. "What in the hell did they do to you?"

I can feel my teeth elongate as I hold back the shift that wants to tear through me. "Maia, open your eyes. Wake up, please!"

I drop my lips to her wet ones and the cold from her skin seeps into me. Her heart is beating, but only barely, and her breathing is shallow. In minutes, I could lose her forever. A hand falls on my shoulder and I spin around to see James.

"Get her into the barn, mate. The wolves say it's clear."

I look up into all of the watching eyes of my friends. "Where are the lupercus? The ones that did this to her!" My voice is morphed between man and wolf, the alpha in me taking control.

Horas runs a hand through his dripping hair. "They're gone, Seth. The entire camp is empty and the cabins have been cleared out. They bolted, man."

Sasha growls, and her eyes blacken. "Should we go after them?"

I shake my head. "We can't. We need to help Maia."

I stand and run to the barn, holding Maia tightly against me. Inside, the place has been transformed into a living area with couches, beds and even a wood-burning fireplace that is loaded with dry logs. I lay Maia onto one of the couches, letting her long white hair flow over the arm.

I point toward the fireplace. "Someone light that, and find a blanket. Maia is freezing."

I'm being demanding, but I can't control it. They listen, though, and Qadira lays a thick blanket over Maia while Bree casts a spell on the fireplace, making it roar to life with flames. The heat reaches me in seconds, and I hope it can warm Maia fast.

James drops to the wooden floor beside me and feels Maia's pulse. "She has lost too much blood, mate." His voice is tight with anger. "The only thing that will save her is a transfusion, but we're out of time to get her to a hospital."

Bree's round eyes are wet with tears as she reaches for Maia's hand. "Can't one of us give our blood to her? Is that possible?"

James looks around the room. "Does anyone here know Maia's blood type?"

All of them shake their heads and I curse under my breath before I realize something. "Wait. I'm O-Negative. Can I give some of mine to her?"

James nods. "That you can, mate. Just give me a sec."

He stands and runs across the room to a long table that looks like it belongs in an operating room. I hadn't even noticed that when I came in. "What the hell is all of that?"

Sasha crosses her arms and scoffs. "It's blood draw equipment and IVs. Looks like they were hydrating Maia just so they could take more blood from her. What freaks!"

James runs back to me with his hands full of equipment. "There are no alcohol pads, so with her human healing, she could be at risk for infection."

I shake my head. "Let's worry about that when we need to. Please, just help me keep her alive."

James nods and reaches for my arm. He rolls one of my sleeves up to my shoulder and ties a band around my bicep. Before I can even flinch, he jabs a long needle with a catheter into my arm. If a human had tried to break my tough shifter skin, they would have struggled, but James does it easily and I'm so thankful to have him here. And to think that I hated him a week ago.

James connects the catheter to a long tube with another needle at the end, and he hesitates before puncturing Maia's skin. "Are you ready, mate? I can't promise this will work while she still has the cure in her. And with your wolf blood, it's kind of up in the air."

I nod. "It's worth a try. I need her, James." The vulnerable words fall out before I can stop them, but I don't even care.

I love Maia, and she is all that matters to me in this world. There's no way I'll leave her to die. I nod to James and he sticks the needle into Maia's skin before messing with the catheter on my end and letting my blood flow into her body.

It's silent for a moment as we all watch the steady flow of red.

"What do we do now?" Bree questions while she continues holding Maia's hand from the back of the couch.

Each of us looks at one another, and James sits back with a sigh. "Now, we wait."

Chapter 31

◇◇◇

Maia

A LOUD CLANGING FILLS MY EARS and it feels like my brain rattles inside my head. I turn over with a groan and wrap my arms around my head. *Worst hangover ever.* Except, I'm almost certain I wasn't drinking.

I take a deep breath through the pounding headache, and the smell of rain and musk is so strong that I cough against the thick scent. *Yeah, definitely a hangover.*

"Snow, I'm here, okay? Just breathe slowly and try to stay calm." Seth's soothing voice floats to me through my covered ears.

Thankfully, the sound isn't as jarring as the clanging, so I slowly lower my arms. I crack my eyes open, but quickly shut them when a blinding light hits me. "What the hell is going on?"

Seth's fingers stroke my cheek gently. "Take it slow, alright? Do you remember anything?"

I shake my head, keeping my eyes closed. I feel like I've been forgetting a lot of things lately, but I don't even know what things I've forgotten. I swallow past the incredibly dry lump in my throat and cough again. "Dear lord, I need a glass of water." *And many, many painkillers.*

Somehow, Seth finds that funny and his soft laughter floats to me. "Dira, can you conjure Maia some water, please?"

Oooh, Qadira's magic water is the best!

Qadira's sweet tone reaches my ears. "Open up, Maia."

I obey, and cool, clean water flows into my mouth. I drink it down and sigh at how good it feels. "Thank you," I say, and try opening my eyes again.

Someone must've turned off the lights, because I'm able to see without the brightness giving me a worse headache. I blink a few times, adjusting to the soft firelit room. I look down at my dirty wrinkled clothes. "Ew. I need a shower."

Laughter makes me turn around and four pairs of comforting eyes are smiling down at me. Wilk and Qadira stand hand-in-hand, making me smile right back at their closeness. James and Bree are beside the faeries, seemingly making a real effort at not touching, but somehow that even makes me smile. *Stubborn asses.*

I look across to the other side of the large room and the two wolves from the Shaw pack are watching me as well. The giant Horas has a cheesy grin peeking behind his poofy beard, and Sasha looks unaffected by life as usual. At least she isn't glaring for once.

Finally, I trail my eyes back to the one I am really aching to see, and I look up at my sexy wolf shifter, Seth. His hair is an absolute mess, and by the looks of his clothes, he found himself in as much mess as me. I feel like I can see him clearer than ever, and his overwhelming pine scent fills me with need.

I trail my eyes up to meet his always mesmerizing ones and as soon as our gazes connect, a shiver runs through me all the way to my toes. Seth's smiling face falls and his breath hitches at the same time as mine. *What on earth is happening right now?!*

It's as if all of the air has left the room, taking everyone with it, except for Seth and I. We are drowning in one another, breathless, panting, and somehow perfectly happy. I feel made for this man, and I can tell he feels it too.

"Maia," he whispers to me as his eyes turn black. "Do you feel that?"

My vision feels like it widens, and everything moves slower. A pinching draws my eyes to my hands, and I gasp at the long claw-like fingernails at the tips of my fingers. "What's happening, Seth?"

My body begins to shake as I reach out for Seth, accidentally scratching him with my long nails. He grips the sides of my face and forces me to look back into his eyes. "Snow, listen to me. I need you to steady your breathing and focus on my voice." I nod as I try to do what he wants. "You lost a lot of blood, and I had to give you some of mine to save your life. I think the cure was mostly gone from you by the time we found you, and my wolf blood cleaned out whatever was left behind. Do you understand?"

I shake my head. "I don't understand at all. What does that mean?"

I don't remember losing blood. I don't even know where we are right now. Seth's thumb rubs along my bottom lip, making me focus on him again. "I don't know how exactly, but instead of fighting my wolf blood, your body fought off the shifter cure instead. It's gone. You are no longer the holder of the shifter cure, Snow. You're a wolf shifter."

My eyes bulge and I look down at where my claws are clinging onto Seth's shirt. "Holy hell! Am I shifting right now?" I shout the question at him, and he nods.

"Damn right you are, babe! And you and Seth are fated mates!" Bree's voice makes Seth and I whip our heads in her direction. She's grinning from ear to ear, and I feel like I might pass out.

I look back at Seth and he nods. "Your nosey BFF is right, Snow. I'm fated for you." He leans forward and presses a searing kiss against my quivering lips. "Forever."

Tears spring to my eyes and I throw myself into Seth's arms, stealing another kiss from his perfect lips.

I swing my arms wide around his neck, so I don't accidentally slice at him with my sharp wolf nails.

Before my arms settle around my fated mate, I catch a glimpse of the multiple needle marks scarring my inner arm... and the past two days come flooding back to me like the headlights of a semi-truck slamming into me.

Rylee's betrayal.
Being taken and tied up.
The lupercus taking my blood.
Leaving me dying in the mud...

I throw my head back as my spine cracks, and I hit the floor, falling from Seth's lap. I can hear Seth and the others calling to me, but the animal in me is in control now. My human voice screams out as a howl leaves my wolf's jaws. I'm lost somewhere deep inside of my wolf... and she's pissed.

Chapter 32

◆◇◆

Maia

I'M GROWLING AND PANTING. *No.* My *wolf* is growling. She isn't just another part of me like I had always thought. She's her own being within my head, controlling everything while I sit back and watch. I am completely helpless.

I watch as my wolf looks down at the strong body we share. Where my hands and feet were, are now massive furry paws with sharp claws. As far as I can tell, our wolf fur is pure white, matching the hair I grew up with.

She's growling again, and I can hear my friends trying to speak to me. *Do they not know I'm not in control of this thing?*

I try to turn my head toward James in the hopes that I can communicate with him in my mind, but my wolf's head turns to Seth instead. She whines when she spots him, and I have to agree. He's *everything.*

My fated mate.

Seth's brown eyes are worried as he watches my wolf with fascination. "Snow, are you in control? The first shift can be disorienting. Just try to talk to your wolf."

James speaks a few feet away and our head whips to him with a low growl. He takes a step back with his hands out in front of him. "Woah, love. Make friends with your furry side before she tries to eat me, yeah?"

Hey, wolf girl. Can you hand over the reins for a bit? I just need to talk to my friends.

A rumbling growl leaves us again as she continues to stare down poor James. He looks over at Seth. "I don't think she's got control, mate. All I'm hearing is a stream of growls inside and outside her head."

Bree steps in front of James and smiles softly down at me. "Hey, Mai. Just keep trying. This is new for both of you."

To my surprise, even Bree gets a growl thrown at her. I try to reach out to my limbs and take a step back but nothing moves. It feels like I'm tied down, unable to do anything but watch.

Okay, my fluffy alter ego. It's time we make nice. I care about these people and I can't let you go all ballistic on them.

I can feel the large body start to relax as she looks around the large room. Our wolf eyes land on a table against the far wall and my wolf sticks her nose in the air, taking a whiff. I try to press myself forward to smell what she's smelling, and I cringe at the scent.

Blood.

It's the tubing they must have used when Seth gave me some of his blood, but my wolf doesn't understand. All she smells is her mate's blood, and all hell breaks loose.

I'm shoved further back again, unable to do any more than watch as my wolf snarls and growls ferociously. She runs forward, slamming past James and ripping her sharp teeth into the couch that's wet with the scent of rain.

She pulls us faster and slams her huge body into a wall, making a crack from the floor to ceiling. An ache covers my side, and it has to be the wolf body that's hurt.

My wilder side continues tearing through the barn with speed and anger. She's confused about why her mate would be bleeding, as images of my capture from the lupercus flash through her mind. All she can see is red and revenge.

"Maia! Try to control her! You can do it!" Seth's voice filters into me where I'm stuck in the back of my wolf's mind.

I pull at whatever energy I have in me and fight against the wolf's control. *Calm down, girl. It's okay. We're safe.*

She understands my words and we slow to a more controlled pace, still circling the barn that now feels way too small for this many people. The large white paws step to the side with ease to avoid bumping into another wall, but something hot rubs against the wolf's hind leg.

A wolfish yelp leaves us from the burn and my wolf jumps, knocking us into the fireplace. Fully lit logs roll onto the ground and a larger fire ignites.

"Maia! Get away from there!" I can't tell who's yelling at me, but I'm unable to respond.

My skittish wolf leaps away from the building flames that threaten to engulf the entire barn. We run from the building, breaking the large door as we dive into the dewy morning air that makes the forest look like a glistening paradise. My wolf pulls in a long sniff of the woods and takes off with one clear word ringing in my mind.

Run!

◊ ◊ ◊

Seth

Maia's wolf is breathtaking. She is white like the snow, from snout to tail, and I can't help but smile. *My Snow White.* Knowing that she can finally feel the strength and freedom of shifting makes everything feel right, although I didn't expect her to shift right now. The full moon is weeks away, but Maia never has been like everyone else.

I watch in horror as Maia's wolf loses control and tears through the barn. Everyone has to step out of her way, and it's clear that Maia is lost inside the wolf's mind. I call for her to take control, and just when I think she has finally found a way, all hell breaks loose.

"Maia!" I yell after her as she bursts through the barn door with a crack.

I start to run after her, not ready to part from my mate after just getting her back. Wilk and Qadira are already pulling moisture from the air to douse the rapidly growing fire, and the others follow me outside.

I turn with my hands raised toward James, Bree, Sasha, and Horas. "Let me go alone, guys. I'll see if I can calm her."

They each nod, and I don't hesitate any longer, stripping down to my underwear and drawing my wolf forward. *Let's find our mate,* I say to him as he searches for Maia's scent.

He is desperate to be by Maia's side, and we take off at a speed I've never seen before. The wind slides through my wolf's fur and the feeling is incredible, especially when Maia's delicious scent finds me.

Come on, Maia. Don't run from me. I won't hurt you.

I know she can't hear me since our bond isn't complete, but I still feel the need to reassure her. My wolf stops running when we spot the gorgeous arctic white wolf standing beside a thicket of aspen trees, blending into the white bark like she belongs with the scenery. Her hazel eyes are wild as she stares back at my wolf with confusion.

I remember that feeling of wildness and being lost inside the animal that we are born with. I had instruction on how to handle it from my father and alpha Nate. Maia didn't know a thing about what to expect, and I wish I could've prepared her better.

I step closer to her and she takes her own step toward me as well. If she feels at all how I'm feeling then she's being pulled in my direction, like a magnet to metal, because of our mate bond. She lifts her nose into the air and draws in my scent. I can see her raised shoulders drop as she relaxes, and mine do the same.

Damn, I love her so much.

Maia's wolf closes the distance and her head drops to rub along my wolf's throat, stroking our fur in a warm embrace. I nuzzle her back, feeling every sensation that my wolf feels. My wolf and I are one, and I only hope Maia is feeling what I am.

She pulls her pointed ears back and looks deep into my eyes, as if she's seeing both of my forms at once. She makes a whining sound and then her long tongue pokes out to slide along the side of my wolf's surprised face. I laugh internally, loving that she seriously just kissed me in wolf form, and then I throw my head back to let out a long howl.

Maia joins in with her own howl that harmonizes with mine, and if I could see myself, I swear my midnight black wolf would be smiling. I nudge Maia's wolf softly and pull my head back to get her to follow me.

She needs to shift, and I can only coax her through it if I'm back in my human form, preferably fully dressed. I'm more than happy to let Maia see all of me, but that'll have to wait until we're completely alone.

But I really don't want to wait.

Maia follows behind me, back to the others. Her wolf is much happier now that she has calmed down and she keeps pushing into my side as we run. My wolf wants to push her back and roll through the woods with her, but I try to reign in his playful side.

Not now, buddy. Soon.

We stop side by side in the opening outside the still smoking barn. Our friends look our way when we arrive, and I stop beside the clothes I discarded minutes ago, speaking to James in my mind.

She's calm now. Would you mind asking the girls to turn around while I get dressed?

James laughs. "But why disappoint the ladies by making them look away? It has been a long few days and we can all use a good show."

Bree gasps and smacks James on the arm. "Ew! Are you talking about Seth right now? My BFF's naked mate is not the kind of show I'm looking for!" She hurries and grabs onto Qadira, turning the faerie and herself around, glaring at Sasha along the way. "Aren't you going to join us?"

Sasha rolls her eyes but turns like the others. "It's nothing I haven't seen before, but whatever."

I'll have to explain that remark to Maia when I get the chance. I draw my wolf to the back of my mind, shifting back to my human form, and I hurry to slide the discarded jeans back on. I smile as Maia's wolf watches my every movement with curiosity, and a sense of pride rolls through me at her focused gaze.

Once I'm dressed, I look toward James, who is grinning like the Cheshire cat as he looks down at Maia's wolf. He laughs like he just heard the best joke.

"What's so funny?" I ask.

He shakes his head. "Oh, nothing, mate. Let's just get Maia back so we can get out of here."

Yes, please.

Chapter 33

◇◇◇

Maia

WATCHING SETH SHIFT FROM wolf to human form looks so smooth. I can't even imagine having that kind of grace. I watch as his snout shortens and his legs stretch as he stands on two feet instead of four paws. The black fur all over him shrinks back beneath his skin and then he's standing… completely *naked*.

Oh, holy mother may I…

If my jaw could drop, it would, but I have no control over my body. It doesn't stop the feeling of heat spreading through me, and desire flaring within my human self. My wolf seems utterly uninterested sexually in the hunk of naked sexy man getting dressed before us. She just stares at her mate with happiness and nothing more.

You could look away anytime, girl. I am incapable of closing my eyes while you're in control, and this is absolute torture.

My wolf's head snaps to James as he laughs and I want to punch him for listening to my private thoughts. He's thoroughly enjoying himself.

"What's so funny?" Seth asks the vampire, and thankfully he doesn't give away my humiliation.

"You're enjoying this way too much," I say to James in my mind and he just winks back at me.

Now, sadly fully-clothed, Seth kneels in front of me and runs his fingers through the white fur on my neck. My wolf drops to her back and spreads her legs wide for tummy tickles, just adding to my wonderful embarrassment.

"Fine," Seth says through a soft chuckle. "One belly scratch and then we're getting you back to your human self. We have a lot to talk about, Snow."

He rubs the extra soft fur along my wolf belly and my wolf's long tongue flips out of her mouth. *Oh, heaven's sake.* Bree steps behind Seth and she giggles as she looks down at my new body.

"You are never going to live this down, Mai. I hope you know that."

I groan, and the sound comes out of the wolf like a soft growl, making everyone laugh. Seth turns toward the others. "Do you think you guys could step away while I help Maia shift back?"

Bree scoffs and pats Seth on his back. Her simple touch causes a more threatening growl to leave me, and she steps back with her hands up. "Hey. I'm not after your mate, beasty." She looks at Seth again.

"I'm going to bet that Maia would prefer I help her shift, instead. She's going to be naked, and even though I'm sure you'd love that, it's not the time."

I'm dead. I'm seriously dying right now!

Seth's eyebrows shoot up and he looks into my eyes. "Is that what you want, Snow? For Bree to help you?"

I try to nod, but it does nothing so I look at James. *"Please tell him yes, and I'll forgive you for laughing at me."*

James smiles but keeps his laughter away this time. "She says to let the little witch do it. Sorry, mate."

Seth smiles down at me. "Just remember to stay calm and you'll do great, okay?" He leans into my wolf's ear and whispers. "I love you, snow."

The group walks away, leaving Bree and I alone. She sits on the ground beside me and tentatively reaches her hand out to pet my back. "Okay. I'm going to do a spell to help you shift, and all you need to do is imagine your wolf-side curling in on itself, as if going into hiding. I learned this from Grandma Em about a year ago. She thought I should know just in case you were able to shift in the future."

Smart grandma.

My wolf stays resting on her side, completely comfortable, and I try to make myself as calm as my furry beast. I just imagine taking slow breaths and lying in the same position as my wolf, resting against the moist ground.

Bree begins speaking in her ancient witchy tongue, and her eyes close as her hands rest gently on my front paws. It feels like something tugs on my body, and I make an effort to pull the wolf back inside of my mind. I have no clue what I'm doing, but it feels right enough.

I look down at my paws as they morph into human hands and I start to breathe on my own again. The earth feels rough against my bare skin as the shift finishes and I'm once again just Maia Collins. But I'll never really just be that again, will I?

Bree smiles at me and wraps her arms around my neck. "I'm so glad you're back, Mai. I've missed you like crazy."

I smile as her sweet scent fills my nose. The scent is a thousand times stronger than it used to be, but it's still the same Bree. "You do realize I'm full on ass-naked right now, right?"

She bursts into a laughing fit as she pulls away and I join her crazy giggles with my own. Someone clears their throat and I nearly scream before I spot Qadira and not one of the guys.

"I can help you with some new clothes, Maia." Her bright pink hair bounces as she steps closer with a sweet smile.

"Oh, please, yes! Jeans would be heavenly right about now."

I stand from the dirty ground and wipe my body clean, realizing that I haven't showered in days and I probably look horrible. Qadira notices my scowl and smiles again as she waves one of her dainty hands toward me. A wave of water washes over my body and through my hair, making me gasp as it cleans all of the grime away.

In the next second a whirlwind blows me completely dry, taking my breath away, and then a dark pair of jeans materialize against my bare legs, while a black tank top hugs my torso tight enough to make a bra unnecessary.

I wiggle around, feeling entirely comfortable in the magic clothes, and I sigh. "What was with the water and wind?"

Qadira giggles and hurries to bring me into a surprisingly strong hug. "You smelled really bad. A nature bath was necessary."

She steps away and laughs along with Bree. I run a hand through my still greasy, but mostly clean hair. "You guys are jerks, but I love you both."

Qadira's pink eyes practically glow with magic, and I realize it's the first time I've ever gotten to talk to her without Wilk by her side. "Hey, Dira. I'm not sure when I'll get another chance for this, so what's up with you and Wilk?"

Bree's eyes widen and she spins on the faerie. "Ooh, yeah! I wanna know, too. Do you love him?"

Qadira blushes a sweet pink, just like her hair. "Prince Wilk is a dear friend, and a powerful role model to the city of Fae. I have nothing but respect for him."

Bree and I share a look of disbelief, and Bree shakes her head. "No way, Dira. The prince cares about you as more than one of his subjects. Has he tried to kiss you or anything like that?"

"Well," she says, looking shy. "He holds my hand when it is unnecessary to do so, and he calls me beautiful when I do not feel so. I think I could love him, if he was not royalty."

I sigh and grab her hands. "You don't choose who you love, Qadira. If you love him, you love him. It's as simple as that. It wouldn't be the first time a prince and a servant fell in love. Humans literally make movies about this like once a year."

Bree laughs and nods. "It's called a forbidden romance, and definitely the hottest kind. Tell the prince how you feel."

Qadira smiles as her skin seems to glow even brighter. "I will see. Maybe when our journey has ended."

Satisfied, and more than ready to leave this hell hole, I look around at the place I have been held captive and nearly died in. My eyes fall on the tetherball pole that held me while I bled for the lupercus. All happiness leaves as a new rage fills me, and I step over to the place that will haunt me for too long, leaving Bree and Qadira behind.

I grip the rusted metal pole in my hands and grunt as I use my new wolf strength to pull until the entire thing comes out of the earth. I throw it to the side and kick at the dirt for good measure. Tears fill my eyes, and I let them fall as I stare down at the empty hole by my feet.

Large arms encircle me from behind, and Seth's warmth spreads along my back, washing my tears away. He kisses my neck and then the tender spot just below my ear.

"They'll never hurt you again, Snow. You're my mate, and we're stronger than all of them when we're together." His whispers tickle my ear, and I want so badly to believe what he says.

I spin myself around in Seth's arms, noticing the girls have left us, and I look up at Seth's perfect face. Every part of him is clearer to me now. The dark chocolate of his eyes shows specks of gold I never noticed before, and I could number the strands of his messy hair if I stared long enough.

He smiles as I study him, and a warm blush fills my cheeks. "Why are you smiling, wolf boy?"

He rubs his nose against mine. "I can't believe I'm lucky enough to have you as my fated mate."

I wrap my arms around his neck and breathe in his musky pine scent. *Yum.* "What does this mean exactly? Of course I'm very happy that fate put us together, but what do we do now? Like… get married?" I feel like an idiot even asking the question.

Seth shakes his head. "Wolves don't really get married. When they find their mate, they claim one another and... complete their bond that seals them together forever."

I squirm in his arms. I know what completing the bond means, but I need to be sure. *Just grow up and ask the question, Mai!* "So, we need to have sex?"

Seth's eyes darken and I think they'll go fully black for a moment. "To complete our bond, yes." His eyes drop to my mouth, and then meet mine again. "But we're in no hurry for that, Snow. We'll still be fated mates even if we don't make love."

Make love? Gosh dang it, he's so cute.

I nod. "But you want to, right?"

His lips curl up into a perfectly happy grin and he tightens his arms around my waist as he drops his mouth to mine. A chill rolls through my body and I have to hold back a groan as he strokes my lips with his tongue. *Oh, I've missed this.*

He kisses me hard and determined while I match him with a new strength of my own. Seth pulls away from me only slightly and his heavy breath flows across my cheeks. "Maia. You have *no* idea how badly I want to claim you as mine forever, and equally be claimed *by* you. I can guarantee it will be the main thing on my mind until that moment."

"Well," I say with a quiver in my voice. "Let's not wait too long, then."

Seth's hands slide over my butt and he hoists me onto his hips as our lips collide again. Thunder rolls above our heads and rain drops cool my burning cheeks, dripping between our lips. I lick the rain from Seth's mouth and his chest rumbles, matching the roar of the thunder. There's a need in me that I can't control, nor do I want to.

Even though right now isn't the time to complete our bond, I'm not about to stop kissing my mate before I'm utterly satisfied… My stomach growls, and Seth's lips smile against mine.

Okay, one other thing can stop me. *Food.*

Chapter 34

✧✧✧

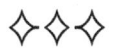

Maia

"DEAR LORD, WOMAN! Will you ever stop?" Bree's wide brown eyes stare at the cheeseburger that I'm currently devouring.

"Never, ever, ever," I say through a mouthful of beef and bread.

We're only a few miles outside of Georgetown, where we're planning to meet with the high priestess of the witches, and I cannot stop eating. It's like my stomach has no limit to the amount of greasy fast-food cheeseburgers it can hold. I've been told that with my new wolf abilities, my metabolism is extremely fast, and I need to eat a significant amount of food to keep my energy up. *And the food is so good!*

Seth turns around and grins at me from the passenger's seat of his jeep as I dig in for a beast-sized bite. *I love that smile.* And I love that he can still smile at me while I look like a rabid animal tearing into a carcass. Can you say *true love*?

We had a long walk to get back to the vehicles the others abandoned when they came to find me. We stopped for a minute where they supposedly tied up Rylee, the fox traitor of our little pack. She was nowhere to be found, and I only hope she finds a better life for herself. She has been manipulated by the lupercus, and I hate that they're the only family she has ever known. All she had to do was give us a chance. Maybe then she could've been happy.

James is in the driver's seat, nodding his head to the classic rock radio station while Seth guides him through the Delaware streets. Bree sits beside me, openly staring at me while I eat, and at this moment, I can't imagine feeling any more content. The other wolves and the faeries follow behind us in Uncle Nate's old trailblazer, and I make a mental note to switch the seating arrangements around on our way back home. I haven't had any time getting to know Horas or Sasha since I met them both, and I feel guilty. They've done a lot for me already, and I owe them both so much.

"We're nearly there. You still want to talk to the old witch?" James eyes me in the rearview mirror.

The high priestess expected us to visit two days ago, but thanks to the lupercus, we got a little held up. I called my dad as soon as we got back to the vehicles. He was freaking out, understandably, along with Uncle Nate and Aunt Lydia. Seth had told them I was taken, but they had no update for the entire night that I was healing inside that barn. Dad was already halfway to

New York by the time I called, and I told him to turn back home. He's only human, and though I wish so badly to curl up and cry in his arms, he's safer with the Shaw pack wolves.

Bree huffs beside me and crosses her arms. "Don't call her an old witch. It sounds like an insult."

"So you're saying your kind is an insult, then?" James teases Bree, and I have to hold back the urge to say *"oooooooh"*.

Bree glares into the rearview mirror at James' wicked smile. "Stop being a jerk, James! Just cause you don't like witches, doesn't mean you get to be rude to my kind, or any other creature for that matter!"

One of James' eyebrows raise, and even though I want to tell him to focus on the road, I just watch curiously as he stares back at Bree in the mirror, his smile falling. "Oh, little witch. You are my *favorite* kind of creature, trust me."

Oh damn.

Bree sucks in a sharp breath and flicks her gaze to the passing scenery outside her window. With my new wolf hearing, I can count the rapid beats of her heart from here. She told me before that she was into the vamp once. I don't think that crush ever went away, and it looks like maybe James is just as smitten with my best friend. *They're so into each other!*

James throws a quick glance back at me with wide dark eyes before looking back at the road where we leave the main part of the city and turn into an old rural neighborhood.

"Great, you heard me. Of course." I speak to him in my mind, but he doesn't react again.

"Well, do you love Bree or not?"

I focus on the tensing of James' hard jaw and his white knuckles on the steering wheel. His eyes turn back to me once more and only a slight nod confirms my suspicions. If it weren't for my new keen sight, I likely would've missed the subtle movement, but it was there all the same. I want to squeal in excitement, but I hold it back so Bree and James can work out their relationship without my meddling.

"That's the house, there." Seth points at the end of the long cul-de-sac, where a large haunted-style house sits, watching over the neighborhood like an old queen surveying her kingdom.

"Wow, somehow it's exactly how I imagined," I say with nerves building in my belly.

Bree laughs and shakes her head. "It's super intimidating."

We pull up to the curb just outside the house and each of us steps out, standing side by side. Seth wraps an arm around my waist, pulling me close to his side and I sigh at the contact. How will I ever have a coherent thought with him touching me?

The others pull up behind the jeep and join us. We stand as a small army staring up at the massive house. The black wood on the outside is peeling, and the high peaks at the top make the house even more castle-like. If I weren't here to find out how to destroy the cure that once flowed through my body, I might take a touristy picture by the ten-foot-tall front door.

"It feels like we're about to sell our souls or something. Should we just leave?" Horas' booming voice breaks the tension. I can't say I don't agree with him.

"Well, we came all this way, didn't we?" I step out of Seth's arms, tentatively moving toward the answers we've been looking for, when the tall door creaks open.

I freeze, but my entire body calms when I see the sweet young woman step out onto the front porch with a beaming smile. Her long blonde hair is the color of sunshine and her pink cheeks are sprinkled with freckles, highlighting the baby blue of her eyes.

She sashays in her flowy pink gown and waves at us. "Hello, friends. Come on in and let us talk of your long journey to my home. I believe you need a lot of rest."

I look back at Bree, who shrugs, and I turn back to the gorgeous girl. "Thank you, but we came to see Priestess Aurelia. Do you know her?"

The young woman smiles brightly and bows to us with a dainty hand on her waist. "That is me, Aurelia Masalis, at your service, Maia Collins."

If my eyes could fall out of my head, they would with how wide I stare at the beautiful young priestess. I turn around to all of the others, and they each have wide stares of their own. James laughs softly and crosses his large arms.

He looks down at Bree by his side. "Well, I'm not taking back the *old witch* comment."

Priestess Aurelia opens her arms to us. "Come, all of you. We have much to discuss." Her eyes land on James and she glares. "The vampire stays outside."

Bree giggles and to my surprise, she winds her arm back and smacks James right on his ass. "See ya later, *old* vamp." She winks and we leave James with his jaw on the floor, dumbstruck for the first time since I met him.

Chapter 35

◇◇◇

Seth

MAIA LEADS OUR LITTLE BAND of travelers into Priestess Aurelia's massive house. The priestess shocked us all with her appearance. I'm not going to lie and say I didn't expect her to be an ancient-looking woman with wrinkles deeper than the Mariana Trench. The small blonde woman with a perky hop in her step is surreal.

Maia reaches back to me with an open hand as we move into the candle lit entryway of the home. I lace my fingers with Maia's and I can feel my heart flutter at the contact. Everything she does makes me crave the feel of her skin against mine, even as she tore those cheeseburgers apart like the ferocious woman I know her to be.

Priestess Aurelia stops just inside a large living room with vaulted ceilings and ornate wallpaper that meets at the peak. Everything about the home screams Victorian age, and I can't deny the magical feel of it.

"You may all take a seat wherever you feel comfortable, but I would like Maia to sit beside me." The woman smiles sweetly and takes Maia away from me to squeeze beside her on a loveseat.

Maia gapes at the woman for a moment. "I'm sorry if this sounds rude, but I'm really curious about…" She searches for the words, but Priestess Aurelia chimes in.

"…about why I look like a seventeen year old girl?" She giggles, only making her seem younger.

Maia grins and I feel my lips mirroring hers. *Gah, I love that smile.* "Yes. I just wasn't expecting the high priestess of the witches to be so young."

"Aren't you supposed to be over a hundred years old, priestess?" Bree asks, not in the know about her own leader.

Priestess Aurelia throws her golden hair over her shoulder. "I am one hundred and sixty-one to be exact, my young witch." We all collectively gasp, and she giggles that twinkling sound again before whispering like she's telling the room a secret. "My magic is connected to all of my people; therefore, I am able to cast a continuous age glamour over myself. I mean, who would choose an aching back and wrinkles when you can have this?"

She waves a hand up and down, gesturing to her young body. She has a point, but knowing there's an incredibly wise elder hidden below the innocent exterior makes me feel uneasy in her presence.

"Thank you for having us in your home, priestess," I say, hoping to make friends with the powerful witch. "Well, most of us." *Aside from James.*

She looks back toward the front of the house and raises an eyebrow. "I am sorry about your friend, but I dated a vampire once and I will forever loathe their kind."

Bree stiffens where she sits beside Qadira and Wilk, and I can hear her heart rate pick up. "Do you think vampires are untrustworthy?"

Priestess Aurelia shrugs. "My Lucian was a pig. I am not naive enough to say they're all the same, but I am also not willing to take the chance. I don't have many days left in this life. I only want to share those days with the best company."

A week ago, I would've loved that James got left out in the night, but he has somehow become one of my most trusted friends. I want him to be treated with respect, but I have no say in a house that isn't mine.

"Well, I'm sure you know why we came to your home, priestess." I'm ready to move forward with this night and be alone with Maia again.

The priestess nods. "I know you originally came to see if the shifter cure could be removed from our young wolf hybrid. It's clear that you've accomplished that on your own." She looks Maia up and down.

Maia twirls her fingers together under the witch's gaze. "Is it really all gone, though? Is there a way to tell?"

She's worried that she could still carry the cure?

Priestess Aurelia grabs Maia's hands in hers. "Oh, dear. It is completely eradicated from your system. You are only a wolf and a human now, no longer a danger to shifter kind in that way."

Maia sighs as if she is finally dropping the weight of the world off of her shoulders. "Thank you. I'm so happy to hear that." She looks my way with a small smile, and I want so badly to run to her and hold her in my arms.

Chill out, clingy wolf.

Priestess Aurelia closes her eyes briefly, still holding onto Maia. "The cure is not in you, but it isn't gone from our planet entirely. Your blood is captive in the arms of the lupercus that stole you away and liberated you from your curse."

Liberated? More like tortured...

I lean forward, resting my elbows on my knees. "But can it even be destroyed? The cure is supposed to be indestructible."

"It was once that way, yes. When the shifter god created the cure, it was with his own blood. Putting it into the blood of a human weakened it, especially after living inside of Maia for all these years. I believe that the reason Maia is free of the cure now is because you awoke her wolf side when you donated your blood to her, and it was Maia's alpha blood that destroyed the remaining poison."

She really does see everything, doesn't she? "How do you know it wasn't my alpha blood that killed it? I'm the alpha heir."

Priestess Aurelia raises a single eyebrow and looks at me like I'm an idiot. "Dear boy. You are not the rightful alpha heir. That honor goes to our Maia here. It was her alpha heir blood that killed the weakened cure, and it will be her blood that kills the rest of it when you track down the thieves." She looks back at Maia. "Be careful, though. You are a shifter now, and the cure could kill you as it can any other shifter."

Bree groans, drawing all eyes to her. "There's no way we can track the lupercus, priestess. They leave no trail."

"Isn't there a spell of some kind? I mean, this is the leader of the witches, is it not?" Sasha asks the questions from where she stands beside a tall fireplace.

Priestess Aurelia smiles back at the shifter. "You need not worry about that. I can find anybody, lupercus or not. But, that is a task for the morning. You have all had a long journey this week, correct?"

I nod along with the others, and two men enter the living area looking like beefy bodyguards. The priestess stands, finally releasing Maia. "My men will show you to your bedrooms. We have many to spare, so you may all sleep comfortably for tonight."

I look toward Maia and she blushes under my gaze. There's no way I'm sleeping away from my mate for a single night. I can't deal with losing her again. I don't mention my worries to the high priestess, though.

"What about James? Will he be sleeping outside?" Bree worries over James' comfort, and I just know he'd have a snarky retort for her if he were in here.

Priestess Aurelia sighs and runs dainty fingers through her hair. "Oh, alright. The vampire may sleep in one of the bedrooms, but he will need a chaperone as long as he is in my home." She points at Bree. "He will stay with you, my witch daughter. Keep him out of trouble."

Bree gulps nervously, but nods without argument. James and Bree are going to share a room for the night, and if I have my say, I'll spend the night looking after my mate.

Hell, this'll be torture.

Chapter 36

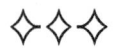

◇◇◇

Maia

SETH GRABS MY HAND AGAIN as we climb the grand stairs of Priestess Aurelia's house. Two hulk-like men lead us down a long hallway of at least ten opened doors. Each room has a large bed, dark Victorian-type bedding, and simple, but expensive-looking decorations. It's like being in a castle on the outskirts of Georgetown, Delaware.

"Our priestess has a large number of witches under her care and guidance. These rooms are for any who need them." The tallest muscled guy turns back to us and then waves to the rooms. "Take your pick. We will keep watch over you for the night."

The two men leave, and everyone hesitates momentarily, but as always, Sasha gives zero craps and flips her hair as she steps into the nearest room, slamming the door.

Horas sighs and shakes his head. "That was an invitation, right? That girl totally wants me."

James smacks Horas on the shoulder. "I'm the only one in need of a babysitter tonight, mate. As much as I'd love to watch that girl kick your ass, it's best you take a room to yourself."

Horas grunts and stalks into the room beside Sasha's. James bows to Bree and gestures toward the following room. "Our humble suite awaits us, little witch."

Bree groans and glares at James. "Don't make me tie you down for the night, vamp."

James' smile reaches his eyes with a wicked gleam. "Oh, please do. I'm happy to beg."

My mouth drops open along with Bree's, and I'm sure she's about ready to smack James across the face. Instead, she stands taller and her red curls bounce as she heads into the waiting room. She turns back momentarily to throw over her shoulder, "You couldn't handle me, James. I would hate for you to break a hip in your old age."

James laughs as he trails after my best friend. I don't know what's going to happen between them in that room, but after that exchange, I'm *not* sharing a wall with those two. Luckily, Qadira steps into the next room and smiles sweetly back at us.

"Good night. My body is quite in need of some rest." She looks over at Wilk longingly and then closes her door.

Just tell him how you feel!

Wilk looks sad as he nods to Seth and me. "I need rest, as well. I have gained much respect for the witches after this kind hospitality. Sleep well."

After the door closes, Seth and I look at one another. His heavy gaze feels like a caress as he smiles down at me. I clear my throat and look toward two free rooms side by side. "I guess those can be ours. Good night."

His smile falls and he nods swiftly. "Right. I'm glad there is enough space for us all. Sleep well, Snow."

He leans down, dropping a gentle kiss against my lips, and I leave him standing in the hall as I close my bedroom door. I drop my head against the door and silently curse myself for not choosing to stay in the same room as my mate.

What the hell, Mai? He's only a wall away! Ravish him!

My inner thoughts are much more confident than I feel, and I shake them away. I don't know the first thing about ravishing anyone. I can't even make the first move! I look down at the only pair of clothes I have, and sigh. I desperately need a shower after the last few days, and Qadira's nature bath this morning didn't do the trick.

The room is large, and my eyes find an attached bathroom hidden in the corner. *Yes!* I turn the bathroom light on and my body instantly relaxes as I look down at the large bathtub and array of soaps and shampoos. *This*. This is all I need tonight. Not a night alone with my mate. Not the chance to complete my bond with Seth. Just a nice warm bubble bath…

Seth in a bubble bath would be heavenly.

I groan and throw my head back at my much too sexy thoughts, as I strip down and turn the hot water on. I climb into the growing bubbles and think about how far I've come. I'm no longer a simple young woman with her whole life ahead of her. I'm a wolf shifter, and my kind is in danger. *And*, I have a fated mate that loves me. Who am I kidding? I don't want to be alone anymore. I want to be in Seth's arms.

I lay my head back and a soft knock sounds at the bathroom door, making me jump. "Uh, yes?" The door swings open and I nearly scream before I see Bree looking disappointed in me. "Bree! You scared the crap out of me! Why are you always doing that?"

She throws her hands on her hips. "Why are you in here, and not in Seth's room?"

I scoff. "What? You want me to sleep in Seth's room?"

"Duh! You two are fated mates, Mai. You love one another, and you need to get in there and complete that bond."

My mouth drops to the water surrounding me. "Are you seriously telling me to go have sex? In a house full of people? For my first time?"

Bree nods vehemently. "Yes!" She pauses and points to the wall where Seth's room is. "Listen. I'm not doing this in a peer pressure way. When you and Seth choose one another by completing the bond, both of you grow stronger and you're able to communicate telepathically. It's supposed to be incredible, all sex jokes aside."

"But, why now? Why can't we just wait?"

Bree crosses her arms and purses her lips. "Because, I made a vow to be your protector, and tomorrow we will be at war with the lupercus. If there is a way to make you and Seth stronger for what's to come, I am all for it."

I shut off the water faucet before the soap bubbles start to pour over the edge of the tub. "This isn't just a boost in power, though. This is a commitment, like a wedding night."

She nods and her face softens. "Is it what you want, though? To do this with him?"

It takes me less than a second to know the answer to that question, and Bree can see it clearly in my mind. She smiles and turns away from me, glancing over her shoulder past her wild red curls.

"I spelled Seth's room. It's totally soundproof until the sun comes up. This is your choice to make, but please know that I love you, and I'm so happy for you and Seth."

With that, Bree leaves the bathroom, and I sink below the water, shutting out the world as my eyes close and I only hear the sound of my own heartbeat. My heart knows exactly what it wants, and Bree was right. I want Seth to be mine forever.

◇ ◇ ◇

Seth

Why on earth did I let her go in that room alone? I should've told her that I want to sleep beside her tonight. I should have promised her that I would watch over her until sunrise. Now, if I go in there uninvited, I'll look like a total creep. *Damn, I'm an idiot.*

I pace the carpeted floor of my room, missing Maia after only twenty minutes away from her. There's no way in hell I'm going to sleep tonight and let Maia get taken again. I just need to remain alert and ready to protect her.

I close my eyes, trying to hear Maia in the room beside mine. She turned on a bath not long ago, but I haven't heard anything since then. *Would it be bad to burst into her bathroom unannounced?*

That'd be sure to scare her away from me for good. I plop back onto the queen-sized bed and kick my tennis shoes onto the ground. A very quiet knock comes at my bedroom door and I hurry over to answer it. I swing the door open and Maia's gorgeous hazel eyes smile up at me with damp brown hair hanging around her shoulders. The white is nearly gone completely.

She's so flippin' beautiful.

I'm clearly struck dumb by her presence, so she looks up and down the hallway nervously. "Can I come in?" she whispers.

"Oh, yes. Of course." I step to the side and she enters my room, her eyes taking in the ornate decor.

Then her eyes find me again as I shut the bedroom door. She slowly steps closer to me, making my heart pound against the wall of my chest. She stops, her body almost touching mine and then she reaches around me to flip the lock on the door.

Holy crap, that was sexy.

Her hands splay across my abdomen and heat spreads through my body. "Seth. I'm ready to complete the bond."

Chapter 37

◇◇◇

Maia

I'M BEING BOLD. It's like my wolf is helping me take control and put myself out there. She's confident and strong, and she knows it.

Seth stares down at me where I wait for his response after telling him that I'm ready to complete the bond. I never imagined saying those words, but they're out there now.

No going back. No hiding away and dying of embarrassment.

Seth swallows hard, and hunger fills his dark eyes. His raspy voice rumbles in his chest. "Are you sure about that, Snow? We have time. The others could hear us."

I place a soft kiss against the front of his black shirt, loving the quick beats of his heart beneath the surface. "I'm very sure. Bree spelled the walls with a soundproof spell." Seth's eyebrows raise at that. "And as for time, I'm afraid we can't promise tomorrow. Our adventure isn't over yet and anything can happen."

Seth's hands slide up my arms and over my shoulders, and I suddenly wish my shirt was gone. I thought about coming over here in a towel after my bath, but I chose the discarded dirty clothes instead.

What on earth were you thinking, Mai?

Seth's hands continue caressing me, sliding down my spine and resting just above my jeans. "Even if I die tomorrow, Snow, I still won't make you do something you're not ready for."

He's too good.

My smile stretches as I stare into those gorgeous eyes, and I slip my arms around his broad neck. "I want you, Seth. No tomorrow, or a thousand tomorrows, I still want to claim you *tonight*."

Seth growls and his eyes turn completely black. "Holy hell, Snow. You talk like that, and you'll have me bowing at your feet."

A chill runs through me as I smile like an idiot. "Just kiss me and let's start there."

He laughs and picks me up off my feet, tossing my legs around his body. His perfect lips crash into mine with so much heat that I feel a fire ignite inside of me. I gasp against his mouth, letting him take control of our kiss.

Seth squeezes my hips, digging his fingers into the fabric of my jeans as he carries me to the untouched bed. His lips trail from mine, across my cheek and to my neck where he nibbles me gently with his teeth. A fever rolls through me as he lays me back on his bed and his body presses into mine, lips never leaving the sensitive skin of my neck.

Seth's tongue darts out to lick just below my ear and I gasp all over again. I tighten my legs around his waist, holding onto him for dear life as his mouth explores my skin. His hands take mine off of his shoulders, and press them into the bed above my head.

One of his hands holds me while the other explores my body with a skill that I didn't expect. He presses a warm palm against my chest and slides his fingers down my cleavage and across my abdomen until they land on the button of my jeans, teasing me.

My breathing is ragged. Seth's lips trail back up to meet mine, fast, hard, and passionate as his fingers pop open the front of my jeans and dip below the fabric. I moan against the feel of his touch and my tongue juts out to taste his, adding more heat to our searing kiss.

Seth's tantalizing touch, his signature smell that covers me, and the taste of him causes the most incredible and overwhelming mixture of pleasure, nearly pushing me over the edge. Seth's hands release me as he climbs off of the bed. I literally almost whine at being separated from him.

He stands like a sexy king, staring down at me, breathing heavily, his hard muscles tensing. "Are you still sure you want to continue, Snow?"

Is he kidding?

I lick my lips and nod, pushing myself to lean on my elbows as my eyes explore him, starving for more. "I have zero doubts, Seth. I never want to stop."

He smiles the happiest smile and grips the bottom of his shirt, pulling it over his head and making his hair even messier. And, damn, he is so incredible. His hands undo the button of his pants and he slides the dark jeans down, tossing them to the side.

Oh, heavens. He's going commando...

My eyes widen and it's almost impossible not to stare at *everything*. But, he's mine, and he'll be mine forever. It's practically my right to stare as much as I want, right? A low and primal growl builds in my chest, completely against my control.

Seth holds his hands out and I place mine in his. He pulls me easily to my feet, chest to chest, and he slides my shirt off of me swiftly. His eyes don't leave mine to explore, though, and it's somehow so much hotter.

I hurry the process, impatient, and I grip my jeans, dragging them down my body with ease, until Seth and I are standing completely exposed to one another. I'm at a loss for what to do next, totally out of my element as he searches my face.

"I love you, Maia Collins." Seth's hands slip around my waist and he pulls my naked body against his, causing every inch of me to tremble. "You're everything to me, and I want forever with you. I hope you know that."

Seth spins us so that his back is to the bed and he leans in to kiss me much softer than before. His lips brush against mine loving and tender, and every part of me sighs against him.

I gently shove him backward so that he sits on the edge of the bed, and I climb onto his lap. Seth groans and his hands slip into my hair, rough and needy. I lean into him, taking my turn to control the kiss.

Seth lets me take total control and I kiss along his strong jaw, and down the muscles in his neck, moving my body against him as I explore his skin, a frenzy building inside of me.

"I love you too, Seth. I'll always love you," I whisper against his lips and grab onto his shoulders. Seth presses my hips down, drawing us closer together, and a wildness overtakes me.

My nails extend into claws and I can feel my wolf threatening to come out. A growl leaves my throat and I begin to panic. "Seth, how do I stop this?"

He grips the sides of my face and looks into my eyes. "Just take a deep breath. Your emotions are heightened, and the wolf has a hard time remaining calm."

I close my eyes and nod, trying to breathe steadily. *Stay back, girl. This is my moment.* The wolf slowly retreats and I can feel my body relaxing again. I open my eyes, and I realize that my claws scraped Seth's shoulders, causing him to bleed.

"Oh no! Seth, I'm so sorry!" I let go of him, feeling horrible for hurting my mate, but he's having none of that.

Seth grabs my waist and flips me onto my back against the soft comforter. He presses his hard body against me and his eyes flash black as he growls.

"Don't say sorry to me, Maia. Do you have any idea how sexy you are when you lose control like that? I can't wait anymore. Please tell me if you need to stop."

I breathe hard, ready for everything he has to offer me, and I nod, suddenly lost for words. I just made the man bleed, and he *still* wants me. And I want him with everything in me.

Seth doesn't hesitate as he connects us, claiming me as his, passionate and wild. I never could've imagined such a perfect feeling as this. Seth is mine, and every part of me is his. My mind is all Seth, and I wouldn't want it any other way.

And thank heavens for Bree's soundproof walls.

Chapter 38

◇◇◇

Maia

"GOOD MORNING, SNOW." Seth's raspy voice fills my half-asleep mind, and a delicious warmth covers me.

My eyes flutter open to see Seth leaning over me, his broad shoulders blocking the world from view. He has an incredible smile just for me, and I instantly crave him all over again.

"Good morning. How is it possible that I'm not at all tired after the many hours we spent *not* sleeping last night?" I dip my fingers into his messy brown hair and can't help the way my body moves to be closer to him.

He rubs his nose against mine and kisses the corner of my mouth, teasing me. He leans back so I can see his mouth is closed while he responds. *"Fun fact, my love. Mated wolves don't need much sleep to feel rested."*

I freeze and my jaw drops open. I'm sure I look like I've lost my mind, and I'm not totally sure I didn't. "Did you just speak into my mind, Seth? Please don't tell me I'm finally going crazy after everything."

He laughs and speaks normally this time. "You haven't gone crazy. We are mated, Maia. There's so much more we can do together now." I give him what I hope is a sexy look and he chuckles again. "Aside from *that*, we can speak to one another in our minds, even from long distances. We should be significantly stronger, and be able to shift in a second, rather than gradually." He switches to his mind-talk again. *"And, as I said, we need very minimal sleep."*

His body presses harder against mine, and I am extremely glad we didn't get dressed before falling asleep last night. I never want to wear clothes around Seth again, though that could make things awkward around the others. I giggle at my inner thoughts, and Seth eyes me curiously.

I watch his raised eyebrow and half-lifted lips. *"Can you hear me, Seth? I hope I'm doing this right."*

His smile widens and he nods. *"Loud and perfectly clear, my love."*

I wiggle my hips against his and wrap my legs around him until my ankles lock behind his back. He responds with a low groan, and I speak through our mate link again. *"Good. Now, stop calling me your love or I'll have no choice but to claim you all over again right this minute."*

He sucks in a sharp breath, and his lips drop to connect roughly with mine. Oh, how I love the way I can drive him crazy so easily. Seth trails his talented lips over my chin, kissing every spot until he reaches my neck. I'm breathing heavily, but my labored breath turns into wild laughter as Seth nibbles playfully on my neck, rubbing his stubble against my skin.

I fight against Seth's torturous tickling, but he's thoroughly enjoying himself. He drops to my belly, blowing a raspberry against my flesh. *"Stop it right now, you devil!"*

He laughs, kissing the spot he just tickled and looks up at me through his stupidly thick eyelashes. *"But your laughter could carry me through anything, Snow. Why would I ever want to stop?"*

I sigh happily, just as a knock on the bedroom door makes me jump. The teasing British voice speaks through the heavy wood. "I thought you should be aware that the little witch's soundproof spell only lasted until sunrise. The sun has risen, so put some clothes on and join us for breakfast."

My face flushes with heat. If I could die of embarrassment, now would be the prime moment.

◊ ◊ ◊

Seth

Of course James would be the one to volunteer to interrupt our perfect morning. That damn vampire loves pissing me off. Maia's red cheeks make me smile. I love that she could be so open and confident with me all night and still get embarrassed so easily.

Hell, I love her so much.

Reluctantly, I climb off of Maia, being sure to scan her naked body from head to toe before tossing the comforter back onto her. I head over to the bedroom door, dragging my jeans on along the way. I pull the door open to see a grinning James looking like he is so utterly proud of himself.

James has become a good friend of mine, and I would never wish harm upon him, but we never settled our business with one another after he kissed Maia, knowing very well how I felt about her. I'm not an idiot, and it was clear he could read my mind when I found Maia in his cabin.

James raises his eyebrows, teasing. "Did you have a restful night, mate?"

Forgive me, Maia.

I clench my fist and swing my arm forward to punch James right across the face. The hit has enough power behind it to make a cracking sound, and I can't help but feel satisfied.

Maia squeals from where she hides beneath the blankets of *our* bed. "Seth! What are you doing?"

James turns his face back to me, the red mark already fading thanks to his rapid vamp healing. He rubs his jaw and nods to me with an easy smile. "I know I've done quite a few questionable things, but might I ask what that particular wallop was for?"

I shake my stiff hand out and cross my arms across my bare chest. "That was for kissing *my* mate."

James clicks his tongue and holds a finger up like *"oh yeah"*. "Ay, I was wondering when you were going to do that, mate. Good on you."

Maia yells behind me again. "Good on you? What the hell is wrong with you two?" Then she mumbles something like "freakin' men."

I laugh and hold my hand out for James to shake. He accepts my gesture and peeks over my shoulder to look at Maia with a quick wink and a smile. "I love the messy-hair-in-bed look."

With that, he runs before I can punch him again, and I spin back toward Maia, shutting the door behind me. She glared back at me just like the day I first saw her in that coffee shop, and I can't help loving it.

"You are so beautiful when you get angry."

She stands from the bed, using her new wolf abilities, and she's in front of me before I can blink. Her finger pokes my chest hard. "You can't just go around punching our pack members, alpha ass!"

I swear I almost miss what she says because I'm so focused on the fact that she is standing naked in front of me with that sexy glare. I grin, happier than I've ever been, which only makes her angrier.

"What's putting that goofy smile on your face?"

I grab her around the waist and hoist her up into my arms, making her squeal again. "You, Maia. Only *you* could make me this incredibly, stupidly happy."

She sighs, all of the previous anger leaving her, and her mouth crashes into mine with a heat somehow rivaling the flame of last night. I growl against her kiss, trying my hardest not to grip her hips too tight as her tongue dips in between my lips.

I pull my head back, amazed at her black eyes as she fights her animal urges. "I seem to recall being called down to breakfast."

Why did I say that? I don't want breakfast!

She nods. "You are absolutely right." She hops off of my hips and runs fingers through her tangled brown hair, no longer white now that she's free of the cure and officially mated. "Well, let's go have breakfast with all of our friends that know exactly what we did all night."

She looks pained, but I smile again. "Well, they may have an idea, but only you and I know the details." I switch to speaking in my mind as Maia dresses in last night's clothes. *"I'm so damn glad you're mine."*

She smiles back at me. *"And I'm so damn happy that I'm yours."*

Chapter 39

✧✧✧

Maia

I SWEAR, THEY ALL KNOW! Why do they all have to know? Seth and I take a seat outside Priestess Aurelia's house. Her backyard is large and beautiful with tall trees and blooming flowers everywhere. The winter cold is fading away to bring the spring sunshine and I want to bask in the feel of it. But I can't, because Bree is grinning at me like she's in on the fact that I am no longer a virgin.

One of the beefy men that showed us to our rooms last night places some steaming sausage and homemade waffles on the long table in front of Seth and I. I thank him as my mouth waters, and I immediately start loading up my plate with as much food as it will fit.

James and Bree sit side by side across the table from us, and beside them Horas is digging into his food like a beast. Seth and I ended up seated between Qadira and Wilk, who normally are attached at the hip. Of course, ever the loner, Sasha sits sharpening a knife at the end of the table. The only one missing from our morning gathering is the priestess herself.

I stare down at my pile of food and drool. *I'm starving!*

James chuckles low across from me. "I bet you are, love."

I snap my head up to his and kick my leg out, connecting with his shin. He grunts and Bree bursts into laughter beside him.

"I don't know what that was about, but I would bet good money that you deserved it," she says through her laughter.

"He did," I say back, taking a bite of my syrup-covered waffles.

Beside Seth, Wilk glows happily. "You look well rested, Maia. I am very glad that you are officially mated. It shall be a strong and joyous union."

I want to bang my head against the table, but I hold myself back. I'm already embarrassed enough. Horas claps his hands together once as he lets out a booming laugh.

"Yo, faerie prince. You're embarrassing little Maia with that kinda talk."

Wilk's eyes grow wide as he stares at me. "I am sorry, Maia. We were speaking of it before you arrived. I thought it was not something inappropriate, or I would not have mentioned it."

Oh, dear lord!

I shake my head and try to calm my nerves, refusing to make eye contact with anyone. "It's not at all, Wilk. At least, it shouldn't be inappropriate to talk about. I'm very grateful to have Seth as my mate forever."

Seth watches me with hunger in his eyes while I take a big bite, and I raise an eyebrow at him. *"You look hungry. You know there's food right in front of you..."*

He smiles and lazily grabs a handful of sausage links while he continues to watch me. *"That's not what I'm hungry for, but it'll have to do until I have you alone again."*

I gulp and am suddenly reminded that James can hear my thoughts. I look up at the vamp, but he's focused on a conversation about fighting techniques with Horas.

"Can James hear us when we talk to one another like this?"

Seth looks toward James and then back to me. *"I guess not. Another thing just for you and I, my love."*

I'm grinning from ear to ear, and I don't even care that everyone knows we had sex last night. I'm happy, dammit.

Everyone sits at attention when Priestess Aurelia steps out into the yard, dressed like a queen in a golden dress that matches her hair and dangling gold earrings. "Good morning, my lovely guests. Great news. I have found your thieves."

◇ ◇ ◇

Seth

"You found the lupercus already? How?" Bree stands in shock, her eyes wide.

Priestess Aurelia grins and flips her hair over one shoulder like an average teenage girl. I would never have thought this young girl could be over a hundred years old, but almost nothing surprises me much anymore.

"I told you that I'm more than capable of finding anyone, young witch. The lupercus are no exception. I woke early for meditation, set my mind on the shifter cure, and I was able to locate the thieves nearly six hundred miles north of here."

"So, Canada? Really?" Sasha groans and rolls her eyes.

Horas leans forward in his seat, causing the strained wood to groan under his weight. "Oh, poor baby. There isn't anything wrong with Canada. It's one of the best places for hunting."

Sasha scrunches her nose. "But the people are so… friendly. It's weird."

I smack my hand on the table, not in the mood to talk about Canadians. "Hey. Both of you, be quiet. We're not going to Canada to make friends with the locals. This is a war." The wolves shut their mouths and straighten their shoulders as a sign of respect. I dip my head to the priestess. "Please, priestess. If you have the coordinates, we will leave immediately."

Priestess Aurelia smiles sweetly with twinkling blue eyes and it's incredibly difficult to see her as our elder. "Thank you, Seth. I do have coordinates, but you all will not be traveling as you have this past week. I have much better ways."

"A portal, then? Dira and I can help." Wilk stands and laces his fingers behind his back, looking like a blue Fae soldier, ready for his commands.

"Yes, young prince. Thankfully though, I have a lot of power to share, so I will not need the help. I have chosen a location just six miles from the lupercus camp. This way you can get your footing, wait until nightfall, and attack. The area is remote, with rough terrain, so be careful."

This witch seriously doesn't procrastinate when she sets her mind on something. I reach my hand out to grab Maia's and she smiles up at me. *"This is happening really fast, Snow. Are you ready to go into battle?"*

She nods immediately, squeezing my hand tight. *"I'm so ready to be done with that damn cure, and to start a life with you."*

That's all the reassurance I need. I turn back to the others who are all watching me with questioning eyes. They're waiting on my answer. I'm suddenly a commander, choosing to send my soldiers into battle. If only I didn't love them all so much.

I take a deep breath and nod to the priestess. "Alright, then. The lupercus made the wrong move when they went after Maia. I think it's about time they pay for their grievous mistake."

The entire table stands, erupting in shouts of agreement. James leans over the table and pats my arm, his sharp fangs flashing. "I'm ready, mate. I could use a good fight, and after that hit this morning, I'd say you're in need of practice."

I smile, despite his teasing. "You've gotten quite funny in your old age, James. Just be careful not to over exert yourself out there."

Priestess Aurelia whistles, bringing our attention back to her tiny presence. "Alright, alright. If you want your revenge, it's about time we get a move on. All of you, gather around."

The eight of us leave the long dining table, still full of more food than we can eat, and we each stand side by side in front of the priestess. She looks us up and down before chanting a few words in her witch tongue. I've never understood the Latin-like language, but it's fascinating to hear from someone so seasoned.

Priestess Aurelia's eyes begin to glow with a silver light and she waves a hand in the air from left to right until it passes each of us. A sudden pressure covers my body and I look down in shock as black and gray athletic pants replace my jeans. A tight black long sleeve shirt covers my torso and to top it off, I'm given a pair of hiking boots and a long blade is tightly secured around my waist.

My eyes bug out of my head as I scan the others beside me. Each of us matches, like an actual team of warriors, or midnight ninja assassins. My eyes take extra long to trail up and down Maia. Her black and gray clothes are skin tight and the knife hanging from her hip makes her too sexy to handle. Seeing her fight like that will be torture of the best kind.

I bow to the high priestess in thanks. "We are grateful for the clothing, priestess. I hope we don't ruin it during the shift."

Priestess Aurelia grins from ear to ear. "Oh, dear wolf. This uniform is different from regular clothing. You may take wolf form to fight or run and return back to your human form, exactly as you are now. The clothing will not leave you until you willingly remove it."

Maia gasps and pumps her fist in excitement. "Awesome!"

The witch giggles gently and steps forward to take Maia's hand like she did last night. "Your future is bright, little hybrid. Just trust in your heart and do not be afraid. Remember that like your many protectors, you are strong."

Maia nods and pulls the priestess into a warm hug. "I will never forget your kindness, priestess. You are a treasure." *That's my loving Snow.*

Priestess Aurelia steps back and looks at each of our faces with a kind smile before throwing her arms out wide and showing us into another place through a massive portal. It's like looking into a television screen, displaying crisp woods with dark browns and vibrant greens.

"Canada awaits. Just be safe, and don't forget my home. You will always be welcome." She pauses, glancing at James momentarily as she sighs. "Even the *vampire.*"

James winks at the witch and is the first to step into the portal. The vast woods are thick with broad trees and the smell of nature. I grab Maia's hand again and together we follow the others into the unknown land.

I turn in time to see the portal, like a big painting of Priestess Aurelia's backyard, folding in on itself behind us. Just like that, we're all standing in the quiet of an unknown forest, only the sound of a whistling breeze. We've been in this same position so many times lately.

Sasha pulls the katana sword off of her back and tests it in the air a few times with a whistle. "So, what now? Attack or wait? Personally, I say attack."

"So quick to die." A slow cackling laugh follows the female voice, piercing the calm around us, and everyone drops into a defensive stance. I whip my head around, searching for whatever made the sound.

"Who are you? Show yourself!" I yell into the woods with my back to Maia.

I need to protect her. She hasn't had time to learn how to fight properly with her new mated abilities. And neither have I, for that matter.

What was I thinking coming out here with her?

A tall dark-skinned woman with short maroon colored hair steps out of the shadows. She is wearing a long black dress and her eyes are completely silver. She has to be a witch.

Before I can ask the intruder any questions, her mouth purses to throw out a high-pitched whistle. In seconds, the thudding of footsteps fills the wide opening, and we are surrounded from all angles by the lupercus.

One thing I notice immediately: they planned this encounter, somehow knowing we'd be in this exact spot at this exact moment. Also, we are seriously outnumbered.

Chapter 40

◇◇◇

Maia

WE'RE SURROUNDED BY LUPERCUS, and some really creepy witch lady is leading the attack. We only just arrived in the forest, and somehow the lupercus saw us coming. All of my friends surround me, shielding me from the threat, but I don't need protection anymore. The lupercus already got what they wanted from me.

"Let me through." I squeeze in between Seth's broad back and Sasha's glinting sword. Seth side-eyes me but he doesn't stop my progression, and I'm grateful. I stare at the silver-eyed woman and try to keep my voice steady. "What's your name, ma'am? And how did you know we'd be here?"

The witch moves her lips to speak, but a familiar face appears beside her to talk instead. It's the thin older woman who kidnapped me and held me while her lackeys drained my blood just days ago. A rage fills me, and I have to focus to control my shaking.

"Your little pack of creatures isn't the only one with a witch on their side. You have Priestess Aurelia, but we have Marian. She's as old as your witch, and every bit as powerful."

Bree steps beside me with her fists clenched around two long daggers. "Nobody is as powerful as Priestess Aurelia. Age doesn't make the witch."

"But experience does, little one," the witch, Marian, says. "I saw you coming the moment your priestess cast the spell to find the cure."

I gasp, and my heart sinks. We have no advantage, and we're trapped from all sides. *"What do we do, Seth?"*

Seth reaches for my hand, squeezing it like he does to comfort me, though this time it doesn't quite hit the mark. *"We fight, my love. But we stay together."*

I nod, and ready my mind to prepare for battle. Before I can act, though, the witch makes the first move. I don't even see her flinch. She whispers something under her breath as she launches a ten-foot-tall wall of fire straight at us. I nearly scream, but the faeries have our backs, using their power to erect an invisible shield.

The witch's fire hits the invisible wall and dissipates upon impact with a sound like crackling fireworks. "Oh, how I hate faeries," she says with a pout.

Wilk snorts behind me. "And I cannot say I care much for witches like you."

Ooh, Wilk-burn.

"Thanks Wilk. I'll take over the smack talk, if you don't mind." Bree sticks her middle finger in the air, flipping off the witch, and turning it toward the surrounding lupercus with a sneer. "Back the hell off now, or you will all die. Final warning."

That's my girl.

The lupercus leader crosses her arms with a cocky smile. "That's sweet, but your words don't hurt us, dear."

Bree sheaths her daggers and scoffs as she flicks her hair over her shoulder. As her fingers slide off the ends of her red locks, a bolt of golden lightning shoots from her fingertips, hitting the lupercus woman square in the chest. The woman drops to the ground, her whole body shuddering as the electricity travels the length of her.

"Was that enough *hurt* for you, *dear*?"

"Ay, that was incredibly sexy," James says with a wicked smile, and he winks at my best friend.

"Enough!" Marian bellows loud enough to shake the ground we all stand on. She snaps her fingers and points to my friends and I, inciting a full-on attack from the fourty or so lupercus.

Everything happens in a blur. The lupercus shift to their animal forms, like large rams with sharp horns on their heads and yellow eyes. They stand on two legs like humans, but their feet are large hooves and their bodies are covered in goat-like fur.

My body begins to shake as I fight back my wolf who wants to take control. Fear floods me as I think about getting lost inside myself during this battle.

"Maia, let your wolf out. It won't be like last time, okay? We're mated now."

Seth's black eyes find me as he calls his wolf forward. I can feel the power from him as he shifts in less than a second, suddenly standing on all fours, large and ferocious. *Holy crap!*

I've never seen him shift that fast. I watch as Seth, Horas, and Sasha charge the lupercus in their wolf forms. Horas is the biggest wolf, but it's clear who the leader is. Seth tackles one of the goat-creatures to the ground and tears its throat out so fast that I gasp loudly, bringing attention to my terrified self.

Dammit!

I decide to trust Seth and open my mind up, welcoming my wolf to take hold of me. The shift is instantaneous, just like Seth's, and I sigh when the wolf's power fills me. I turn my head from side to side, assessing the incoming threat and I smile internally. I have control, right alongside my wolf. We are one, powerful and strong.

We got this, girl.

My wolf growls in response to my encouragement and together we leap away from the lupercus man that charges us with his sharp horns. He runs right past us like a bull running through a red cape, but he quickly turns to try a second attack.

I press my wolf claws into the dirt and jump right at the creature's chest before he has time to bend forward again. My canines chomp down on his flesh, and I'm filled with the coppery taste of blood.

Hey, that's not too bad.

My wolf likes the taste, and it spurs her on. She takes another bite out of our attacker, dropping his lifeless body to the ground, and then she whips our head around for more. I spy a dome of magic holding back a hoard of lupercus while the faeries face off back-to-back against five of them. They're trying to control the attack as they keep throwing the elements at the creatures, but it's not fully clear who has the upper hand.

Bree and Marian stare one another down, looking like they're fighting in their minds, and James fights off the lupercus surrounding the witches, protecting Bree.

I find Seth and the other wolves tearing into lupercus, taking down one at a time while helping each other like the pack mates they are. It seems that the fight is surrounding my friends and nobody is paying much attention to me. Of course, they're all protecting me again.

I spot the lupercus leader, recovered from Bree's electric shock. She steps out of the fight to face me, and I growl back at her. My wolf flashes our fangs at the woman, and she snarls back at us with her creepy goat face.

"Come here, little wolf. I know we got off on the wrong foot back at my camp, but I won't hurt you."

I laugh internally at the psycho chick, and I charge toward her, fast and strong. The woman surprises me as she does nothing to stop my attack, and it's not until I'm in the air, aiming for her neck that I see the glisten of metal in her hand.

A sharp needle pierces my wolf's side and I let out a pained howl as my old, poisoned blood enters my body once more. I'm still able to knock the woman down as I fall, and I use the last of my strength to clamp my sharp teeth around her skinny neck.

I hear a crack as I tighten my bite, and then I fall to the earth with a thud. A faint screaming fills my ears, and it takes me a moment to realize it's me that's screaming.

I look down at my human body, and I already begin to mourn my wolf as I feel the shifter cure burning through me, killing my shifter side once again.

No, no, no!

I grab at the magic clothes that cover the puncture wound from the shot. Tearing the clothing off of my hip, I rub at the small hole, but it's useless. I can feel the heat burning through my veins already, like liquid fire.

My head whips from side to side, watching my friends in a life-or-death battle against the advancing lupercus. They're amazing as a pack, but it's not enough.

"Maia! I can't feel you!" Seth shouts at me as he shifts back into his human form, pulling the sword from his hip. He slices through a lupercus fighter, and then turns to me with wide eyes. "Maia! What happened?"

I want to cry from the pain traveling through my body, but I try to keep the tears back. "It's the cure, Seth. It's inside me."

My voice is quiet, but I know he heard me. Seth's face hardens and his eyes turn black again. Two more lupercus appear behind him and I scream for him to turn around. He whips his head around just as both of the lupercus attackers are blown back by a gust of wind.

Seth spins to his left and a dozen faeries fly into view, covered in shining armor. Wilk shouts over the sounds of battle. "Brethren!"

Relief floods me, even through the miserable pain of being burned inside out. *We're safe. The faeries have saved us.*

I watch as the Fae army attacks the last of the lupercus with a force like none other. Blasts of wind and water tear through the goat creatures as the earth bends to the faeries' will. They defend their prince with so much power. I don't know how they knew we'd be here, but I'm grateful nonetheless for our incredible allies.

Exhaustion fills me, clouding my mind, and I drop my head back to the ground, trying not to look at the dead body beside me. My vision blurs, but I can still hear shouts around me, or maybe *at* me.

"Step back, mate. I'll drain it before it reaches her heart."

Silence, and then, "Are you sure you can handle it?"

"We'll see, won't we?" *Is that James?*

Silence fills my mind as another stinging pain hits my hip. *Another shot?*

I'm not sure what's happening, but a comforting warmth covers me like a blanket and I drift off into a dreamless sleep.

Chapter 41

✧✧✧

Maia

"IS SHE GOING TO BE OKAY? She's still a shifter, right?" The voice that wakes me is Sasha's, and she sounds panicked, not at all like her usual snarky self.

Someone grunts and Horas says, "Careful, Sash. You might give us the impression that you care about our little Maia."

"Shut up. I have a heart just like everyone else."
Sasha cares about me? Ha, yeah, right.

Someone moves beside me and I reach out to grab onto them like a lifeline. It's clear that I'm positioned somehow on Seth's lap, and when I finally open my eyes, I'm staring right at his neck.

I smile at the sight of my mate and the yummy scent of him that fills me. I moan as I snuggle in deeper and I lean forward to kiss his warm skin.

Seth flexes underneath me and clears his throat. His voice is hoarse when he speaks. "You better stop that, Snow. We have a bit of an audience."

Someone laughs, and I turn my head away from Seth to see at least twenty pairs of eyes watching me. My friends are smiling down at where Seth and I sit on the ground together, and behind our little group are the faeries that saved us from an attack we were sure to lose.

I reach down to the spot on my hip where I was injected with the shifter cure. It's sore, but I feel fine otherwise. *Oh no.* I try to call on my wolf, but nothing happens and panic floods me.

"Is my wolf dead? Did the cure kill her?" Tears fill my eyes and I want to go back to sleep to escape the thoughts of not being a shifter anymore.

Seth squeezes me tighter and shushes me. "Hey, let's not think about that right now. Time will tell, and I'm just glad you're still alive." He kisses me gently, and I can feel the sorrow he has dealt with for the past hours.

It's dark out, so I had to have been asleep for at least two hours. I turn to the small Fae army and slowly rise to my feet, still feeling weak. "You all saved us from the lupercus attack. I want to thank you for your kindness, and for whatever you did to stop the cure from killing me."

Wilk speaks for his people. "The witch priestess, Aurelia, called upon my father after we left her home. I think we must all thank her. My warriors fought bravely and killed the last of the lupercus, but they did not heal you, Maia. That was James."

I spin my head to the right, where James is standing with a handsome smile, looking wicked with his fangs glistening in the moonlight. "James? How on earth did you save me from the deadliest thing known to shifter-kind?"

"By doing what I do best, love…"

"Sucking," Bree interrupts with a goofy smirk and the group laughs at her joke, though I still feel pretty lost, like I missed the punchline.

James shakes his head and glares down at Bree. "Oh, little witch. I think it's best we keep the dirty remarks to the bedroom, eh?"

Now it's my turn to laugh at the bright blush in Bree's cheeks, matching the color of her hair. Seth steps close to me and lifts the torn hem of my tight black tank top. There are three puncture wounds on my pale skin, and I swear my eyes look like saucers.

"You *literally* sucked out the poison, James?" I look up at Seth who nods, and then to James.

His usual smile is softer, and he shrugs, very unlike the sexy vamp that once kissed me. "Turns out that wolf shifter blood with a hint of deadly cure is entirely intoxicating." He winks.

There's the devilish vamp.

Seth growls quietly beside me, and I snap my head to him. "You okay, there?"

He nods and rolls his eyes, but his loving smile returns as he stares at me. "I'm just so glad that the lupercus are gone for good."

"You mean, they're all gone? Like extinct? They said there were hundreds of them, but we didn't fight that many."

Bree speaks again. "Well, they lied to you. That old witch chick tried digging around in my head during the fight, so I reversed her spell and saw everything. The lupercus were a dying breed, and these were the last of them all. No children in the whole species anyway, so they didn't have much of a chance for continuing on."

"Wow. I can't believe it's over." A sinking feeling fills my chest. "But, wait! If they're all gone, how will we find where they hid the cure? We can't let it sit somewhere for anyone to stumble upon!"

Bree waves her hands at me, as if wiping my worries out of the air between us. "Mai, I don't think you realize how far I went into that psycho's mind before I killed her sorry ass. I saw the actual moment that she lost her virginity… like a hundred years ago. I know exactly where the cure is, and we can walk there from here."

◊ ◊ ◊

Seth

It takes us less than an hour to get to the spot where the lupercus hid Maia's blood. Of course, the hike is rough in the dark, but not impossible thanks to all of our abilities to see at night, aside from Bree. Of course, James is more than happy to hold her hand along the way.

Maia even makes it through the dark with ease, and it gives me hope that her wolf is still intact. Our small group stands under the stars beside a rocky cliff side, minus Horas and Sasha. I sent them to go back home to Stowe and tell Alpha Nate about the battle. Maia also asked them to hurry before her dad ends up in Canada. Knowing Mathew, it wouldn't even be a surprise.

The Fae soldiers were dismissed by Wilk after Maia woke up. We each thanked them, and I promised the faeries a lifelong alliance with the Shaw pack. I don't know where we'd be without Wilk and Qadira, and luckily they chose to stay with us until we returned back to the pack lands.

Maia releases my hand that she has been holding during our hike, and she looks around for any sign of the cure, desperate to end this chaotic mess. "This is the place? Where's the blood?"

James steps toward the smooth rock and smells the air around an overgrown bush. He lifts the thick leaves of the plant, and at its base is a small pile of disturbed dirt.

"Jackpot," says James with a click of his tongue.

"Anyone got a shovel?" Maia's voice trembles slightly, and I know it's not from the cold. We're right back with the cure that kept her hidden from the world for eighteen years. She doesn't want to be anywhere near it.

"It'll be okay, Snow. Let's end this." I speak to her through our bond, and she looks at me with a beautiful smile.

Wilk rubs his glowing hands together as he looks down at the pile of dirt. "We have no need for a shovel, Maia. You should know this by now."

Wilk stretches his hands out, and his blue hair lifts slightly as his power pulls the loose dirt from the ground. He continues to pull dirt out of the hole until a wooden box appears two feet below the surface.

I drop to my knees and tug the rectangular box out of the hole. I move to open the lid but Qadira grabs my arm.

She stares down at me with her bright pink eyes. "Wait. Please let one of us do that, Seth. The cure is in that box, and it is still capable of killing you."

I nod and step back, letting the others take charge. Maia loops her arm with mine, and her shaking subsides. Bree and Qadira kneel side by side and lift the wooden lid to reveal three mason jars full of red liquid.

"Eww. I'll never be able to look at homemade jam the same way," Maia says with her nose scrunched up.

Bree pulls out each jar and struggles to open the lids. "Seriously? Why do jars hate women?" She hands them, one at a time, to James. "Make yourself useful and open the poison blood jars."

James laughs but obliges. As the lids pop open, his eyes flash red, but his control is incredible. There is no other vampire capable of restraint like that. Bree lines the open jars up beside the pile of dirt, and the six of us stand around in a circle with no clue what to do next as we stare at the jars.

Qadira looks at Maia and touches her arm. "You are an alpha heir, Maia. It is your wolf blood that will kill the poison."

Maia shakes her head slowly. "But, what if my wolf is dead? It won't work, will it, if I'm just a human mated to a wolf?"

I reach out and touch her soft cheek. "Snow, at this point, I believe you are still the rightful alpha heir to the Shaw pack, wolf or not. You will make an incredible leader."

Her lower lip quivers and it takes everything in me not to capture it in my mouth, erasing all of her worry with my touch. "Okay, I'll try. Is that it, then? I just bleed into the jars and my blood should attack the old blood?"

Bree holds up a hand and gasps. "Oh, I almost forgot! When I was in that witch's head, I saw that the destruction of the cure takes more than just your blood. I think it's why your body didn't immediately kill the cure once it was injected into you earlier. We have to burn it."

"Just burn it? That's easy," I say.

Bree shrugs. "Well, it has to mix with a rightful alpha's blood and then be burned with a witch's flame. It was created by the shifter god and a witch, after all. Priestess Aurelia must not have learned that half of it. I guess you have to be super evil to know all the deets."

James grunts. "Well, good thing we have a little witch here." He smiles down at Bree and she rolls her eyes.

"Will you ever stop calling me little?"

James grins wider. "Never."

"Okay," Maia says, nodding her head. "We can do this together, then." She sticks her wrist out to me, and her eyes show a perfect determination. "I figure it's your turn to bite me. Team work, right?"

Damn, she's so hot.

I nod. "As you wish, Snow."

I take her delicate wrist in my hands and call my wolf forward just enough to cause sharp teeth to extend in my mouth. I bite down against Maia's racing pulse, and she holds her dripping blood over the open jars.

It's instantly clear that her blood has an effect on the cure, as it mingles together and turns black. Maia pulls her hand back and I tear a piece of my shirt to wrap it around her wound.

"Bree," Maia says to her best friend. "I think it's your turn."

Bree closes her eyes and holds her hands in front of her. She chants in words I don't know and each jar lights up with a blue flame. Maia gasps beside me as she stares in awe at the blue witch fire.

A sizzling noise comes from the contents of the jars and we all hold our breath as the flame completely burns away the black liquid until it's gone. The flames die down and all six of us look from one to the other, only the moon and stars lighting our bemused faces.

"So, is anyone hungry? My treat," Wilk says with his small wings rising and fluttering excitedly.

We all burst into laughter, and I don't hesitate to lift Maia into my arms. I spin her around as she laughs in my ear, lighting my heart on fire. *"You're mine now, Maia. Forever. And there's nothing left on this earth to take you away from me."*

Chapter 42

✧✧✧

Maia: Six Months Later

I STEP OUT FROM THE TOWERING TREES of the thick woods, and the land opens up to a vast field of frost-dusted heather, warming under the spring sunshine. I bask in the warmth with the flowers as I dance in circles. My chocolatey-brown hair flows behind me, letting the breeze tickle my neck, and I giggle. I know I've been here before, in a vision once. Only, this time it's all real and the musky scent in the air has my body flushing with desire. Seth.

Large arms circle my waist and Seth's prickly face drops to my neck, kissing my skin. I spin in his hold and let my lips crash against his. Yup, very real. Seth growls against our kiss and he tips me backward until I'm lying in the wildflowers as he covers me with his hard body.

"I love you so much, Snow. I want to stay here with you forever." He nuzzles my neck with his nose and his tongue swipes against my collarbone.

"But, what about home? The wolves will be missing their alpha heir." The words come out breathy as Seth continues his trail of kisses all the way to my belly button.

He looks up at me and the sun highlights his dark hair and high cheekbones perfectly. "Well, I certainly would miss you, too, if I were them."

He raises the hem of my shirt and kisses the sharp peak of my hip bone. I grab his shoulders and pull him back up to look at me. "Do you think the pack will accept me as their alpha? They've never had a female alpha before."

Seth's eyes explore my face and he sighs. "They will love you. Just because it hasn't happened before, doesn't mean it can't happen. You are what they need..." his forehead lays against mine and my eyes close. "... what I need."

I wrap my arms around his neck and raise my lips to meet his. My wolf stirs in my mind, whispering to be free and I freeze. "Seth, I can feel her. My wolf!" I shout in excitement, reveling in the fact that the other half of me isn't gone.

Seth grins down at me as he searches my eyes. "I knew she couldn't be gone. She's strong and stubborn, just like you."

I giggle in excitement as Seth's teeth nibble on my bottom lip teasingly. I pull him to me again, a new urgency overcoming me. His hands explore every inch of me, hungry and urgent as we get lost in one another *under the warm sun. I know our future is bright, as long as we're together.*

"Daydreaming again, Mai? We need to get going!" Bree takes me from the beautiful memory.

It has been six months since that perfect spring morning, after defeating the lupercus and getting rid of the cure. James, Bree, Qadira, Wilk, Seth, and I spent the rest of that hectic night eating junk food and sleeping in a hotel at the edge of the woods. It was a night of peace, and I took an early morning walk to say goodbye to the gorgeous Canadian mountains.

Seth told me then that the Shaw pack needed me. Today, I am officially being accepted by the pack as their alpha heir. For the past six months, I have learned the way of the wolves. I've befriended them, celebrated with them, and fallen in love with them all.

Apparently, a traditional ceremony is necessary to officially declare the alpha-to-be. I just can't believe that I'm the person to take on that role. Most days, I still feel like little Maia hiding from the mean bullies at school.

I turn to Bree and she looks me up and down with a grin. "You look so gorgeous, Mai. Like a true princess."

I turn back to the full-length mirror while Bree sticks pearl earrings in my ears. My long hair is darker brown than ever, not a hint of white left behind. I'm wearing a sleeveless, floor-length forest green dress that hugs my torso tightly, and flows out from the waist, though it doesn't feel as comfortable as Qadira's magic clothes.

The dress pushes my breasts up, leaving nothing to the imagination, but I've learned that nudity isn't a big deal in the shifter pack, so a little cleavage is nothing. My hazel eyes are highlighted by dark eyeliner and thick mascara. I look like a woman, maybe even a leader.

I sigh and spin back to Bree, pulling her into a tight hug. Her red curls smother my face like always, filling my nose with the scent of vanilla, and I love it. "Thank you, Bree. I don't know where I'd be without you."

She pushes me to arm's length and shrugs. She's dressed up as well, in a long blue silk dress that hugs her thick curves. "Who knows, babe, but my life would certainly be way too dull without you in it."

I roll my eyes. "Oh, really? You'd still have James, so it couldn't be that bad."

Bree scoffs and runs a hand through her hair. "That vamp really does keep me on my toes. But he might just be *too much* entertainment at times."

"Are you sick of dating him already? Do I need to get my wolf pack to kick his ass?"

She laughs at that and shoves my shoulder. "Sadly, I don't think I could ever be sick of calling him mine." She smiles like an idiot in love, and I completely understand that feeling.

The day Bree came to me and told me that James finally kissed her and told her how he feels, I practically screamed in excitement. All I wanted for her was to be happy, and James gives her that, even though they have their own obstacles. Who said obstacles can't be conquered?

"Speak of the devil," I say, smelling James before he enters the room.

James swings open the front door of mine and Seth's little cabin. *Our home.* "I heard my name. I hope it was an entirely naughty conversation."

Bree runs to James and jumps into his arms. Their lips crash together in a steaming kiss and I have to look away. "Holy hell, you two! Get a room!"

James drops Bree back to the floor and smiles his signature sexy grin. "Are you offering up yours?" He tilts his head toward my bedroom and I glare at him.

"That bed is for Seth and I only, and I will not let you two wild animals defile it!"

"Says the *actual* wolf," Bree says, practically glowing with happiness.

"Yeah, yeah. Let's get out there before Dad comes looking for me. I don't need a lecture. Remember how psycho he got when we were home late from the senior homecoming dance?"

Bree's eyes go wide, and she drags James outside in a hurry. Even the big bad witch fears my overprotective father. We step out into the chilly fall air and I'm grateful for the breeze. Every part of me feels too hot with nervous energy, and all I want to do is jump into the nearest lake to calm myself down.

It's only a short walk to the center of the neighborhood, and Horas is the first to greet us with his towering frame. Without hesitation, he lifts me off the ground and into a bear hug. I wiggle in his arms, not really using my strength because I actually really love Horas' hugs.

"You can struggle all you want, little alpha. Nobody can escape my wolf hugs!"

I laugh and swat at his chest. "Just because Sasha likes me now, doesn't mean she won't skin me alive for getting too close to her boyfriend."

Horas drops me and quickly scans the area for his blonde Barbie doll, a hint of panic in his eyes, causing Bree to laugh behind me. "Are you really that afraid of her, Horas?"

He looks at Bree like she's an idiot. "Are you kidding? I'm terrified!"

We're all laughing again as we step out into the pack gathering area. It's a large circular opening in the trees with stadium-like seating built into the earth with thick green grass, and a small wooden stage at the front.

As far as I can tell, every single Shaw pack member is seated along the grass benches, causing my heart rate to pick up even faster at the two hundred plus people. Bree kisses my cheek and drags James to an open seat.

My smile lights up when I see the faeries seated in the front row. Qadira, Wilk, Wilk's sister, Princess Evin, and King Faren himself. I wasn't expecting them to be here.

Qadira and Wilk jump up and run to embrace me. It has been a few months since I saw them last, when I was invited to their wedding. It was hard for them in the beginning, to start a relationship with the obstacle of Qadira's servant status, but when the king saw how loyal and brave Qadira was after helping me, he upgraded Qadira to a royal soldier. Apparently, it's a high honor and worthy of marrying a prince. It was amazing to be back in the city of Fae, and a faerie wedding is one of the most miraculous things I've ever witnessed.

"I'm so glad you guys are here! Why didn't you tell me you were coming?"

Wilk grins at me, his blue eyes glowing. "We wanted it to be a surprise. Are you happy?"

My eyes land on the stage where Seth stands in a stream of sunlight, waiting for me, and I sigh. "I'm so happy, you guys."

I hug them both once more and wave to the Fae king and his daughter. Evin still doesn't like me much, but I've learned that she doesn't like many people, so I try not to take it personally.

My eyes focus on Seth again as I climb the two steps up to the small stage. Everything about him excites me and also somehow calms me to my core. He turns to me with a warm smile, and his dark eyes trail up and down my body, changing from happiness to complete desire.

"You are the most beautiful thing I have ever seen."

I swing my arms around his neck and breathe in his delicious scent. *"Thank you. How do you so easily make the rest of the world disappear?"*

He looks down at me and kisses my nose. *"I can't help that you're obsessed with me, Snow."* He grins and I shake my head at my adorable mate.

"I'd argue with that, but it's actually so true that it's embarrassing."

Seth laughs out loud, drawing the attention of the crowd awaiting my big moment, and I blush under the gaze of my loving pack members. *"I guess it's time. Let's hope I don't fall on my face."*

Seth chuckles softly as he nods and kisses me swiftly on the lips. He turns and leaves me on the stage to sit in the grass beside his father's wheelchair. I smile at the man that made my mate, and he nods back to me with a grin that wrinkles the skin around his eyes. Seth looks so much like him, and it makes me love the man even more.

Faolan Lowell has become a second father to me since I came to the Shaw pack. I was told by Seth that his dad was once closed off and somewhat of a recluse, but this year he has come out of his shell and become lively again. I love that his son's happiness did this for him.

I'm only alone on stage for a moment before Uncle Nate and Aunt Lydia join me, both of them pulling me in between them to get sandwiched in a warm hug. Dad follows them with tears in his eyes and I sigh at the sight of him.

"Come on, Dad. Why does every big event make you blubber like that?" I wrap my arms around him, and he squeezes me tighter than ever.

He steps away and wipes at his eyes. "I just had such a hard time imagining this future for you, baby girl. It was hard to have hope that you could escape the curse I put on you. I'm just so incredibly proud, and your mom would be bawling just as hard if she were here."

I can feel my own tears coming and I wave my hands in the air, trying to dry the moisture. "Geez, how do you always do that to me?"

He laughs and kisses my cheek before stepping off the stage and settling beside Seth. Aunt Lydia rubs a hand on my back but stays silent as her husband calls for silence in the crowd. Of course, everyone instantly goes quiet, ever loyal to their alpha, and I take a deep breath, trying to settle my nerves.

"Welcome, Shaw pack, our faerie friends, witches, and even vampires. This is a first for this pack. Not only do we have alliances that we never could've imagined, but we have an alpha heir unlike any other in our history." He touches my shoulder. "Maia Collins will be the first female to lead our wonderful pack, a new generation who I imagine will even outshine the last, and she is more than worthy of the task."

My eyes find Seth's and he nods along with Nate's words. *"Stop checking me out and just enjoy the moment, my love."* He winks and I have to hold back an eye roll.

Nate continues, "Maia isn't just another wolf shifter. She alone carried the shifter cure in her blood for eighteen years. She was born of a strong human man and one of the greatest wolf shifters that our pack has seen. What union was once unheard of, and at the time seemed impossible, gave us the miracle that is our future alpha, Maia. My niece."

Lydia steps up beside her husband and stretches her arms out to the crowd. "Now is the time to accept Maia as your future alpha by raising your voices in a howl."

Nate drops his head back and lets out a long deep howl. Immediately, Lydia joins in and Seth follows with his low howl. It's Sasha who leads the rest of the wolves in a chorus of howls that are like music to my ears. Somehow, she has become one of my biggest supporters, and I am constantly in awe of her. I look around the large gathering as each shifter follows suit, and the entire forest fills with the sounds of the wolves' howls. Even Bree, James, and the faeries join in and it's as if I can feel the immense power behind each individual voice.

My heart swells with acceptance and love, and I can't imagine a better feeling than this. I draw my wolf forward as a show of my power for the pack, as is tradition for these ceremonies, and in half a second, I'm standing on all fours in front of my people. Only months ago, I thought I had lost this feeling forever, and now the wolf and I are one again.

I throw my wolf head back and release my own long howl that overpowers all of the rest, and my eyes fall on my mate again. He watches me in awe, pride written across his handsome face, and he speaks to me in his mind. *"You have been accepted by them all, Maia. This is your pack, and just like me, they will always be your home."*

The End

Review This Book

It means so much to me that you bought my book! Writing is such a passion of mine and I look forward to your feedback.

So, if you liked this book, whether it be the characters, settings, or adventures, I'd like to ask you a small favor. Hop on over to Amazon and leave a review with your thoughts. It'd be so great to read what YOU have to say!

From your friend, Abigail Grant

Other Books by This Author

Exclusive Freebies:

A Vision in Thessaly

Shifter Cure

The Intended Series

The Rescued Series

Hidden Cure Series

The Kingdom Trials

About The Author

Bestselling author of the Intended Series, Abigail Grant has always found herself lost in a good book. Whether it be as a teenager sprawled out in her upstairs bedroom reading all hours of the night, or more recently as a wife and mother of three small children, excited for bedtime when she can tell imaginative bedtime stories of magical realms and fierce creatures.

Follow Abigail on Facebook, Instagram, Goodreads, Bookbub, and Amazon

Printed in Great Britain
by Amazon